THE OUTLAW'S ENIGMA

Book One of Two

C.A. CLEMMINGS

For Krishna

Chapter One

THE ROAD TO THE CABIN was invisible from above through the thick cluster of trees. Thirty miles from the nearest town, the cabin was hidden even from the offshoots of roads that sprang from the main road like branches only to end abruptly or be cut off by an unexpected slough or the harsh, unmovable woods.

Isabelle Bartley only needed to know one route, and she had marked it clearly over the past four months. Her own disposition was smooth, much like the tranquil appearance of foliage from a distance. At times soft ruffles of emotions were evident, shifting quickly across her face like light and gray shadows. Beyond that, Isabelle was as still and as secretive as the woods she plunged toward. She alone knew of the dark fissures that originated and spread like branches from her heart. With silken brown skin and an exquisite yet virtuous face, her smoldering amber eyes were a glimpse into the depth of her inner world.

She had left the guesthouse she owned in rural New Jersey on this Sunday morning in late-April. Over an hour later she turned off the narrow back road onto a lane barely the width of her car. Dense hemlock flanked the dirt-and moss-covered pathway. The cabin was lumpy and stagnant in the distance like a swamp creature. In the front and on one side, a gravel embankment led to a dried-up pond of rotted branches and debris. To the right and back the woods crept in. Twigs crackled under the tires of the Mercedes as Isabelle pulled up. She sat for a moment and considered turning around. The windows were sealed shut. The lights were off. The cabin was a ridiculous ramshackle house under a cloak of trees.

Isabelle retrieved the box from the trunk. A dull light came on inside at the first creak of the porch boards. She held her breath as footsteps approached, hesitated, and then stopped. The door opened. Round amber eyes the same as hers stared at her. They were wide with apprehension for a moment, until a relieved smile spread across her mother's face. Marcia Bartley-Gillespie reached her arms out and pulled Isabelle, who was still holding the box, into an awkward embrace.

"Why did you take so long to come?" Marcia asked.

"I was here last month," Isabelle said.

They stepped into the shadowed room, lit only by a kerosene lamp on a table. The furniture was over-sized and out of place. Marcia and Haughton had gathered much of what they could carry in haste from their house in Nutley. One piece of leather sectional filled half the room, its company kept by two solid cherry coffee tables, a swivel chair, a grandfather clock in one corner, and a chest against the wall. Marcia had laid out family pictures since the last time Isabelle had visited.

"Come in here," Marcia called out from the kitchen.

Isabelle registered the smell of bread pudding and coconut. She went in with the box and unpacked the groceries. Marcia had lost weight and gained new stress lines in her face. Her hair was pulled up into a bun on top of her head and it had gone gray at the temples. Her beauty was fading with worry.

"Take these back with you." Marcia packed freshly-baked *gizzardas* into a plastic container.

"I can't take those back with me." The pastries, made of sweet coconut filling in a round crust, were unique, and Isabelle's meddling staff at the guesthouse would find them curious.

"Just say you got them from a friend," Marcia insisted.

In the months Isabelle had been running the guesthouse she had never mentioned having any friends or much about her past.

"You and Bastian used to love these," Marcia said.

Isabelle stacked canned goods into the cupboards. She disliked the way her mother referenced Bastian as if their childhood in Jamaica had been idyllic.

"Go in and see Haughton, especially if you won't be back for another month."

Isabelle stiffened her shoulders and went toward the back of the house. The hallway was unlit, but a column of light emanated from the half-open door at the end. Haughton "Hacksaw" Gillespie was standing over a table with a knife, which he stuck into soil in a large flower pot. A row of smaller pots was lined up on the table and a long florescent bulb hung from the ceiling over them. Her stepfather was tall, with gargantuan hands. Hands shaped out of cement and slapped on, his shoulders a large block of rock carved into the shape of a man. He reached out and clasped the stem of a Begonia flower, perhaps to caress it or to strangle it. Isabelle went back to the kitchen without being seen.

"I have to head home," she said.

"Don't forget these." Marcia smiled and placed the bag of baked treats in her hand.

❖

Isabelle's mother and stepfather were behaving like fugitives. Marcia believed her husband was losing his grip on reality, but despite his apparent paranoia she followed him wherever he led. Haughton was not paranoid. The truth was his enemies were nipping at his heels. In the last couple years Haughton's department stores in Kingston had been robbed repeatedly. Months before he went into hiding in the woods, three stores were burned to the ground. Isabelle's store – which he said was his gift to her for going to boarding school after they moved to New Jersey – remained untouched. Her stepfather was being targeted years after his retirement and relative solitude in the United States. A long time ago he had the means and the power to punish anyone who crossed him, but these days his power had waned.

Haughton had been a constant figure through much of Isabelle's life, yet she could not summon any sympathy for him. Even when her parents were still married, Haughton hung over her family like a vulture. Her mother carried on an affair with him for years when they lived in Kingston, and Haughton sunk his claws into her brother, Bastian, steering him toward a lawless life of extortion, intimidation, and murder. Isabelle suffered silently at home throughout her mother's betrayal and her father's growing helplessness.

She'd had spurts of rebelliousness, but she survived by making herself pliable and indifferent. She did her chores without complaint, excelled in academics, and stayed away from boys as required. The latter rule she had no real desire to challenge. As she got older she kept her romances hidden. Her college flings were one thing, but when she came back home to Marcia and Haughton's gilded coop she could only discuss her girlfriends in hushed whispers with her mother. She had dated Caye Wauburg, a business analyst from New York City, on and off for two years and never even considered introducing her to her stepfather.

Four months ago, when Marcia and Haughton first moved to the cabin and Isabelle had left them behind, the world truly opened up in front of her. She was twenty-nine years old and away from her family for the first time. She was free of Haughton's heavy hand and Marcia's selfish whims. She had driven along the lonesome back roads in the remote woods of Northeast New Jersey, where the houses were separated by the winter forest and were shrouded by great oak and hickory trees. The parts that were visible hinted at a stately and historic flair in their design.

Isabelle had come upon the Romanesque mansion retreating from the icy road. The exterior of the house was deceptively off-putting with its massive stone structured walls and Gothic-arch windows that took on the quality of omnipotent faces. A conical tower roof pointed skyward, intersected by smaller towers on the front and side. The house was steadfast and defensive under gently swaying trees, hidden from the placid roadway in its solitary enclave.

A *For Sale* sign listed an address but no phone number. Isabelle had to drive another fifteen miles south, then west at the fork as directed by her GPS, then north toward the center of the town. The region had been built up to encircle the oval-shaped lake.

The stores and restaurants along the main avenue were closed, shuttered as if they had lost their battle with winter. The streets were white from salt and brine. A woman went by slowly on a motorized scooter with a basket on the back. Isabelle imagined a once vibrant and idyllic town now having lost its inhabitants and its luster.

The city hall building was flat and rectangular with no redeeming charm. When Isabelle arrived it looked both vacant and hostile and was covered in a glob of white paint, obviously painted over numerous times without removal of the existing coats. A man with a wide midsection looked Isabelle up and down as she entered. His black hair was thick and stiff with gel, with visible comb lines that had transported the lump of it from one side of his head to the other. He was seated at an old metal desk in the center of the low room.

He took his time before he replied to Isabelle's greeting with a stern, "Good afternoon. I was just leaving for the day." She suspected he was the only employee there.

"I'm looking to buy the Romanesque house," Isabelle announced.

"It was sold to the town by its previous owner."

"Does the town still own it?"

"Yes, of course."

"I'm looking to buy it."

"Why would the town sell it?" Even as he said this he was already turning away as if losing interest in the conversation. "Anyway," he went on before Isabelle could respond, "You can look at the documents here." His right hand was on the computer mouse while his left hand fiddled with a folder in a file tray on the desk. Isabelle moved toward the computer.

"Here," he said, and pulled one of the folders from the stack. "The previous owner ran a guesthouse. Take a look at the documents and be quick. I'm going to the hunting lodge."

It was ten minutes after two.

"The sign on the door said this office closes at three," Isabelle pointed out.

"I had begun the process of shutting down this machine when you walked in." He blinked slowly. The computer made a last murmur as it powered down. Isabelle took a seat beside his desk. They sat in an awkward silence. His hand still rested on the mouse. The nameplate on his desk read, RAVI HOLDER.

Isabelle read for several minutes. The file contained glossy color photos of the house, which had a dark oak interior. Beyond the arched entryway, the wide staircase made a sharp, polished ascent. Limestone accents and stairways made of smooth stone ran throughout the house. Fourteen rooms were listed, and though most looked modest in the photographs, they still possessed an air of aged-opulence.

Something dawned on Isabelle.

"Are you considered 'the town'?" she asked.

A self-satisfied smile stretched across Ravi's lips. He turned to face her, the inner arch of his lips stained brown. Inside his mouth was equally dark.

"I am the town."

"You are the town?" She had to admit she was fascinated.

Ravi smiled again. "I own most of the property here, including the house that is of interest to you."

"It says here it's fully furnished."

"Yes, everything remains as it was before."

"Why did the previous owner sell it?"

"He went abroad, and not because of bad business. The town appears sleepy, but when the warm weather rolls around it has a good deal of visitors. There's hiking trails up Norvin Green and a shop that rents bikes. You can also get a boat to go out on the lake. Fishing is big, and of course, the hunters always come."

Isabelle wasn't concerned about the town. She was looking for a refuge, and the property appeared big enough to get lost in. She needed time to reflect on what she truly wanted to do with her life. She had spent the last few years working in the family restaurant with her mother before Marcia and Haughton sold it and headed for the woods.

"Is it available immediately?" she asked.

"Have you looked at the price?"

She had looked at the price. She had stopped writing over two years ago, but she had a large back-list of detective chick lit novels out there earning a modest return. Tales about ill-fated quests to solve mysteries had been her specialty. She wrote under a pseudonym and used to churn them out like bread from the oven. After a while, her writing became uninspired and unremarkable, much like her life. So she stopped.

Her store in Jamaica was managed by her Uncle Boyd, who transferred revenue to her bank account whenever he felt like it. That irked Isabelle, but she had decided a while ago to let it slide. She only communicated with her uncle when absolutely necessary. She liked to pretend this piece of property did not exist, for it had been given to her out of guilt, perhaps because of Haughton's treatment of Bastian and her father, and his role in the destruction of everything she cared about.

"Have you looked at the price?" Ravi repeated.

She snapped out of her musing. "Yes. Can you arrange a tour?"

She *was* truly on her own for the first time, but all she wanted to do was bury herself in this backwoods town.

Chapter Two

LATER THAT SUNDAY MORNING after she had dropped off Marcia and Haughton's groceries, Isabelle had come home and showered. She blew out her lustrous medium-brown curls and flat-ironed her hair into long wisps that fell against her back and framed her face with subtle highlights. She left her room wrapped in black – stockings, skirt, and a wool sweater whose fluffy turtleneck concealed the lower half of her face. She carried herself as if submerged in a shrouded, agile aura. She glided down the freshly vacuumed runner, pausing for a moment to glance at a bouquet of yellow silk carnations on an accent table. The two housekeepers were at the end of the hallway with their cleaning carts and Isabelle could sense them huddle together once they saw her.

"Where is Anita?" Isabelle asked.

"She's in the kitchen," one of them said.

She went past them down the stone tile steps that led to the basement, her boots unleashing a drum of echoes in the hollow stairwell. She came around through the small conference room on the first floor and out to the empty foyer where James Reginald, a retired jeweler, sat reading the newspaper on one of the burgundy suede couches. He was the first guest to arrive and had paid in advance for the whole summer. The season hadn't officially started, but Isabelle discovered he had nowhere else to be.

The closing on the house had gone quickly, and it turned out Ravi Holder was not the town after all. He had bought up real estate and preened about like Master of the Boondocks. He put Isabelle in touch with the previous guesthouse manager, Helene Keane, who had been disobliged when the former owner shut up shop. Helene accepted the job without hesitation and hired a staff of six, a few of whom had worked with her before.

Looking sharp and buttoned up as if cast in wax, the clerk, Evan Roy, stood behind a sleek walnut front desk. He stood sharper the moment Isabelle entered, his frame resembling an emaciated basketball player's. On the day of his interview with Isabelle and Helene, he had shown up with a fro-hawk frosted with green tips. They had liked him enough despite the wild hairstyle, and encouraged him to cut off the color. Isabelle gave him a slight nod of approval without breaking her stride to the kitchen.

Benny, the chef, had a square face, square fingers, and thick square bifocals propped up across his nose. He tamed his wiry hair by plastering it onto his scalp. As soon as Isabelle entered the kitchen, he led her over to the lunch special with a subdued flourish of his hand.

"Beef stroganoff with rice," he said. He had pressed and formed the rice into a "Hello Kitty" head with oregano eyes and a spinach flower in her hair.

"What is this?" Isabelle asked. She had an inkling she would need to inspect the meals before he served them.

"Lunch." Benny smiled.

"Benny, are you planning to serve this?"

"It is for you." He presented the dish as if it were a rare jewel.

"But you don't plan to serve this?" Isabelle repeated.

"It is only for you." He gestured again and grinned a wide grin of square teeth. Benny was amused by her and she knew it. He always wore an expression that implied he had just discovered a mischievous secret about someone.

"I'm not hungry." Isabelle allowed a half smile to etch across her small, full lips. "Where is Anita?"

Anita came forward as if she had been seeking cover, dreading the moment when her name would be called.

"Mr. Reginald complained that dinner was cold last night," Isabelle said. "Please don't let it happen again."

The girl nodded and retreated then caught herself and waited. But Isabelle was indeed finished and was already going out the door to the courtyard at the back of the house. The ground was covered in cobblestones that looked like each one had been placed in its exact position by dozens of careful hands. The area was vacant except for the fountain in the center and the three tables arranged around it. The water rose up and danced as if possessed, only to fall back within itself over and over again, enclosed in an indifferent slab of concrete.

Isabelle's stoicism had helped her get through high school during the difficult period. After Bastian left home and Marcia continued to spend all her time with Haughton, Isabelle found herself playing a maternal role for her father, Robert. Robert had always been disconnected and unsure of himself, and he spent most of his time in his work shed beside the house, sanding an unvarnished piece of wood. He was frail and tended to wear a threadbare shirt over khakis. Sawdust would collect in the folds of his pants legs and on the ground around him, and he was oblivious to it. His sole focus was always the task at hand – the rhythmic scratch of the sandpaper across wood.

Robert owned a small wood factory, *Bartley's Furniture and Wood*, which had been in his family for generations, passed on to him in his father's will. He spoke of the pride he would feel to one day leave it to Isabelle and Bastian. Beyond this, Robert was emotionally barren. Isabelle had always said the greatest conflict of her father's life was deciding which wood to choose for a piece of furniture.

Isabelle walked along the courtyard under the shade of the building. She had left most of the house uncovered, and from the start of her journey had merely done a loop, slipping inside and up the stairs leading from one end of the yard to arrive back at her suite.

The season would start in two weeks and already she was weary. She plopped down onto the couch and looked for something to do. Hers was a spacious suite, located at the far end of the second floor, separated from the guest area. The other room across the hall had been assigned to Helene. She was the only member of staff who lived on the premises.

Isabelle had all the comforts of home in her suite, including a small kitchenette and a desk by the window overlooking the lake. It was the first place she had truly lived in by herself, not counting her college dorm or the hotel she stayed in for the first few weeks before she moved into the mansion. She had decorated the suite herself with contemporary style furnishings – a flat beige leather sectional with an espresso hardwood base and a coffee table and accents with an espresso finish to match. She needed nothing else, but Helene Keane had been threatening to color her walls with art.

She checked her cell phone voice mail. She had two messages from Ravi Holder asking if she was ready for the start of the season and what he could do to make things easier for her. The third message was from Caye Wauburg. She was the only person Isabelle had told about the guesthouse and now she wanted to visit. It was a testament to how insensitive and self-centered Caye behaved sometimes. Isabelle wanted to kick herself for spilling the news.

During the course of their relationship, Caye saw her only when she had time in between building an empire with her father, Alexander Wauburg, at his business consultant firm. Their romance had been easy and mostly drama free, but Caye was a spoiled daddy's girl who never felt the need to explain herself. Six months ago she had disappeared on a business trip and when she returned, she took Isabelle out to lunch and told her she'd met someone else. Isabelle had hardened her heart and moved on. Caye lost the privilege of an invite or even a return phone call.

Isabelle wanted a clean start. She wanted something whole and true with a woman who was devoted, brilliant, and uncomplicated. A tender pillar of strength and a safeguard to steady her tottering existence. Where could she find a woman like that in these backwoods? Where could she find any women here?

What she didn't want was a life where chaos seethed beneath the surface. She could do without the shadowy, slithering intentions of everyone around her. Isabelle had witnessed this behavior in her brother, her stepfather, and even her mother, whose darker tendencies were more nuanced.

She went over to her desk and looked out at the lake. The surface of the water was dull and white, holding and reflecting nothing but the bare sky.

❖

Opening day arrived in Mid-May and guests trickled in. Isabelle relinquished control to Helene, who took everyone on a tour of the house and property after Evan checked them in and carried their luggage to their rooms. At first it was jarring to see strangers milling around in a house she had lived in primarily by herself for months, but Isabelle adjusted once she learned Helene was quite capable of running the show on her own. The woman floated throughout the house, putting out metaphorical fires and sharing a charming laugh with everyone. This gave Isabelle the opportunity to retreat to the solitude of her suite or to rummage around in the basement, where boxes of old knick knacks from the house had been stored. She sorted worn notebooks and unraveled maps. She found the wooden stock of a shotgun and had spent the better part of an afternoon looking for the rest of it.

Isabelle was opposed to the idea of a Grand Opening party, for it conjured up nightmares about mingling with guests and putting on the welcoming air of a hostess. Even when she worked in the restaurant with her mother she spent most of her time in the office balancing the books and managing the wait staff. She had no patience for social pleasantries. Nevertheless, Helene got her wish and the Grand Opening party was scheduled for the end of May. Isabelle took comfort in the fact that only a third of the rooms were booked, which meant fewer people she would be forced to socialize with.

On the day of the party Isabelle awoke with a groan. How had she been tricked into agreeing to it? Helene was a retired school teacher with far too much energy. Her children were grown and her husband was deceased. *She has nothing better to do.* Isabelle just had to get through the day. She put on a pair of black skinny jeans and an old gray Eric Donaldson T-shirt she had stolen from Bastian when they were younger. The front of the shirt featured a cartoonish drawing of one of his album covers, with the words "Cherry Oh Baby" written across it. She finished the look with a pair of black flip flops and left her room in time to see Helene coming up the stairs. She had been singlehandedly lugging stands, frames, and artwork she had collected from local artists to the library on the second floor. Several pieces were already dispersed throughout the house, and Helene had decided the library would be an impromptu gallery for the rest of it.

"Oh," escaped her lips when she saw Isabelle, but it sounded more like a gasp. Her eyes went directly to the outfit. "Today you dress down?"

Isabelle smiled and tried to get past her to feign her usual rounds. "I have to check on Benny," she said. "Who knows what kind of concoction he's putting together."

Helene held her by the shoulder. "Come, let's look at this one."

They went out to the balcony overlooking the courtyard. Helene's bristle-straight silver hair was cut sharply across the nape of her neck and shone in the open air. She had light blue eyes and a small face, and was several inches shorter than Isabelle. She pulled away the brown wrapping paper and turned it to Isabelle. It was a painting of a golden candelabra with a flow of curling vines dancing around the stem and up and out from the holders. Isabelle had barely looked. It was a random piece of art to which she was sure Helene would attach some random, intangible meaning.

"This one," Helene said, "goes in your suite."

Not only was the painting forced upon her, Helene was also forcibly picking out an outfit for her to wear to a party she was forced to host.

"It's at least six hours away," Isabelle protested. She was more than capable of picking out her own outfit. Helene was hardly listening, for she was deep inside the folds of Isabelle's closet examining the options. Finally, she emerged with a silver pencil skirt and a silver ruffle front blouse. Isabelle grimaced. "God, no."

Helene chuckled and dug into the closet again. She stepped out proudly and held up a white wrap dress that stopped above the knees. She looked Isabelle up and down and smiled.

"This will show off that slender figure."

Isabelle was sure Benny and Helene were conspiring against her. It was one thing to have to put up with the rest of the staff gossiping about her, but they both flittered around like over-enthusiastic servants poking at a wretched princess.

The party was in full swing, but Isabelle was fully dressed and hiding in her room. She was wearing the outfit she had been ordered to wear, but that was as far as she would go. She stood at the window and watched a small fishing boat on the still water. Dusk was approaching, and her attention was held by the brisk light of a solitary lantern inside the boat.

Something moved closer in her line of vision and she looked down to see a dark-haired woman with her back to the house. She was standing on the lush front lawn, which sloped downward to the beech and black maple trees that were the last buffer from the lake. Isabelle had the same view of the water as the woman did, but from higher up. Even though she had not memorized the names of guests the way Helene had, Isabelle could still recognize them all by face and physical features. The woman outside must have just arrived.

Isabelle glanced at her watch. She strolled over to her desk and slowly sorted through her mail. Along with her subscription to *Bon Appétit* and *Food and Wine* magazines, which were more for Benny's benefit than hers, the stack included a bill from the landscaper and a series of invoices from the exterior lighting company Helene had hired to "festively prepare the house for season." There was also a postcard with "Isabelle Bartley" printed on the back in large block letters. No return address. The rest of the card was blank, except for an image of a single black rose on the front. Isabelle thought of her brother.

She hurried downstairs to the front desk with the postcard now splotched with moisture from her hands. Evan was directing a drunken James Reginald to the courtyard. He had apparently gone in and out of the conference room several times, only to come back and inform Evan that he could not find the party. After he had been successfully ushered in the right direction, Evan returned and immediately stood at attention with his gangly frame. He was a few years younger than Isabelle and she was somewhat tolerant of his awkwardness.

"Just lock that door," Isabelle said.

Evan rushed over and locked the door to the conference room. He sprinted back when he realized she was still standing at the desk.

"Did you bring the mail up to my room?" she asked.

Evan mumbled. "I . . ."

He looked unsure, like he thought he had forgotten to bring the mail up.

"This was in the pile from today. Do you recognize it?" She held up the postcard. "I need to know where it came from."

"Today . . . I didn't handle the mail," Evan said, brightening. "Mrs. Keane did."

Isabelle went out to the balcony to find Helene. A few guests stood off in a corner talking and sipping cocktails, but most were down below in the courtyard. The energetic clinking of beer bottles and glasses accompanied the sound of Frankie Valli's voice coming through the speakers. Yellow glow from the overhanging lights threw the faces into a mystical gleam.

"There she is," Evan said. "Should I ask her about the mail?"

He was pointing to a table where Helene sat with two women.

Isabelle was surprised he had followed her outside. She had barely had a need to speak to him before and now that she had, he thought he had committed a grave error.

"No. But thanks." She smiled to reassure him. "I'm required to make an appearance anyway."

Halfway down the stone steps that led from the balcony to the courtyard, Isabelle stopped abruptly. Evan was still behind her.

"Who . . . ?"

"I believe that woman is Caye Wauburg," he said. "And that's her friend – a woman who introduced herself as Harper."

Isabelle knew it was Caye, but Evan provided confirmation she was unwilling to believe. "Did she have a reservation? Because I would like to have been informed . . ." She stopped when his brows furrowed. She had never once shown any interest in the reservations.

"No, but she told me she was a friend of yours," he said. "I thought it would be okay. They just arrived."

Isabelle considered high-tailing it back to her room and pad-locking herself in. As she was about to make her escape, Helene's eyes met hers. The older woman flung her arms up and exclaimed something that made the other two turn around. Then Helene traipsed across to retrieve her.

"You didn't tell me your friends were coming," she said, as she led Isabelle over like a prisoner to the guillotine.

Caye had apparently stood only to smile and say, "Isabelle" in a tone that suggested they had merely run into each other at the grocery store. She looked as she always did – dressed for business even at casual affairs. Her sun-tinted hair hung loose around her shoulders, accented by the glass of champagne in her hand and in perfect coordination with the cream-colored skirt suit she wore. Caye let the silence hang, perhaps for the pleasure of it, until Helene roused herself into action and motioned Anita over.

"Bring us more champagne please," Helene said. She turned back to the women. "I was just telling Isabelle I didn't know her friends were coming."

"*We* didn't quite know we were coming," Caye gushed. "It was decided on a whim." At that moment she remembered her companion, who had been quietly observing the non-introduction. "Harper, here is the owner of this odd little refuge. Isabelle, meet my girlfriend, Harper."

Chapter Three

ISABELLE FOUND HERSELF alone at the table with the two women. Helene had been called inside to attend to other matters, leaving Isabelle to stare into her untouched champagne or out at the hedge that formed at the perimeter of the courtyard.

Finally she said, "This is a surprise."

"I said we might drop by," Caye announced, as if Isabelle had somehow been neglectful of their itinerary. "Besides, we won't stay more than a day or so."

The issue of course wasn't about how long they were planning to stay. Caye had not only shown up uninvited, but had also brought her girlfriend along.

"I need a real drink." Isabelle didn't bother to conceal the annoyance in her voice. She pretended to look for Anita then rose quickly from the table.

"We haven't even had a tour," Caye said. She rose and Harper rose with her like a shadow. Isabelle had avoided looking at the girlfriend, and now the first thing she noticed was her height. She was an inch or two taller than Caye, and her black hair was swooped to one side so that it flowed down over her shoulder. Her eyes were dark and shining like impenetrable stones that followed Caye's every movement. At first she was strangely unperturbed, but now Isabelle caught the woman's weighty stare in her peripheral. A curious and scrutinizing look that bore into Isabelle as she walked away from the table.

Much to Isabelle's dismay they followed her inside to the small bar. Caye immediately offered Harper a refill of champagne, which was refused. She turned to Isabelle. "Martini?" Before Isabelle could respond she was already signaling Anita, who had left the bar and was headed outdoors. Anita stopped in front of her boss with a tray and Isabelle picked up a fruity cocktail. She wanted a Martini, but she wouldn't give Caye the satisfaction of ordering for her. It was her house and her bar and she could drink whatever she wanted. So she did.

By the time she was on her third cocktail she was less irritated. Isabelle stood off to one corner, studying the room in a forlorn way. She had managed to put several yards between herself and Caye and Harper, and they did not pursue her.

Ravi Holder was there, pinching off little sandwiches from the spread of hors d' oeuvres, and gesticulating among other locals with his mouth full. He still carried that heavy aura of winter and isolation.

"Oh, Miss Bartley," he called, approaching her. "I'm putting on a play as I have done for the last several years. It's not terribly complicated, and I think you might find it quite fun."

Isabelle made affirmative signals toward him to suggest she was listening, but she was distracted by Caye and her spirited arguments about politics, the stock market, and start-up companies with the people who had slipped in and out of her circle throughout the night. Much like her father, Caye hawkishly sought new ways to make money at every turn.

"People really enjoy it," Ravi continued, patting the sides of his belly as if he were about to devour a banquet meal. "I wrote it myself and scripts are available at my office if you're interested in a role."

"You're multi-talented," Isabelle said dryly. "I don't think I'll be able to."

"Well." He paused and lowered his torso in a short bow. "If you change your mind, you know where to find me."

He spun and strutted to the other side of the room, Isabelle assumed, in search of livelier company.

Isabelle turned her attention back to Caye and Harper. Harper seemed content with monitoring Caye's conversation, and greeted everyone else with a shrug or a half smile. As the night wore on, Isabelle detected an unusual disconnect between the both of them. A layer of superficiality wrapped around Caye and Harper like a cloak, and awakened inquisitiveness within Isabelle. She strolled over to them, tired of avoiding her unwelcome company, and emboldened by her drink. She came up to Harper, who was startled by her appearance.

"So what do you do?" Isabelle asked, with a plastered smile.

"Me?" Harper stuttered on the one syllable, as if she had been presented with a quandary.

Isabelle nodded, realizing she derived joy out of making the woman uncomfortable for an instant.

"I'm a philanthropist," Harper finally said. Her voice was melodic but firm, and she seemed to be straining to control it, to take the edge out.

"A philanthropist?"

"Yes."

"Full-time?"

"Yes."

"What kind of organizations do you work with?" Isabelle's interest rose despite her annoyance at what was a clear refusal on Harper's part to discuss her work.

"Several." Harper shrugged. She avoided eye contact, but her glance roved over Isabelle's face at opportune moments.

"I hope you're not required to give any speeches," Isabelle said, half-joking.

"Luckily I'm not."

It was difficult to detect any nuance to her tone, or to determine if she was upset or joking in return. They remained in a sort of suspended state, staring each other down, as if the already awkward circumstances had abruptly become laden with another layer of perplexity.

Still, Harper was oddly expectant, as if she thought Isabelle might ask her more questions, but Isabelle had given up. The party was winding down and all but a few people had dispersed.

Isabelle excused herself, not quite scampering, but her boldness had dissipated. Harper's peculiar energy had knocked her off-balance.

She ran into Benny outside the kitchen, who smiled and greeted her pleasantly.

"Happy to see you out and about," he said.

She ignored his little dig at her reclusiveness, because he was carrying a tray of what looked like tiny chickens. Some had red tails, red combs, and red beaks. Some had yellow and green.

"What is it?" She lowered her face uneasily toward them.

"What do you think it is?"

"Is it egg? Boiled egg?"

"Could be," he said, grinning. She was swaying slightly, and he held onto her with his free hand. "Or it could be chicken."

Isabelle laughed. "Tomorrow I will get to the bottom of this." She wagged her finger at him as if to suggest he would be punished.

"Ooh," Benny teased as she walked away.

She climbed the stairs, holding on to the banister and replaying the events of the evening in her mind. This place was as remote as could be, yet somehow her solitude had been intruded upon. She shook her head and muttered under her breath. How could Caye have left her for such a confounding woman?

Her suite was at the far end of the hallway, and as she neared her door she sensed someone behind her. Isabelle turned to see Caye slithering up to her in the dimly-lit space.

"Why did you come here?" Isabelle asked, surprised. She tried to inject a forceful tone to her voice, but she was thrown off by Caye's sudden nearness.

"I needed to see you," Caye said.

"Why?"

"I didn't plan to bring her," Caye pouted. "She was out of the country, and then she returned unexpectedly."

"She's so wooden." Isabelle then remembered a distinct moment that night when Harper's eyes appeared to brim with a secret pleasure.

"She's a mystery even to me."

"Don't worry about it." Isabelle shook her head, attempting to dismiss that line of conversation.

"Do you miss me?"

"No."

"Well, I missed you." Caye bit her bottom lip. "Looks like you need some help. Why don't you open the door?"

"I don't have my key."

It was supposed to be an excuse, but Isabelle really did not have her key.

Caye's warm breath brushed across Isabelle's face. Her cobalt eyes held an excited glimmer, and she had a strong face, dominated by fervent eyebrows and eagerness and ardor. Caye was the kind of woman who would always be on the hunt for rousing adventure.

Isabelle leaned against the door, feeling cornered, exasperated.

"Caye, you can't just show up like this."

"It's not that big of a deal." Caye shrugged. "I just longed to be close to you again."

"Keep longing." Isabelle let her words and tone sting. "You're with her now."

"Don't be like that. Let's go inside."

Helene's door opened across the hall and she peered at them, looking concerned. "I thought I heard voices." She was still dressed, and perhaps was headed back down to monitor the remnants of the party.

"I don't have my key," Isabelle said. "Can you let me in? Caye was just saying goodnight."

"Of course." Helene retrieved a jangle of keys from her pocket.

They had to move aside so Helene could get to the door.

Caye hesitated, until she realized Isabelle was serious. She sighed. "I'll see you tomorrow." She slid her arm around Isabelle's waist and down toward her buttocks, which she gave a squeeze before disappearing back down the hallway.

❖

The old wooden bench in the garden sat under a canopy of untamed fargesia hedge, which ran along the side of the house and formed its own border at the edges of the garden. The garden itself was haphazard, although the landscapers had been trying to restore order for a few months.

Isabelle sat in the quiet of early morning examining the postcard she was sure had come from Bastian. She was trying to decipher his intention from the image. At age eighteen he had fled Kingston. They thought he had gone to London to a distant relative of Robert's, but that turned out to be a lie he had told to throw them off. Robert's relative had not seen him. No one could pinpoint his exact location. Her brother wanted it that way, Isabelle realized as time passed.

She was alienated and isolated after he left. Her family was being decimated from the inside out and she needed her big brother more than ever. Bastian had been her protector and had provided a sense of security during her formative years. Then one day that security had been taken from her, like a once cozy blanket ripped off, leaving her to shiver against the night chill.

When Marcia began her affair with Haughton, Bastian was fourteen and Isabelle was only nine. Besides being a girl, Isabelle was much too young to be of any interest to Haughton, but in Bastian he saw potential. He groomed him in the ways of handling business: blackmailing, carrying out threats, and beating and killing if it came to that. Powerful people depended on Haughton to maintain law and order in the constituency, to make sure capital flowed the right way, and to ensure that when election time came people voted as they were supposed to. It was a tightly managed operation and Haughton needed soldiers.

Bastian had been transformed into a soulless creature brainwashed by Haughton. He was a child soldier committing monstrosities beyond the scope of imagination. He had always been clever and intelligent, but the violent activities he was involved with took a toll on him. He changed. He became a hardened criminal, an exactor carrying out orders. Perhaps he could also see the terrible change in himself and knew the only way out was to flee, even if he had to leave his family and his little sister behind.

Marcia acted concerned for her son, but the financial gain from Haughton's work was too enticing. She was giddy with excitement over her new adventures with this powerful man. Whenever she came home, she would take Isabelle out to the guava tree in the backyard to talk about her excursions. Isabelle listened with detached interest, digging her fingers into overripe guavas to check for worms. Marcia would go on relaying romantic details about her trips, while Robert was inside studying the horse races.

She whispered about how Haughton took her to explore the North Coast. How they had moved on from Boscobel to a cottage in Montego Bay so she could stretch her limbs out half-naked on the veranda. About how she would go for a stroll down the narrow country road running parallel to the sea and that the sound of the sea was all she needed.

"Just to know it was there," Marcia would say. "I wanted to feel the earth beneath my feet."

Marcia always had her beauty and certain ferocity to her. She was an older version of Isabelle, with intense amber eyes and warm terra cotta complexion, unbothered while others melted under the Kingston sun. In her younger years, she wore her hair brushed back, which left her face open. Much like Isabelle, her features were vibrant and inviting, her lips plump and small.

It occurred to Isabelle how much younger her mother looked than her father. They were the same age, but Robert always wore an intangible burden that perhaps Marcia never quite understood, even though they'd been married for twenty-two years. Isabelle understood her father's burden. It was an amalgamation of the early death of his parents and ill-treatment he endured as a child, the hard labor required of him as a boy growing up in the country, the feeling of vagrancy that permeated his soul, and a tainted mass of fear and cowardice that remained within him even as he became a man.

Robert was a timid craftsman. Marcia was ruthless and fanciful. Such juxtaposition in her mother unsettled Isabelle. She never understood how a person could be filled with such whimsy and lightness, yet coldly execute whatever their heart desired no matter who got hurt in the process.

Robert had died two years after Bastian left home. Isabelle was fifteen at the time, and the day after the funeral she received an anonymous letter. It contained an ink drawing of a single black rose.

While she had sensed Bastian's presence before when they lived in Nutley, his correspondence now via the postcard was baffling. Isabelle had long suspected that Haughton's growing "paranoia" was a result of Bastian secretly taunting him. She remembered the champagne-colored Cadillac with tinted windows that had hung around outside the restaurant on and off for two days. One moment it would be there then the next moment it was gone. Haughton had caught on after a while and had summoned his former right-hand man, Jay Broderick, who had been his "lieutenant" for over two decades. Jay drove down from his home in Connecticut with a resigned air, as if he was merely there to ease his friend's worries. By then the car was long gone and Jay could not pick up the trail.

The postcard was sent to Isabelle at the guesthouse. Her new home. She held no doubt Bastian knew where they were. Isabelle had a hard time deciding if she was also hiding or merely living her life. That could be said about her entire adult years, but figuring out what reason she would have to hide required a certain depth of self-analysis she was not prepared for or willing to allow.

"That has to be some letter."

Isabelle heard Caye speak before she realized someone else was present in the garden. Caye joined her on the bench.

"It's nothing," Isabelle said. She slipped the postcard into her skirt pocket.

"Are you still upset Harper came here with me?"

"I'm not upset." Isabelle watched a small lizard skitter across the grass.

"I still care for you, you know." Caye reached out and smoothed over Isabelle's hair, which lay neatly, voluminously down her shoulders.

"That certainly explains why you moved on," Isabelle said.

Caye shrugged. "She keeps things interesting . . ."

Isabelle got up and strolled through the garden. "Where is she now?"

Caye followed. "She went for a ride with some of the locals."

"Really?" Isabelle chuckled. "*I* don't even know the locals."

"You're not the type to get to know the locals."

Isabelle made a wry face and moved away from her. She pretended to study the newly sprouted flowers. It was a peculiar collection of peonies and clematis clinging to a wire trellis in the center, then a wide bed of yellow and red hyacinths that overwhelmed everything. In a small corner the last of the daffodils remained, shaded by the hedge and the shadows of other plants nearby. It was a solitary flower, and Isabelle bent to look at it closer.

"Isabelle," Caye said impatiently. She held Isabelle's arm and eased her up.

When Isabelle shifted, her heels sank into the soft ground. Caye grabbed her as if mounting a daring rescue, which made them both laugh.

"Those are not exactly shoes for the garden," Caye said.

She kissed Isabelle before she could answer, hesitantly at first then more deeply when Isabelle did not resist. A familiar flicker of excitement flared then petered out inside Isabelle's chest.

When Isabelle opened her eyes a woman was standing by the garden's edge. Harper. Isabelle blushed and pulled away. Caye froze. Then she stepped toward Harper but said nothing.

"Looks like you girls had a better morning than I did." Harper's voice was cool and controlled. "My horse had a stubborn trait."

"I can explain," Caye finally said, but she did not go on.

Harper was wearing shiny high boots and a black chiffon blouse tucked into tan breeches. Her body was lithe and strong, like an athlete's. She held both hands behind her back as if she were a Headmaster sizing up the naughty kids.

Mostly she was watching Isabelle.

Chapter Four

"IT WAS A PRETTY LOW moment." Isabelle sank back against the leather couch in her mother's cabin later that afternoon.

"And she said nothing?" Marcia asked, incredulous.

"Something about having a hard time with her horse. She was so smug, as if she meant to punish us for sneaking around behind her back."

"Which begs the question," Marcia said as she took a sip of her mint tea. "What's going on with you and Caye now? Are you getting back together?"

Haughton had gone outside, and Isabelle knew her mother relished the moments when she could discuss her daughter's love life openly.

Isabelle wouldn't classify her relationship with Haughton as one on a Cold War level. He'd always been terse in his commands whenever he spoke to her, and she spoke to him in a halting style, choosing her words carefully. When she did live at home they co-existed in relative silence. It was a Tepid War.

Marcia was always the buffer between them, which meant she had them both to herself. She served as a steady confidante for Isabelle as she explored dating. In turn, back in the days when it was an extra-marital affair, Isabelle had served as a captive audience for her mother's tales about romance and adventure with

Haughton. Something had always bothered Isabelle about those tales, but she could never quite figure it out. They were over-wrought and superficial, as if to cover for something else.

"I really don't know when it comes to Caye." Isabelle sighed. "She hasn't changed at all."

"Pity," Marcia said under her breath.

"I know you've always liked her."

"She's smart. But relationship-challenged."

"Did I mention that creepy girlfriend of hers wants us to meet for lunch?"

"What do you mean?" Marcia sat up.

"Caye told me Harper wants the three of us to have lunch tomorrow," Isabelle explained, watching closely for her mother's objective reaction.

Marcia thought for a moment. "She wants to have lunch with you after she caught you locking lips with Caye?"

"Told you she was creepy." Isabelle waited. "What do you think?"

"I would be careful. I also would be curious."

"It is intriguing."

Isabelle rested her empty tea cup on one of the coffee tables and looked around. Not much had changed since she was here in late-April.

How much longer did her mother plan to be holed up here with Haughton?

Haughton came out into the clearing from the woods as Is-abelle was walking to her car. He had a machete in one hand and in the other a long satchel with a variety of weeds poking up through the opening. He stopped when he saw her.

"Everything well?" he asked.

"Yes," Isabelle said.

"What have you been up to?" He put down the satchel and rubbed his shoulder.

"I opened a guesthouse." It was old news now, but she had never discussed it directly with Haughton. Right now, the guesthouse was a relatively safe topic of conversation.

"Your mother told me." He nodded. "And how are you managing?"

"I . . . we are managing well," Isabelle admitted. She was hesitant to mention she had a guesthouse manager. "I have a staff helping out."

"That's wise." He paused. "This was a long turn around."

"What do you mean?"

"I haven't seen you in a while."

She had only come to see her mother and to vent about Caye and Harper. Isabelle's skin pricked with embarrassment. Haughton was well aware of when she visited, and she had not gone in to say hello to him on her last trip.

"Last time I was rushing," she said hastily.

"And this time?"

"You were in the woods."

"I guess I was," he said, pensive.

His brown face was broad and intelligent. His beard was patchy along the jawline and he scratched at it. Otherwise, there was symmetry to his features: a clump of gray hair in the middle of his goatee was aligned with a similarly-shaped distribution of grays above the center of his forehead.

Isabelle could tell he was upset. Guilt struck her like a slap to the face. She was the only visitor they allowed here, and she had come by twice in the last month and had intentionally avoided Haughton.

"So you're doing okay?"

"Yes," she said. He had already asked her that.

"Have you heard from your brother?" His eyes narrowed.

"No." She shook her head for emphasis. She had no intention of bringing up the postcard.

Haughton walked over to the porch and sat down, much to her dismay.

"I never had much time to talk to you about life," he said. "It was hectic back then, you know."

Was this confession time? An Hour of Great Regrets? If so, it was too late for any of that. She half-nodded, not wanting to encourage him.

"I could have taught you to be tougher," he said, contemplating. "But you were a girl and I thought as long as you were inside and safe you would be okay."

"I was okay."

"No, you have your father's nature. Smart, but unsure of yourself. Timid."

A bubble of rage rose up inside her. She swallowed hard to push it down.

"Don't talk about Robert," she said, stunning herself. Then she clamped her mouth shut. She had never spoken to Haughton like that in the two decades she'd known him.

He was taken aback, but he smiled a tight smile and looked away, first down at the gravel before him then out at the trees.

"I won't talk about your father," he said finally.

"Good."

"I was better with you than my father was with me," he said in an abrupt manner, as if he had been injured by her unusual defiance. "My father was a preacher. My mother a preacher's wife. Five times a week I had to sweep and wipe the church floors. Every day I got a beating from him – for speaking, sometimes for simply breathing."

Isabelle stared at him. All she had ever heard him say over the years was that his father was a tough man. Restless and tormented, as if he thought his life should have been about so much more than children and a small country church.

"Not one day went by without my father putting his hands on me. So-called man of God." Haughton swatted at a beetle inching its way across the wood railing. "He was a lover of his own damn words. Lover of worship. The congregation were lovers of an idea of God and being saved through singing and shouting and clapping their hands. That's how I saw them as a child."

He clenched his fist. "The first time I held a piece of chrome in my hand I felt truly powerful and I thought, from now on my gun is my God."

Uneasy, Isabelle shifted. She drew a blank on any kind of response. She searched her heart. Should she pity him?

"By comparison." Haughton met her eyes. "You had a damn good life. Regardless of how things shaped up for Robert and Bastian. At least Bastian was a survivor."

At that, Isabelle turned to walk away.

"Don't turn away from me," he said, standing. "I was good to you. I was never a hypocrite. I was the same person out on the street and at home. You remember that."

He picked up the bag and threw it across his shoulder. "Enjoy the rest of your day, Isabelle."

He waited on the porch as she got into her car. After she spun around and headed back down the path, she watched him in the rear view mirror and thought of the time she once plotted his death.

❖

The next afternoon Isabelle went to the Grand Machiné restaurant in town. The streets were much livelier in the warm weather. Storefronts were bright and prominent, and people basked in the atmosphere along the plaza. They stopped and sampled offerings the restaurants had set up out front to lure diners inside. The sidewalks had been hosed down, and vehicles pulled boats along the avenue on the now visible blacktop.

The whole place had awakened, as if someone had blown the dust off a stale photograph and magically brought the town to life.

Isabelle was driven by an impulse not entirely clear to her. She dressed defensively, though she was not conscious of it. She wore her skinny jeans tucked into rugged ankle-high brown boots, with a loose brown blazer. Her leather messenger was slung across her shoulder. She had allowed her hair to have its own way this morning, to show how unimpressed she was with this meeting. Now she was beginning to regret that, for her long curls moved with the wind and with every step she took. They fell across her face, so that she had to grab a fistful and swipe it away.

She went through the spacious bar of the Grand Machiné, where men and women hunched over and spoke languidly, their conversation low. The restaurant had the same match-lit atmosphere as the bar, but only a handful of diners. Caye and Harper were already seated at the table.

Caye was wearing a navy dress and a gray tartan blazer with the sleeves pushed up to her elbows. Her hair was a little unkempt and she looked refreshingly casual.

Harper looked up first – an intriguing expression flashed across her face. Caye stood then sat back down.

As Isabelle walked toward them she was struck by a disconcerting notion. What if this was a sort of kinky game orchestrated by Harper? Were they toying with her?

The waiter came over and took Isabelle's drink order as they exchanged pleasantries. She settled for sparkling water with lemon. She meant business and was not here for wine or cocktails.

Caye cleared her throat, but said nothing. She adjusted her dress and squeezed the lapels of her jacket together.

"I thought we should clear the air," Harper said.

"We should," Caye replied, keeping her gaze on the table.

"Is there something between you two?" Harper asked calmly, her eyes on Isabelle.

"Not anymore," Isabelle said, and was sure of it.

It occurred to her that Harper was the kind of woman Caye's father would have picked for her. She was a rigid, emotionless android who would fit into their cold empire. Alexander Wauburg had once told Caye he thought Isabelle was "too soft." When Isabelle had pressed Caye for an explanation of what he meant, the best she could come up with was that Isabelle was not naturally an aggressive person. If this lunch meeting was any indication, Harper was certainly not the soft, shrinking type.

Harper hesitated for a moment. "Good."

Isabelle relaxed, satisfied she had seen them for what they were, and she had placed her card firmly on the table.

"Did they say rain today?" Caye asked, looking around at nothing in particular.

"We'll get a light drizzle tonight," Isabelle said. "But it should remain like this all day."

"I might go biking on the trail." Caye's cell phone rang. She got up and stepped toward the far corner of the room to answer it.

Harper's eyes followed Caye for a while, but her conversation was out of earshot. Harper fiddled with her wine glass, holding the stem and twirling it back and forth between her fingers.

Finally, she looked up.

"Are you in love with her?"

"What?" The question startled Isabelle.

"Are you in love with Caye?"

"I used to be," Isabelle admitted.

Harper smiled. Warmth diffused across her face. She was wearing an elegant black sleeveless dress with a high neckline. A gold necklace with a brass bulb pendant hung against her chest. Her hair was slicked back into a ponytail, and she had firm cheekbones and a sultry face. Her ethnicity was ambiguous. She looked Mediterranean, and she brought to mind places like Jordan and Lebanon. Isabelle considered asking.

"This is a strange place to vacation," Isabelle said. "Surely somewhere less remote would have been more suitable?" She wanted to figure Harper out.

"It suits me." Harper glanced around the room. "And I've been to many places."

"Where have you traveled?" Isabelle pressed.

"Everywhere." She pursed her lips. "Do you travel, Isabelle?"

"Not since college."

"Where did you go?"

"England, France with college friends."

"Are you adventurous?"

"Not like you, I'm sure."

Harper laughed, but her intense eyes locked onto Isabelle's. "What's the most adventurous thing you've done?"

In the early days of high school, Isabelle had curated raunchy stories written by her friends, and as a result she got sent to the school chaplain for regular counseling sessions. The forbidden kiss she'd shared with her female art teacher was unforgettable, and could have gotten her expelled. Because of that kiss Marcia managed to convince Isabelle to move to the States and finish high school here. She had also taken a liking to weed during that period, purchasing it from Aiden Grant, one of Bastian's old schoolmates. She had put herself in danger every time she went to the shadowy side of town where Aiden lived. But she clamped down on her wayward ways as she got older. Perhaps with age came fear, and she had lost the guts to take chances.

"Nothing worth mentioning," Isabelle said, coming back to the present.

Harper knotted her brows. She didn't believe her.

"You're good at keeping secrets then?"

"Secrets?"

"Yes," Harper said. "The kind that require you to hide things."

Isabelle's face grew hot. She reached up instinctively and touched the side of her face, which was burning.

Before she could respond, Caye came back to the table. "I have to go."

"For what reason?" Harper studied Caye with more intensity than Isabelle had seen from her before.

"My father wants me to meet with a client," Caye said. "I'm sorry."

Harper stood. "Can he not find someone else?"

Now it was Caye's turn to study Harper. It was as if an unspoken secret lay between them. An unpleasant one. Caye leaned in and gave Harper a kiss on the cheek. "Stay and have lunch." She smiled at Isabelle and quickly rushed out.

Harper's eyes followed Caye and remained fixated in that direction long after she had left the room. She was contemplative for a while, until she turned back to Isabelle and clapped her hands together in a resigned way, but her demeanor was far from resigned.

"Just me and you then." She sat back down. "Should we order something?"

"Is this a good idea?" Isabelle asked. This lunch date was odd enough to begin with, and now she was alone with the woman Caye had left her for.

"We can be civil." Harper smiled and her eyes gleamed.

"Since we're already here." Isabelle picked up the menu and stared at it absentmindedly. She had already decided on a salad. Something that would take the least time and effort and would get her away from here as soon as possible.

"Have you decided?" Harper looked at her menu. "I know what I want."

"A garden salad." It was the first salad on the list.

Harper looked up. "Is that all?"

"Yes."

"Well, the duck in Chianti and cherries looks divine."

Isabelle half-chuckled.

"What is it?" Harper asked, looking confused.

"Chianti always reminds me of Hannibal Lecter," Isabelle said, attempting to be funny.

Harper stared at her. Her dark eyes searched for meaning in Isabelle's comment.

Does she not know who Hannibal Lecter is? Or is she offended?

"Hmm," Harper said, looking down again.

Before Isabelle could right any possible offense, the waiter came and took their orders.

"You didn't order a drink," Harper said, after he had left. "How about a glass—"

"I shouldn't," Isabelle cut her off. "I have to go back to work after this."

"They won't know. Besides, what would happen if they did?"

"It's not about anyone knowing."

"You don't drink with your enemies?" Harper's mouth curled at the edge.

Why wouldn't she let it go?

"I'm not in the mood." Isabelle fell silent. She was close to offending her again. Harper likely wanted her to say she was not her enemy. Maybe she thought Isabelle had unfinished business with Caye. That would be why she followed Caye here. That was the reason for this meeting. Isabelle would not use the word enemy, but Harper was clearly jockeying for position.

Harper twirled her wine and Isabelle looked at her phone. They remained like that for a long time, until Harper talked about art: the unexpected ways in which it could capture an emotion or a feeling. How subjective it was; that you could look at a painting twice and come away with a different meaning each time.

"You have wonderful pieces at the guesthouse," Harper said.

"That's Mrs. Keane's art," Isabelle said. "Not mine."

As a way of conceding in the spirit of conversation, Isabelle told her how it had been an all-spring-long project that involved Mrs. Keane diligently meeting with local artists and curating every single piece herself.

Harper indulged her for a while, and then asked pointedly, "Why did Caye describe your place as a refuge?"

"You've been there," Isabelle said dryly. "How would you describe it?"

Harper stared again, as if genuinely stumped. She recovered and met Isabelle's eyes. "Are you hiding from someone?"

Harper had kept her voice light, but her words carried an incisive weight, as if she was trying to get to the essence of Isabelle's being. Isabelle's tongue tripped as she was about to respond. She shook her head instead of answering.

Their meals came and they ate in silence. Harper watched her as if enraptured. Isabelle had made up her mind that the woman was odd, and found comfort in telling herself that once this lunch was over she would never have to see her again.

Harper reached out and pulled on a wisp of Isabelle's hair. The shock of it left Isabelle dumbstruck.

"A piece of lettuce," Harper said, smiling.

Isabelle flipped her hair back quickly, trying to ignore the fact that Harper's gaze followed her every movement, and was now fastened to Isabelle's face.

"Thank . . . thank you," Isabelle said. A flush crept across her skin.

"My pleasure." Harper sliced into her duck and topped it with cherries before forking it into her mouth. Red cherry juice smeared across her lips. She licked it off and smiled again.

"Isabelle Roberts."

Isabelle started. "What?"

"That's you, isn't it? Isabelle Roberts. You write under that name."

"Yes," Isabelle admitted. "But it's not exactly common knowledge."

"I have ways of finding out things."

"Things that are completely irrelevant to you?"

"Not exactly." Harper did not continue.

"I gave up writing," Isabelle said, feeling rattled.

"Why?"

"I don't want to talk about it."

"Perhaps I could—" A message beep sounded on Harper's cell phone and she combed through it eagerly. Her face darkened.

"You won't believe this," she said, regretful. "I have to run."

She dug into her purse and placed cash on the table, signaling to the waiter as she did so.

"I believe it." Isabelle was puzzled by the haste to leave, but it was just another twist in this strange afternoon.

"Let's continue this conversation?" Harper stood. Once again, she had that expectant air to her, as if she wanted *more* from their interaction. As if she wanted to say more even though she was the one leaving.

"I don't think that's necessary." Isabelle waved her hand. "What's there to talk about?"

Harper parted her lips as if to say something else, but instead she nodded and skipped out of the restaurant. And if Isabelle were to allow herself, she would admit that a tinge of disappointment grazed across the back of her neck.

Chapter Five

ISABELLE PACED AROUND the desk in her suite. The exchange between Caye and Harper at the restaurant yesterday still weighed on her mind. They were oddly suspicious of each other, and she found it unsettling. Isabelle considered what she knew about Caye – anything that could cause Harper's hypervigilance. Caye was resourceful and driven. She was her father's true confidante and right-hand woman, and rarely acted outside of Wauburg's directive. Strong rumors a few years back claimed Wauburg had been entrenched in mafia activity when his business was starting out. Over time those rumors died, having been squashed by good public relations and the detoxification of the Wauburg image.

As far as Caye herself was concerned, there was no great secret to uncover, no puzzle to unravel. She loved women and she loved work. Did Harper suspect her of cheating, or was there more to it than that?

Harper and Caye had checked out of the guesthouse, not that Isabelle minded. She was relieved the air was clear between them. She didn't want Harper to believe she was cozying up to Caye again.

Isabelle stopped pacing and tried to return to work writing a copy for an advertisement Helene said would help attract more guests. She quickly gave up on that and rummaged through a cardboard box she had left unopened after moving in. She poured herself a glass of Cabernet and laid the contents out on the floor: a small mustard-colored blanket she'd kept since childhood, an unpublished draft of a novel, and a metal box. She unhitched the little latch on the box and pulled out a stack of documents bound together by an elastic band. It was a hodge-podge of items that were at least fifteen years old: fake birth certificates and passports, fake IDs, bank account details, and several printed emails and letters. Haughton had used this collection, among others, to carry out his operations many years ago. He had kept them hidden in Isabelle's room when she was young, since it was the last place anyone would have thought to look.

It was preposterous to hang on to this stuff for all these years, and Isabelle had an inkling to take the contents outside and incinerate them.

She pulled the .357 Magnum out of the metal box and turned it over in her palm. Its chrome finish was pitted, and the synthetic grip was worn. It had sat beneath the stack of papers unused for so long, Isabelle doubted it still worked.

She had thought about offering her father this gun once, shortly before he died.

Robert had been dressing to go meet his colleagues at the bar one Saturday evening, when one of the workers from the wood factory called him. Haughton Gillespie and his men had come in as they were about to close the shop and "took over the whole place." Isabelle, who had been quietly watching her father ready himself to go out in that stuporous manner he had, saw the alarm in his face, and the inner workings of his mind as he considered what to do. Should he carry on with his evening? Go on with his plans to drink the night away amongst an equally placid crowd?

Should he call the police? That would do no good. The police were on familiar terms with Haughton. Should he go and see what's going on? He nodded to himself.

Isabelle had come up with a solution. She went to her room and slid her storage chest aside. She used a pencil to jiggle the loose floorboard, and once she got it up she saw the box. The .357 Magnum handgun was amongst the small cache of documents, which all belonged to Haughton. Isabelle held the weapon in her hands. It was cool and had the webby smell of the cellar.

She would give it to her father and tell him to tuck it in the waist of his pants. That would take Haughton by surprise, to discover that Robert had showed up packing.

Isabelle went back to the living room. "Dad."

Robert turned and looked at her, still deep in thought. His eyes held a distance indicative of the places he must travel to in his mind.

"You should take precaution," Isabelle said. "Don't you think?"

Robert only sighed. "I should have a talk with that man."

The way he said it frightened Isabelle. A talk about Haughton invading his place of business? Or a talk about Haughton usurping his family and stealing his wife from under his nose? A talk about the destruction of Bastian's future? Her father had so many grievances to hash out with Haughton. He was not up to the task and would never be.

"I'll go with you," she had offered.

"You will stay here." He looked around the room. Marcia had taken off after dinner. "I will be back soon."

With that he put his fedora on and stepped through the door.

Around one o' clock in the morning Marcia called home to say Robert had been shot. Isabelle was numb. She had been awakened from a turbulent dream and stood in the hallway gripping the phone as her mother spoke.

"He came to the factory and demanded that Haughton and his men leave. I don't know why he did that. Lord, I don't know why."

Her whimpering angered Isabelle.

"Who shot him?" Isabelle's voice was as cold as her shivering skin.

"One of the guys," Marcia said, through muffled tears. "Jay Broderick or Royal. I don't know."

Robert spent several weeks in the hospital. He'd been shot in the abdomen, the bullet penetrating vital organs. When they sent him home, Marcia stayed with him for a couple days then she hired a young lady from the neighborhood to look after him. After a week, Robert dismissed the young woman, chasing her off for not cooking the way he liked or for not changing his bandages the way he thought she should.

A month later he died from an infection. Her father, with his meager frame in a sunken bed, had willed himself toward death. He had been willing himself toward death all his life.

A knock at her room door startled Isabelle. She threw the gun into the bottom of the metal box, replaced the documents, and latched it quickly before going to the door. It was Evan.

"I have a message for you," he said.

"What is it?"

"Ms. Harper called." He held out a piece of paper. "She said to give you this and to ask you to call her."

It was Harper's phone number.

"I don't understand," Isabelle said, puzzled. "Why do I need to call her?"

"She didn't say." Evan retreated.

"When did she call?"

"Just now." He shrugged.

Isabelle nodded her dismissal and drew back into her suite. This Harper woman certainly was intriguing. First she refused to even make conversation at the party, then the odd interrogation at lunch, and now she was making unusual overtures Isabelle couldn't quite understand. Isabelle folded the note and slid it between the pages of her agenda book. She wasn't interested in whatever game Harper was playing.

Helene was sitting on the concrete slab that encircled the courtyard fountain. Isabelle went over to her and stood for a while. The early June weather was warm and still carried the newness of summer.

"Beautiful day," Isabelle said, awkwardly trying to break the ice.

Helene kept her eyes closed. "Are you initiating conversation with me?"

Isabelle had to laugh. She rarely interacted with Helene and the rest of staff.

She watched the water dance for a minute. "I've been wondering for some time now. Caye and her friend Harper – what did you think of them?"

Helene opened her eyes. "Aren't they together?"

"Yes," Isabelle said.

"They make a strange couple."

"Why do you say that?"

"There's no real warmth between them." Helene shook her head. "It seems like a relationship of convenience."

So Isabelle was not the only one who had picked up on their strange dynamic.

"I thought the same." She took a seat next to Helene. "Harper arranged a lunch meeting between the three of us so I could promise not to interfere with their relationship. Still, I had the sense that was not what the meeting was about."

"What do you mean?"

"It was as if she was feeling me out, trying to determine what to make of me."

"As competition?"

Isabelle had not made any declarative statement to Helene about her sexuality, but clearly the woman wasn't stupid. She squinted as she waited for Isabelle's response.

"Not quite." Isabelle chewed on her lip, thinking. "Maybe she doesn't see me as a threat. It's more like she decided she wants something from me."

Helene wrinkled her brows, deep in thought.

"Well," she exclaimed dramatically, "whatever could that be?"

She got up and walked absentmindedly toward the back gate. Isabelle followed. She had seen Helene out on her daily walks around the premises. The older woman genuinely loved the place.

"She wants me to call her," Isabelle said.

Helene turned to face her. "Why?"

"No clue. She left her number with Evan."

"How strange."

"And absolutely random, right?"

They went through the gate. The champagne colored Cadillac was parked in the nook of road behind the guesthouse. Isabelle had seen it in town as she strolled the avenue shopping. The windows were tinted, but it was the same car.

"What's wrong?" Helene asked, following Isabelle's gaze.

"That car."

"Who is it?"

Both women stood across from the vehicle, making no attempt to hide their curiosity. The driver's window descended slowly.

"My brother," Isabelle said.

Bastian stood in the guesthouse garden like an oddity, next to the small Redbud tree that was the centerpiece of the whole arrangement. He was rubbing one of the petals between his fingers as if feeling its texture, but soon he rolled it into a red wet speck and flicked it to the ground. He looked up.

"This yours?"

Isabelle was seated on the bench across from him. She decided he was referring to the guesthouse, but when she opened her mouth to speak she realized she'd been holding her breath from the moment he came across the road and they walked into the garden together.

"Yes," she said finally. "We just opened."

"Going well?"

"Yes, so far."

"I've been here."

"Where?"

"In town."

"This town?"

"And other towns."

Isabelle considered. "You mean you've been in the States."

"Yes."

"For how long?"

"Long enough."

Six months? A year? Several years? His cryptic responses did nothing to settle her nerves.

"What were you doing all this time?"

"Living. Planning."

Planning what?

She was afraid to ask. His voice was so hollow and so devoid of heart. It had to be a dream. A childhood fantasy come to life – the resurrection of her self-exiled brother coming home to deliver her from a light-less destiny.

"Didn't you see me that day in Nutley?" His narrow eyes studied her. "Outside the restaurant?"

He pulled out a string of silver magnetic beads from his pocket and pinched at them as one would with a rosary.

She had seen him but had kept quiet, pretending all she saw was a suspicious car like everyone else.

"I did," Isabelle admitted.

Bastian removed his sunglasses and wiped his face with a khaki-colored handkerchief. Isabelle caught the little monogrammed corner that contained his initials: BB. Bastian Bartley. Their father had called him BB when he was little. No one else did.

He wore a short-sleeved khaki bush jacket like the Rastafari-ans tended to do, and navy blue denim. His hair was shaved low, and worry lines creased his forehead. He had a neat face with sharp features and always had the look of a fresh-faced athlete in-stead of a street soldier or a dealer. Now he resembled a hulled out fashion model, as if the essence of him had been excavated by something brutish.

He slid the handkerchief into his back pocket.

"Just greeting you," he said quietly and turned to leave.

"Where are you staying?" Isabelle asked, stunned he would leave so abruptly after having shown up without warning.

"At a motel."

"Nearby?"

He didn't respond. His gaze swept across the garden and at as much of the house as he could see from this vantage point. Then it settled on Isabelle.

"You okay?" he asked, eyes narrowing again.

Isabelle nodded.

"Any of your guests causing you problems?"

"No."

"Your friends?" He broke the magnetic beads apart then squeezed them into a ball. His fist flexed around the mass as if he was ruminating on a hostile memory.

She shook her head no.

"Just checking." He looked at her as if he wanted to say more. "Alright."

He walked away so quietly Isabelle was struck by how surreal the moment was. It was the first time she had spoken to her brother and had seen him face to face in sixteen years.

Chapter Six

THE COCONUT-FILLED pastry whirled across the surface of the water, tilted sideways and sank. One by one Isabelle sent them flying. The disc-shaped gizzardas had stayed hidden in the trunk of her car for the last several weeks, ever since Marcia had forced her to take them home.

Bastian's presence irritated Isabelle. Or rather it was his appearance, because she had always been aware of his presence. Now he had stepped out of the shadows but wouldn't say why. She replaced the lid on the plastic container, now empty, and strolled back toward the house. She went up the little slope of the front lawn then veered left to the parking area. Her Mercedes was parked closest to the house and she reached into the passenger side to retrieve her purse. Then a thought occurred to her. She never found out why Harper wanted to speak to her.

Isabelle leafed through her agenda book and pulled out the sheet of paper with Harper's phone number. She took a deep breath and dialed the number.

"Yes?" Was that how she answered the phone?

"Hello," Isabelle said in a subdued tone. "This is Isabelle Bartley. I'm calling for—"

"Isabelle! I didn't expect to hear from you."

Isabelle frowned. "You left your number for me to call you."

"Oh, I don't mean I didn't expect you to call," Harper said hurriedly. "I thought you wouldn't call, since so much time has passed."

"One day."

"What?"

"One day has passed."

"Well, yes . . . but," Harper stuttered.

"You thought I would return your call immediately." Isabelle smiled to herself. She found Harper's discomfort amusing.

Harper chuckled, relieving the tension. "I must admit I did."

They both fell silent until Isabelle said, "How can I help you?"

"Well, yes okay," Harper started abruptly. "I mentioned my project, didn't I?"

"No."

"Okay, I'm working on a project, a memoir of sorts, but not quite. It's a collection of events in my life, but right now it's all in disarray."

"You're working on a book?"

"I'm not sure. It will be a collection of data . . . I guess I could say. I would like your help to organize everything."

"Well, it's either a book or it's not." Isabelle was being curt but she couldn't stop herself. She was reeling from Bastian's visit and not wanting to think about his motives for showing up. Now she found herself dealing with just as much vagueness from Harper.

"Are you putting together a film?" Isabelle tried to emote patience. "I can assure you I know nothing about that medium. Not that I'm an expert on books or memoirs for that matter. I'm also not agreeing to whatever this is."

To halt her rambling, she took a breath. "What I'm saying is I don't know how I can be of any help."

"I can't go into further details right now," Harper said. "Are you willing to meet with me?"

"Listen, I only came to lunch the other day to set the record str—"

"This has nothing to do with Caye."

"Well now I'm even more confused."

Harper sighed on the other end of the line. "I know it's hard to trust me given the circumstances. You don't know me, but I am a proud person. I wouldn't be asking my girlfriend's ex for help if I didn't think it was," she paused, "important."

"Why me?"

"Oh, gosh." Harper laughed. She sounded nervous. "You are difficult to bargain with."

Isabelle waited.

"Aren't you curious?" Harper asked, an easy allure coming into her voice. "Anyway, I had another thought too, about the guesthouse."

"What about the guesthouse?"

"Well, I told my friends about your hinterland and they think it sounds cool. Wouldn't that be nice? To have more guests coming. Drive up business?"

"Mrs. Keane will be happy to hear that, but why are you helping us?"

"To put it bluntly, so you'll help me."

"With your project?"

"Yes."

The woman was determined, and Isabelle's curiosity had been stoked, though she would not readily admit to it. It was the effortless charm Harper had switched on that did the trick. She wasn't stiff and unfeeling – that much lunch at the Grand Machiné had revealed. Harper was seductive and clever when she needed to be and definitely persistent.

Furthermore, if Bastian was planning to make repeat appearances, mysterious as they were, then she needed to be busy to discourage him. Anything that would get her out of this town for even a few hours was welcome. Even Harper's memoir-slash-life-anthology-slash-convoluted project.

"Okay," Isabelle said heavily, as if agreeing to embark on an arduous expedition or a leap of faith.

"Great," Harper said. "Come up to Chester and I'll explain everything."

❖

Isabelle parked on West Fourth and walked to the Washington Square Diner. The atmosphere was comfortable and familiar, like stepping back into a time when meals were served promptly and without fanfare. Her meeting with Harper was at one in the afternoon, and she had cut across to New York City to grab brunch. She was surprised at how much she relished the opportunity to get away from the confines of the guesthouse, and being able to spend a couple hours alone before her audience with Queen Harper. She of the convoluted indescribable memoir. She of the-I'm-recounting-my-many-great-adventures-to-call-attention-to-myself project. Of course she would be lauded for her ground-breaking vanity piece. As the inevitable wife of Princess Caye and the daughter-in-law of the Great Wauburg of New York, lauded she would be. What did she need from Isabelle? What good was the backing of a self-defeated novelist? Someone who once wrote formulaic junk but no longer had the heart for it?

"Ahem . . . coffee?"

The diner waiter stood over Isabelle's table with a coffee pot.

Isabelle nodded, embarrassed. She had been sitting there sulking as she demonized Harper in her mind. The waiter was proficient and nice enough, and soon she was able to settle into her meal of home fries and a spinach and feta omelet.

Her cell phone buzzed in her purse as she had a second cup of coffee. Caye. Isabelle hit the ignore button and turned to her copy of the daily papers. She glanced at articles about sports stars, celebrities, and the crime story of the day. The overall tone was bitter and sensational, and she lost interest in reading it.

Blithe yellow lighting around the room imbued her with a sense of reverie, and the heaviness that had dogged her for so long abated. She had a view of the street from her table by the window, and the rush hour foot traffic had dwindled. Small gusts of wind carried pieces of trash down the avenue. A man in a gray New York Yankees hat stopped and searched his bag. He pulled out his wallet and counted a few dollars. When he looked up his gaze met Isabelle's and she looked away. He continued up the street past the diner, but when Isabelle looked up again he had turned and was coming through the door. Isabelle picked up the paper and pretended to read in case he had any intention of approaching her. When she turned the page to the gossip section, she forgot about the man entirely.

Two large pictures of Caye took up a quarter of the page with the headline: *NY Socialite Parties with Airline Heiress*. In one picture, Caye walked arm in arm with a wispy blonde, and in another picture she walked slightly ahead of her as photographers surrounded them on the street. The little write-up went on to detail their night at the club:

Gorgeous blonde businesswoman Caye Wauburg let her hair down over the weekend. The daughter of business mogul Alexander Wauburg was spotted dancing the night away at Club Boardroom in the city with airline heiress Gergina Piers. Unnamed sources said the two were "all over each other" and even "made out on the dance floor." We can't help but wonder what Papa Wauburg thinks about his straitlaced heiress frolicking among the commoners, much less allegedly locking lips with a woman so publicly.

Isabelle stared at the page, re-reading the article several times. It was heedless. It was brash. It was incongruous with the woman she knew Caye to be. Despite her shortcomings, being careless was not one of them.

Her phone buzzed again. This time Isabelle picked up immediately. She half-expected to hear the familiar nonchalance in Caye's voice, but instead she was shrieking, at first unintelligibly, then when Isabelle finally got her to calm down she said, "The paper! The fucking paper!"

"I just read it," Isabelle said, lowering her voice. She was afraid the other diners might hear Caye's high-pitched voice on the other end.

"Do you have any idea what this could do?"

"Some . . ."

"This is a fucking mess. They have to print a retraction. Where are you?"

Isabelle told her where she was. "What good will a retraction do? The damage is done."

"Oh my God," Caye groaned. "My father is going to kill me. This is not a good look at all. Our clients are going to think I am a loose party-girl type."

"What about Harper? What will she think?"

Caye fell silent.

"Oh my fucking God," she then exclaimed. "It is going to be much worse than I thought. My father . . . I need you to come with me."

"Where?"

"To Papa Wauburg's office. I need to explain."

"I have an appointment upstate. I can't."

"You have to come with me," Caye insisted. "We have to do damage control before he reads the article."

"There is no 'we.'" Isabelle frowned. "Can't you just pass it off as a fluff piece? What were you doing with that woman anyway?"

"I didn't think you were one to hold a grudge."

Isabelle rolled her eyes. "Don't try to guilt trip me."

"Please, Isabelle. I need you."

Before Isabelle could reply, a black Lincoln Navigator pulled up in front of the diner. The back windows slid down to reveal Caye's worried face. Isabelle paid the check and went outside.

"I'm going to see him now," Caye said.

Isabelle sighed and slid in beside her.

They drove up Fifth Avenue to the gray towers where Alexander Wauburg kept his offices. Caye paced in the elevator with her arms akimbo. When the doors slid open on the eighteenth floor she took Isabelle by the elbow and they walked out together.

Alexander Wauburg's chair protruded above his head like a leather throne, and he looked preoccupied behind his mammoth desk when they entered his office. The windows behind him offered a panoramic view of other skyscrapers, and people hunched over their desks in the building across the street. The drudge of corporate life had never appealed to Isabelle.

Wauburg wasn't a large man, but he always held his shoulders back stiffly and carried himself with surplus dignity and pride that made him look expansive. He had thinning salt and pepper hair and a South Beach tan. His facial expression usually conveyed a practiced pleasantry that was aimed at securing deals and advantageous relationships.

He came over and took Isabelle's hands in his. He kissed her cheek. She had gotten along with him during her tenure as Caye's girlfriend, but they had never gone beyond expected courtesy and acknowledgment of each other's existence. She was surprised to see him so effusive.

"I ran into Isabelle on the street." Caye had a way of making announcements. "I thought she might like to say hello."

Isabelle feigned a smile and took a seat in front of Wauburg's desk as he gestured for them to sit. "I wasn't exactly *on the street*." She raised her eyebrows in a suggestive way and he laughed.

"How are your parents?" he asked.

"They went abroad," she said, without skipping a beat. Every once in a while she would run into an old acquaintance of her mother and stepfather. Her answers had become routine. "They went on a cruise of the Caribbean. Then they made their way to Europe."

"That's superb," Wauburg said glumly. "I live for the day I can retire and sail away."

Caye interjected and prattled on about a report for several minutes. At last she said, "We were just reading one of today's papers, and Isabelle and I came across something rather unfortunate."

"What?" Wauburg in fact had several newspapers lined up on his desk, still waiting to be read. He made no moves toward them.

"Over the weekend I met with a client at the Johnstonian. As you can imagine I took them for a drink after – to show them the pleasures of New York City of course – and here comes this nasty little paper embellishing a night of entertainment."

Wauburg sorted through the stack. After Caye pointed him in the right direction he read the article carefully.

"Hmph." His mood shifted from genuine curiosity to surprise to displeasure all within the few seconds it took him to read it. "This is fucked up."

Caye apologized.

"And . . . well?" He took a cigar from the case on his desk and tapped it against his fingers. "Where is my mysterious friend?"

"She is attending a charity event."

They were talking about Harper.

"I don't know where your head is at." Wauburg stared at the cigar in his hand and shook his head ruefully. "You lost your grip on reality."

"I haven't," Caye said quickly. "I know exactly what—"

Wauburg put his hand up to silence her. He walked over to the window and shoved his hands into his pockets.

Isabelle shifted uneasily. The gravity of the potential impact of Caye's little night out made her uncomfortable. There were things they were not saying and would never say in front of her. She was also sure whatever they were not saying had something to do with Harper.

"I must get going," Isabelle said. "I have an appointment."

Wauburg came over and kissed her cheeks again, smiling with the thin edges of his lips, while his gray eyes remained distant and glazed.

As soon as Isabelle was on the other side of the door he said, "Stop bullshitting around!" She imagined him pointing his thick, ill-shaped finger at Caye as the veins tightened across his face.

She hurried away before he could sniff out her presence behind the door.

Chapter Seven

ISABELLE HEADED UPSTATE on I-87 with a web of thoughts clinging to her brain. She tried to make sense of the conversation between Caye and her father, but couldn't extract any clear explanation. Had she misinterpreted the exchange? Maybe they weren't talking about Harper at all. Still, the strange tension between Caye and Harper at the restaurant made her suspect they were.

When she arrived at the address Harper had given her in Chester, New York, she doubted she had come to the right place. She didn't see an office building or any building for that matter. She had exited off the highway onto a beautifully paved country road flanked by wheat fields and acres of farmland. The directions led her to a number on a gate post and not much else. A long fence stretched out around both sides of the gate and trees hid much of anything that lay beyond.

Isabelle parked outside the narrow gate and went in. She had walked about six hundred feet before the house appeared. It was a simple Georgian structure painted asparagus green. She rang the doorbell three times before Harper opened it. She was wearing a camouflage military jacket with black jeans and Wellingtons. Her hair was pulled back in a loose bun and her dusky dark eyes inspected Isabelle.

"Where is your car?"

Isabelle pointed back toward the direction from which she had come.

"I was expecting you to come from that end. Next time come up the side road. It's easier."

Isabelle was thrown off guard. She wasn't sure if it was Harper's disarming appearance or the allusion to "next time."

"Come in."

Harper led her through the house without stopping to make an introduction to the place. The furnishings were unpretentious and plain. A couch, a book stand, an area where a television might be concealed, lonely accent tables without pictures or flowers, nothing on the walls.

They walked through the kitchen. Standard utensils and appliances, all sparkling clean, two wooden stools around an island in the middle.

Out on the back porch was a table with a pitcher of lemonade and a plate of cookies. Next to that sat two pistols, a rifle, and a basket of apples.

Harper caught Isabelle's train of thought. "My hobby," she said. She handed Isabelle an extra set of ear protectors and picked up one of the pistols. "See that apple there?" She pointed to a single red apple on a post out in the yard. "Watch this."

Harper moved close to the porch railing and brought the pistol up to eye level. She squeezed the trigger and in an instant the apple exploded. Isabelle flinched and almost knocked over the tray of treats next to her. Harper turned and gave her a casual wink. A strange mixture of fear and excitement flowed through Isabelle's body. She couldn't stop herself from blushing.

Harper flushed, and she quickly grabbed an apple and walked out to the post. When she came back she was composed again.

"Have some lemonade." She filled two glasses.

Isabelle took a sip of the cool drink and tried to relax. Had Harper been in the military? A label on the right breast of her jacket read *"V. Harper."*

"What's your first name?" Isabelle asked, wanting to find normalcy in this moment.

"Victoria."

"Victoria?" She had assumed Harper was her first name. In fact, she hadn't given it much thought before now.

"Yes." Harper cleared her throat. "So why did you give it up?"

"Give up what?"

"Writing. To continue our last conversation."

Isabelle frowned. "That really isn't your business."

"Someone broke your heart?"

"Why would that cause me to stop writing?"

"I don't know." Harper shrugged. "You're the one who stopped." Then she looked bashful and kept her eyes averted. "How long did you and Caye date?"

"What?" Isabelle was confused by her topic hopping.

"How long?"

Isabelle was compelled to answer. "On and off. Two years."

"How'd you meet?"

"At a party in New York City."

"You don't seem like the party type." Harper sat up. "Did you stop doing that too?"

Isabelle didn't answer and instead stared out at the expanse of the backyard. The yard was vacant apart from a small storage shed in the back, the target post and a narrow table hitched to-gether with two planks of wood for the top, and two slender beams for the legs. The rest was barren brown grass that ran into oat-colored wheat fields beyond the fence. There were no oth-er houses for miles. Isabelle was struck by the sense that Harper must not spend much time here. It was a refuge. Perhaps it was a hideout.

"What do you think of Caye?" Harper asked, pulling Is-abelle's attention back to her.

"Are we still playing this game?" Isabelle shot her a disap-proving stare.

"What game?" Her tone suggested innocence.

"Where you interrogate me as if I owe you an explanation for something."

"Well," Harper twisted her lips into a guilty smirk, then smiled. "About my project."

"Right."

"I already have the story. I need you to help me package it. I sense that you . . ."

"Why don't you start by telling me about yourself?" Isabelle said quietly.

The guns, the locale, and this arcane project were making her queasy. It might have been a mistake to come here, to meet with Harper at all.

"What would you say if I told you I belong to a defunct vigilante organization that now wants me dead?" Harper held her gaze. The look in her eyes frightened Isabelle, but Harper laughed and said, "I'm only joking."

She crossed her legs at the knees and leaned back in her chair.

"I guess I should begin at the beginning. My family is from Newport, Rhode Island. That's where I grew up." She paused, considering. "I never enjoyed being at home when I was a kid. My family liked to bicker over money, and I always wanted to be somewhere else. So I went abroad as much as I could." A wry smile curved her lips. "Finally, once I was done with school, I went to live with my Aunt Roslyn in Turkey. I spent time modeling across Europe, attending parties, and doing things that misguided young girls in their early twenties do." She paused again. "I met a man named Steven Smyth who taught me about charity and being selfless, so my life took shape. I learned how to find fulfillment through helping others."

Harper got up slowly and walked to the edge of the porch, lost in her thoughts. Then she sat on the railing, facing Isabelle. "This is where youthful idealism got the best of me. An organization called The Maramaxe Relief Fund, based in Turkey off the Black Sea, provided food and tent materials at refugee camps across the Middle East. Steven Smyth had been aware of this group and told me about it. I worked with them. We would go out and serve food to the refugees based in Turkey, and bring them medicine and so on. I met . . . people whose lives had been ripped to shreds. Families separated from each other. Children." Harper pressed her lips together. "We kept biographical documentation on them for records. Six months into working with this charity, I noticed files were going missing from our local headquarters at Maramaxe."

"The records on the refugees?" Isabelle asked.

"Yes, and at first I attributed that to a faulty and disorganized filing system. I installed a lock and distributed keys to my colleagues. When the files were still being tampered with, I concluded someone was taking them or taking information from them."

Isabelle exhaled audibly. Tension rose inside her body.

"I went to my superiors and was met with silence," Harper said. "So over the course of several months I kept notes on the files that went missing, and when they did, I tracked the person whose profile had been stolen. They had all left the refugee camps and ended up at various construction sites in Turkey, Syria, or even back in their own war torn land."

She came back to the chair and took a drink of lemonade, before turning to face Isabelle.

"I learned through sources that a few of those people had disappeared from the job sites they'd been shipped off to. I became extremely fearful for them. I told my Aunt Roslyn that their abrupt disappearance probably meant they were dead. She told me to leave it alone, but I couldn't."

Harper ran her hands across her face and sighed. "I compiled an exposé on the Maramaxe Relief Fund, detailing the missing files, the illegal construction site labor, and the subsequent disappearance of those people. I mailed this report to high ranking officials at Interpol and boarded a flight back to Rhode Island."

"When was this?" Isabelle asked.

"More than ten years ago."

"What did you do when you got back?"

"Nothing. I buried myself in my family's business and charity work."

"What became of the exposé? Was anyone arrested?"

"There was brief mention of an investigation, but you know how these things are. The authorities don't publicize their case before they have wrapped it all up."

"So you never learned of charges being brought? Did you ever find out who was funneling the refugees out of the camps illegally?"

"Later on, I managed to gather details about who was responsible." Harper paused. "But that is something I cannot divulge."

Isabelle didn't disbelieve Harper's story entirely. She was sure part of it was true, but it was riddled with pockets of omissions and distortions. She suspected Harper had not given her the full scope of what happened.

"Why didn't you remain in Turkey and go directly to the authorities?"

"I couldn't. I was smart enough to understand the danger. It was . . ." She paused and looked down. "It seemed to be a massive operation. The charity was infiltrated somehow, and people were being trafficked for slave labor." Tears pooled in her eyes and she looked away. "Or worse."

When she had sufficiently recovered she continued. "How does one begin to tackle all that? I did the best thing I could think of, and that was to alert the authorities. I left it in their hands."

Isabelle's mind was racing ahead before she could reason with herself. Finding the people responsible shouldn't have been difficult. Who had been running those construction sites? What were they building and who was paying for it? That would have been a strong start to the investigation and would have led to a few indictments. The only way an investigation like that could have stalled was if the law enforcement officials were somehow implicated or the criminals were too powerful, and too connected.

"What if they were indicted and you were not aware of it?" Isabelle asked, considering a less cynical view.

"Not one person was arrested," she said flatly. "That was when I knew I had put myself in deep shit."

Over ten years ago. Yet she had come home to the states and presumably resumed a normal life. Had she lived in fear? In hiding?

"Did they try to find you?" Isabelle asked.

Harper's face tightened and grew pale. A passing cloud of terror and confusion darkened her expression. "Many times." She took a sip from her glass, but before Isabelle could get a good study of her face she got up. "Wanna shoot?"

"No." Isabelle shook her head.

"Are you afraid?"

"I have no interest in guns."

"This is something you need to experience," Harper whispered. She leaned in and held her hand out. The shift in her was magnetizing. Was she done reminiscing about her ill-advised exposé? Isabelle's imagination had been playing out images of risky whistle blowing scenarios and complicated political crimes. She was trying to get a handle on who this woman was and what she had done. And now she had switched gears and was inviting Isabelle to shoot at red apples in the middle of nowhere.

"How did you meet Caye?" The question popped out before Isabelle could stop herself.

Harper was perplexed at the question. She didn't respond. Instead she pulled Isabelle up gently by the arm, leaving behind a warm sensation at the spot she touched. "Let me show you how to shoot."

She brought one of the pistols and ammunition and laid them out on the table in the yard. Even though they were closer to the apple, Isabelle had no chance of hitting it.

"I should find a bigger target," Harper said, looking around.

"That's not necessary. I'll just watch you."

She did not insist, and for that Isabelle was grateful. She had no desire to fire a gun. Harper loaded it slowly and meticulously, as if her mind had wandered elsewhere.

"We were introduced," she said finally.

"You and Caye?"

"Yes. At a bar somewhere. An acquaintance thought we would make a good match." She turned. "Does she talk about me?"

The day had started off strangely with Caye and her father dancing around the Harper subject before Isabelle had fled that tension-filled room. It was even stranger now, and she wanted to keep information between these two groups of people, at least where that information intersected with her, at a bare minimum.

"No," Isabelle said. "She hasn't said much about you."

"She has never spoken to you about me?" Harper's brows furrowed.

"We haven't had occasion to." Isabelle stood her ground. "That apple still looks small from here."

"You've met her father, Alexander, right?"

"Yes, of course."

Harper was pensive as she held the pistol. "Go on." She brought the gun up and aimed, but did not fire.

"Haven't you met him?" Harper made her nervous.

"Briefly."

"Then you should have an idea . . ."

"I never accept anyone at face value," Harper said. "There is always a part of us that is hidden. Locked away. How involved is Caye with his business?"

"You might say she is his right hand."

"He might confide in her and she in him?"

"You could say so." Isabelle waited. It was as if she could detect Harper's thoughts pinging across her brain.

"And does she do his bidding?"

"Bidding?" Isabelle feigned confusion.

"If he needs something done, and it is within her power to do it, would she?"

"I get the sense you're not talking about business."

"I don't mean to be so coy." Harper smiled coyly then. "You have a deeper connection to Caye. Though we are strangers I trust you for some reason."

"Is your relationship with her serious?" Isabelle asked, attempting to steer the conversation. Whoever introduced them thinking they were a good match was misguided.

"It's hard to say," she said. "Caye is neither here nor there."

"Caye does what her father tells her to do."

"I've always thought so." The wind ruffled loose strands of Harper's hair and they twirled across her face. She brought the gun up again and her eyes darkened with intense focus. When she pulled the trigger the noise rattled Isabelle even more than before. Harper turned and held her shoulder to steady her, but that only increased Isabelle's nervousness.

"Why did you invite me here?" Isabelle fought to regain her composure. "You don't even know me."

"You seem goodhearted. Is that not true?"

Goodhearted. It sounded so simple.

After the chaplain of her high school had discovered her propensity toward girls, he had once told her she was like an ornate tomb. That enclosed within her, beneath rather pleasing features, lay moral decay and a scanty collection of foul bones. He had a real way with words.

"You said you never take anyone at face value," Isabelle reminded her.

"I believe I know exactly who you are."

The certainty in her voice shook Isabelle to her core. She turned away, avoiding Harper's eyes, and made her way back to the porch.

Harper followed closely behind her.

Isabelle took a seat, and without looking up said, "Tell me how I can help with this project."

Back in her room, Isabelle opened her laptop and did a Google search. She typed "Victoria Harper" into the search bar and scrolled through the results. She came across a blog titled: *The Harpers of Newport*. Harper's mother, Patricia, was a politician and a third-generation American descended from Indian immigrants; her father, Edward, of Scottish-American descent, was a social magnate and former playboy. Throughout their history the family had amassed a conglomerate of newspaper and magazine companies, as well as a radio show. There was brief mention of a family clothing store. Isabelle glossed over all of that. She found little details on the woman herself.

Before she left Chester, Harper had told her the end game was to get justice against the human traffickers and murderers. Isabelle questioned whether that was still possible after so much time had passed. It seemed farfetched, unless there were subsequent crimes and a plethora of evidence existed against the perpetrators. Harper would not confirm whether this was the case. She said she would gather the data and all she needed from Isabelle was a promise: that when the time came Isabelle would be willing to compile the story in whatever format she saw fit, a book or an article. It was an obscure plan and Isabelle told her she could not commit to the project until she had a firmer grasp on the details of the story. Harper had reluctantly agreed, offering to set up another meeting to fill Isabelle in on the "nuances" of her life.

Isabelle was trying to fill in the nuances on her own. One of the search results brought up the website for the Eugenie Bradford-Harper Foundation, which was named after Edward's grandmother. The site highlighted philanthropic work they had done over the years, working with children's charities and providing support in war torn places. There was nothing about the organization Harper mentioned.

Isabelle typed "Maramaxe Relief Fund" into the search bar. The first result was a link to a vacant website featuring a small paragraph in the middle of the page:

In 2007, The Maramaxe refugee organization disbanded due to lack of funds and resources to properly execute management and monitoring of displaced people. We have closed our doors, but our hearts remain open and with those who have suffered hardship at the hands of others.

So it was true at least that the organization had existed. Had it been shut down because of the report Harper sent to Interpol? Isabelle clicked through a few more results, but found no further details about the organization. No news reports? No blog commentary from volunteers? Where were the articles?

Equally frustrating was the lack of information on Victoria Harper. It was as if she did not exist on the Internet, which was next to impossible in this era. One page delved into the exploits of Edward Harper and the long list of women he romanced during his heyday. A blurb at the bottom of that article, apparently about Victoria, read: *Another failed attempt at reform for Edward's daughter, Crashes out of West Point after six months.*

The line contained a hyper link, and when Isabelle clicked on it another window popped up. This one displayed the error message: *Page Not Found.*

What was Victoria Harper hiding, and why was she so adamant about involving Isabelle? She must have friends to call upon – people with skills and experience who could help her. Had Harper even broached the topic with Caye?

Sure, Isabelle had been snared by the woman's persuasive skills in the moment, but now with the benefit of reflection, she had her doubts. How could she agree to have anything to do with this, whatever *this* was?

Isabelle had been in the basement for the last hour, not rummaging, as Helene liked to put it, but working on something tangible. She was repairing a broken table. Yesterday she had glued the top back on, and now that the glue was dry, she had decided to paint it.

Helene came downstairs as Isabelle was selecting the sandpaper – one with fine grit to remove the existing layer of varnish. Helene wore a crisp polyester blend frock in quiet brown and teal. Today, a red beaded necklace added a pop of color to her church matron ensemble.

Isabelle watched as Helene stopped in the middle of the staircase and studied the scene: Isabelle in baggy light blue jeans and a tight white T-shirt tied at the waist to reveal her taut midriff, surrounded by a few disheveled boxes, the healed table in her lap, and several swaths of sandpaper laid out on the floor like an unfolded fan.

"Do you think that would be useful?" Helene stared at the table.

"I'm sure there's a place for it upstairs."

"There are people who can do that sort of thing for you." Helene had a pleasant face, but her brows knitted in bewilderment, as if Isabelle were a riddle she was trying to solve.

"It's a good way to pass the time," Isabelle said.

"Have you managed to find inspiration here?" Helene came to the bottom of the stairs.

"What do you mean?"

"With your writing. I find it peaceful to be surrounded by all this greenery. You should try the fresh air."

"I went for a drive Upstate." Isabelle ran her fingertips across the sandpaper. "It was one of the strangest things I've ever experienced."

"Upstate?"

Isabelle laughed. "I had a meeting of sorts with Victoria Harper."

"Really now?" Helene's voice had a cautious tone to it, as if she was leery of what Isabelle might say next.

"She asked me to meet with her to discuss a project she's working on." She set the table aside, stood, and dusted off her jeans. "Thinks I could help her organize her life story."

"Why you?"

Isabelle shrugged. "That still isn't clear to me."

"What made you decide to meet with her? I thought at worst her presence at the party was inappropriate and unwelcome, and at best you found her odd and unfriendly."

"It's hard to explain." Isabelle did not want to tell Helene she found Harper alluring, exciting even. "I was nervous about my brother's visit. Or maybe I was bored."

Helene gave Isabelle her trademark confounded stare.

"Anyway," Isabelle said, before Helene could reveal what was on her mind. "She's got quite a story. About how she tried to bring down an international crime syndicate."

"Beg your pardon?"

"She did," Isabelle went on. "More than a decade ago and now she has plans to write about all of it."

"You're not joking." Helene looked incredulous.

"I'm telling you what she told me. She was quite serious."

"Isabelle, this isn't making much sense." Helene perched on top of a box and shook her head. "You have no idea who this woman is, yet you gobbled up an outlandish tale she fed you."

"I don't believe every word of it, but I do think the gist of the story is true."

"That's even worse." Helene widened her eyes for emphasis.

"You're right." Isabelle rolled up the sheet of sandpaper she was holding and wrung it around in her hands, smooth side out. "You're absolutely right."

"You said she 'tried' to bring them down. Was she successful?"

"Not quite, by the sound of it."

"Alarm bells are ringing in my head." Helene narrowed her eyes. "Tell me you're not going to help her?"

"I suggested I would, but now I don't know."

"I can't tell you what to do." Helene stood. "But you should stay away from her. I'm not saying that because I am a worrisome old lady. It's prudent."

Isabelle nodded, but it wasn't convincing.

"It's not normal for you to be friendly with this woman. I find it hard to believe you considered helping her."

"This may sound strange, but I felt compelled. I find her unsettling, yet . . ."

Helene looked at her closely. Then the older woman's face fell open, as if she'd had an awakening. She drifted toward the stairs, lost in contemplation.

"What is it?" Isabelle asked, as Helene went up a few steps. "Mrs. Keane?"

Helene stopped and half-turned to look at Isabelle over her shoulder.

"Be careful," she said quietly, as if she was already thinking of the things that could go wrong.

"I haven't even committed to it." Isabelle held her hands up to reassure her. "I'm still gathering information."

Helene nodded and gave her a faint smile. "Okay," she said, before going back upstairs.

Isabelle sighed and dropped the sheet of sandpaper onto the table. It's not like she had signed a contract to work on the project. She was merely fascinated by Harper's story and the glaring holes in it. The woman herself was shrewd, and that, Isabelle had decided, was the main factor fueling her own curiosity.

Chapter Eight

THE CABIN LOOKED VACANT as always. Dried shrubbery appeared to be rooted in the same spots Isabelle had last seen them in, as if they were frozen in time. The familiar creak of the porch boards announced her arrival. She stood by the door and waited. She knocked. No sound came from inside the house and Marcia did not appear.

Isabelle knocked again.

Silence.

Darkness from within the house expanded and enveloped her on the porch. She looked toward the woods. Its own darkness moved toward her like a mist. Isabelle circled around to the back of the house where the trees pressed in.

She knocked at the back door.

No answer.

She went back to the front and sat on the top step of the damp porch for several minutes, considering. Then she descended the steps quickly, willing herself, and walked to the edge of the woods filled with jersey pines and grand oak trees. She peered in, took a few more steps, and scanned through the low hanging branches. Isabelle looked back at the still cabin and hoped to see the dull light come on inside. When it didn't, she stepped onto the dense path before her, in the same direction she had seen Haughton come from the last time she had visited. The narrow light from the flashlight application on her cell phone led the way over the moss- and bramble-covered ground. Every surface was slick from rainwater, and the foliage glistened with perfect little dew drops.

A soft wind whispered, but all else was quiet. She moved further into the trees. Isabelle sought out areas that might show signs of a clearing from where Haughton might have collected plants for his greenhouse. What could be gleaned from that she did not know. A reaping, cutting, clearing of sort would indicate the presence life in this dense darkness.

She was chilly. Coming in here alone to search for her mother and stepfather when it was obvious they were not here was illogical. She wanted to call out, do something to calm the nerves that had flared up. A rapid tapping sound drew her attention and she brought her cell phone up quickly, startled at the disturbance. A red-headed woodpecker was nipping away at tree bark. She lowered the light again and retreated toward the cabin. A plank of wood was on the ground under a sprinkling of leaves and twigs. Isabelle didn't have the courage to investigate further. She jogged back to her car, and as she reached the clearing at the cabin the sound of crickets pierced the air. It was a shrill, lonely sound in the dark.

Marcia and Haughton were gone.

Isabelle remained in her car on the grassy shoulder of the quiet back road. Ten minutes had passed since she'd left the cabin, but she was rooted to the spot a few turns down the road. Neither her mother nor her stepfather had a cell phone. They did not have a land-line. In this day and age, Haughton had once said, it was unwise to have a phone if one did not want to be found. So they had cut themselves off from the world.

Now they were cut off from Isabelle too.

She should go back and find a way inside the cabin to search for clues. To figure out where they could have gone. What could have persuaded them to leave so suddenly, without telling her? She had been their only connection to the world since they went into hiding. Her chest tightened. They were afraid. Something or someone must have scared them off.

Bastian was the only thing that made sense. He must have contacted them with threats. He had always been brash and vengeful, and once Haughton took him on as an apprentice those traits came to the forefront.

Haughton had taken the family out for ice cream one afternoon, and Marcia and the children sat together outside the ice cream parlor as Haughton chatted with two men. Isabelle could not hear what they were saying, but those two men always gave her a sense of trepidation. One of them was Jay Broderick, who had a habit of winking at her whenever they made eye contact.

As they talked and gesticulated, Haughton was becoming more agitated. Isabelle could tell from the way his shoulders jerked back and forth. He turned and found Bastian with his eyes.

"Come," Haughton said. Bastian was fourteen at the time, and he walked over to the men with his ice cream cone. "Get rid of that."

Bastian hesitated and Haughton slapped the cone from his hand.

"Time to handle some business," Haughton said. "I want to find this Eric."

The three men and Bastian got into the car. Marcia called out. Haughton had forgotten about her and Isabelle in his haste.

He thought for a moment then said, "Come on."

Marcia and Isabelle had squeezed into the car and they drove through the low, blue-green hills of St. Andrew until they came to a house barricaded by pink iron grills around the veranda. The place was isolated from the shanty cluster closer to town and was secluded by orange trees and thick banana trees spread across the property.

"Go get him out," Haughton commanded.

The other man, Royal, went to the trunk and pulled out a hacksaw. He cut through the iron bars that caged the house, and the shrill sound made Isabelle scream. Hunched up against her mother on the back seat, Isabelle could clearly see from the way the padlock dangled that the grill was already unlatched. Royal could have walked right in.

A rumbling sound came from within the house, and then the men realized what was happening. Isabelle caught sight of the in-habitant, Eric, as he charged out through a door at the side of the house. Before he could right himself they were after him. They chased him up a grassy slope that leveled off onto a cement pave-ment, wet with water pouring from a standing pipe. They caught Eric and flung him to the ground. He fell into a bucket of cloth-ing sitting in rinse water. They slammed him several more times until his clothes were soaked and a splatter of blood appeared on his forehead and lips.

"Where you put it?" Haughton huffed, his breath ragged from the chase. "You take me for a fool?"

Eric yelped something. "No" or "don't." It was hard to tell through the anguish in his voice.

"Bastian, bring the saw."

Isabelle then remembered her brother. Bastian had been staring at the man, mesmerized, terrified. Somehow the front of his shirt was soaked too. Water slid down his forearms and face. He was shaking.

"Bring the saw," Haughton told him again. This time Bastian trudged back down the small hill to the front of the house. He hesitated to pick up the hacksaw.

Then Marcia was beside him. She held on to it, supporting Bastian's lanky arms. Isabelle had not seen when her mother got out of the car, but now she was there, a member of the team of assassinators, leading her son to take a man's life. Her expression was oddly focused and cold.

Tears formed in Bastian's eyes and Haughton studied his face long and hard.

"Get to work," he had said.

The smooth chimes of Isabelle's ring tone brought her back to the present. She looked at her phone. Harper was calling while she was in the bushes having a terrible reminiscence.

"Isabelle?"

Isabelle had picked up but was not speaking. She was crying.

"What's wrong?" Harper asked. "What happened?"

The concern in her voice was comforting, like a pocket of warmth in a cold room.

"My parents," Isabelle blurted. "They're gone. My brother took them."

Isabelle drove back to the guesthouse, showered quickly to comport herself, and brewed a pot of Chai tea. She tried to let reason take over, tried to calm her nerves before Harper got there. She had insisted on visiting Isabelle after her freak out over the phone earlier. Now Isabelle felt silly, like she had been melodramatic or would come across as weak.

To Isabelle's surprise, when Harper arrived she looked even more agitated and alarmed than Isabelle felt. She swung into the suite, wearing a long khaki trench over black jeans and high brown boots. It had rained on and off for most of the day and gloomy darkness hung in the atmosphere. Harper brought the turbulence with her into the room.

She threw her bag down and turned to Isabelle, sizing her up. Then she reached out stiffly and touched Isabelle's arm. Heat radiated from the spot and across Isabelle's skin.

"Are you better now?"

"Y-yes, much better," Isabelle mumbled. "You really didn't need to trouble yourself."

"It's no trouble." Harper looked around the room. "Nice place."

"Thanks." Something else was on Harper's mind besides Isabelle's dilemma. "Would you like tea or something stronger?"

Harper thought for a moment. "Tea with something strong."

Isabelle poured two cups of Chai and added a dash of Appleton Estate rum to each.

"I'm sorry for my hysterics," Isabelle said, as they sat on the couch. She took a deep breath. "Not sure what came over me."

"What's this about your parents? You said your brother took them."

"I . . . misspoke." Isabelle didn't want to get into her family drama. "It was dark and they weren't answering the door. I thought the worst."

"So your parents are fine?" Harper took a sip of her tea without taking her gaze off Isabelle's face.

"I believe so, yes."

"Are you just saying that to keep me out of your business?"

Isabelle nodded. "Sorry, this is all just . . . a lot seems to be happening right now."

"Including me being here?"

"Yes."

"I just came to have a cup of tea." Harper pulled her off trench coat and sat back, crossing her legs.

"You didn't know there was tea until you got here." Isabelle met her eyes then quickly looked away. It was as if Harper was trying to see into her soul.

"True," Harper said, letting her leg dangle playfully.

"So?"

"So what?"

"What made you show up here this evening?"

"I missed your place. I missed your 'little refuge.' How's that?"

"Bullshit."

Harper laughed. "I get that you're afraid to talk about your family, but I assure you I mean no harm. In fact, I came because I was worried about you. You sounded so upset."

"And what were you planning to do about my upset?" Isabelle went to great lengths to keep the flirtation out of her voice, because she suddenly had a strong urge to *flirt*.

"Try to calm you. Maybe console you." Harper's eyes flicked up. "In platonic way, of course."

Isabelle was skeptical, but she had to smile. "I don't want you to think this is appropriate," she said, affecting a serious tone.

"There's Caye for starters, and our complicated short history because of her."

"Well, like I said at the Grand Machiné – we can be civil."

"Why do you want us to be civil?"

"The better question is, why not? Just because on the surface we're supposed to be arch enemies doesn't mean we have to be. I think we get along well. Don't you agree?"

"We do."

"And I . . ." Harper took a sip of tea, as if to shut herself up. She fell silent.

What was she about to say?

Isabelle wasn't brave enough to ask. The energy between them was precarious, like the lines could become blurred if they weren't careful.

Isabelle shook off the feeling and cleared her throat. She owed Harper an explanation for crying over the phone like a weakling and for letting her come all this way.

"I feared the worst because of the type of person my stepfather is," she admitted. "He's made some enemies over time."

"Who hasn't?"

"He was a brutal man," Isabelle continued. "Not to me, but to a lot of people, and certainly when it came to dealing with my brother, who was thrown into the old man's world head first."

Harper nodded.

"My brother, Bastian, never recovered and despised my step dad for the shitty way his life turned out." Isabelle drew a sharp breath. "Now Bastian is back in town. Who knows how long he has been here actually, watching us."

"You think your brother wants revenge?" Harper brushed back a few wild strands that had escaped from her ponytail.

"If I had Bastian's nature I would be hell bent on making the old man suffer, even just a little bit."

"Is that what he came here for? For them?"

"Yes. He certainly didn't come for me."

The moment Isabelle said it a cloud of doubt shifted across her mind. Then she shook it off. She had done nothing to harm Bastian or to hinder him. She was an innocent bystander. If anything she had cause for resentment too, the way Marcia and Haughton had brushed her father aside. They were to be blamed for his death. It also hurt her that Bastian had not come to the funeral, even though he must have known.

"You don't?" Harper asked.

"Don't what?"

"Want to make the old man suffer?" Harper furrowed her brow. "Your step dad has never done anything to make you want to punish him?"

"My brother and I are not the same." Isabelle lowered her gaze, aware of the dark emotions welling up inside her. She disliked Haughton in the early years, when he first shadowed her mother like a hippopotamus. As time passed, Isabelle had developed an enduring rancor toward him. Of course she wanted to make him suffer for what he did to Robert.

Isabelle kept her emotions hidden from Harper, who sat back and was lost in her owns thoughts for a while. She was much calmer now, and Isabelle relaxed as well.

"Wait and see what happens," Harper said quietly. "Your parents might have gone somewhere they don't want you to know about. Perhaps they decided on a whim."

When she saw the confusion on Isabelle's face she added, "I think it is premature to blame your brother."

"What makes you think they wouldn't want me to know where they've gone?"

"Because they sound far from naïve." She held Isabelle's stare. "In my very worldly opinion."

Isabelle wanted to inform her she was the only person who was entrusted with knowledge of their whereabouts. They needed her.

"I bring them groceries," was all she said.

Harper's brows arched up sarcastically.

Isabelle looked away. She was being whiny and artless. Harper was acting like she had a better understanding of Isabelle's own parents than she did. As if she was an expert on this sort of behavior.

Harper got up and went to look out the window at the water. Isabelle watched her and waited. Something about her was familiar. She was the woman Isabelle had seen from her window the night of the opening party. She was also the woman who had remained grave and brooding all night, while Isabelle had struggled with the awkwardness of seeing Caye again.

Now here she was, still grave and brooding, yet so much more.

Isabelle had reflected on the story Harper told her about the corrupt charity in Turkey, and the more she thought about it, the more certain she was Harper had not told her everything. If the house in Chester was an indication of anything, it said Victoria Harper was a dangerous woman. She was a woman with secrets, but she was also powerful and vengeful. Though the reason for possible retribution was not yet clear.

Isabelle recognized vengeance in Harper's heart, for she also carried the stain of vengeance deep within her. After Robert died, she had dreamt of ways to kill her stepfather. She imagined waiting till nightfall when he gardened in the backyard. She'd take the gun from the box under her floorboards and sneak outside. In her fantasies she'd point the gun at his back, but she couldn't pull the trigger. Isabelle had seethed and plotted for months, but never spurred herself into action. Not in a way that really mattered.

She lacked the steely viciousness and determination she saw in Harper, from their one meeting in Chester, and she was in awe of the fact that Harper possessed qualities she herself did not. She had been rattled when Harper claimed to know exactly who she was, but now Isabelle was assured. She could sum up who Harper was as well: She was a woman who could finish you with one decisive shot of lead. A woman who would not waver when the time for retribution came. Victoria Harper was a woman who righted wrongs against her with violence and aggression.

". . . past might catch up to you?" Harper had begun to speak so softly that Isabelle missed half of what she had said.

"What?"

"I sometimes think about the past." Harper turned around. "Okay, I think about it a lot."

"Everyone does," Isabelle offered, unsure of where she was going.

"When I was younger," Harper said, "In my teens and early twenties, I lived for fantasy. I had a foolish, self-righteous idea of what my family legacy was. I did everything I could to live up to that misguided fantasy."

"What did you think your family legacy was?"

Harper stared, considering. Isabelle suspected she had asked a question her enigmatic acquaintance was not ready to answer.

"Complicated." Harper's eyes flicked away. "In my view, we sometimes find ourselves on a wretched course without knowing how we got there, or how to choose a better path. I see the similarities when it comes to certain elements of our families."

"My family and your family?"

"Yes."

"You mean there's a washed-up Jamaican Don in your family as well?"

She laughed. The darkness in her eyes dissipated.

"Maybe not a washed-up Jamaican Don, but I had a great-grandmother who was probably just as vicious as any killer."

The moment she said it her face flushed then grew sallow at once. She had said too much. Isabelle remained quiet, sensing this was a moment where the blank pages could be filled in.

"I know I asked for your help," Harper said quickly. "And I do need it – I need some semblance of measured-ness. I need someone who is at a safe distance who can memorialize the mess in some way. Even if I never get what I'm after in all this, I still need for it to be known. To be chronicled."

Isabelle nodded. Harper was struggling.

"There's so much to tell you, but I can't right now."

"What are you after?" Isabelle asked, finally.

"Resolution." Harper slid her hands into her back pockets. "It might not come easily and it might not come peacefully."

She held Isabelle's stare, ensuring that she understood the gravity of what she had said.

Isabelle nodded. She was swept up by the grand complications of Harper's life: what she did as a young kid to try to live up to her "family legacy," what she did during her time in Turkey, and what was the extent of her family's involvement, perhaps even her "vicious" great-grandmother. It was as Isabelle had suspected.

Harper must be going after someone who had wronged her.

She walked over to the painting of the golden candelabra that hung on the wall across from Isabelle's desk. The finish on the metal stem was worn in certain places, with dark spots eating away at the shine. The areas that retained the gold color were pristine, and the true glory of the metal shone through. The vines, of a deep forest green shade, were so thick and so full of texture and life they were better suited to the Amazon jungle and not entwined on a delicate household item such as a candelabra.

"I'll tell you this much," Harper said, staring at it. Isabelle herself had stopped and stared at the painting several times since it had been bestowed upon her. "In my life, there is chaos. There is loss . . . and the nasty smudge of betrayal and envy. But our destiny is sure." She turned to Isabelle. "Our true nature shines through in the end. Don't worry about your brother or your family. Face them. Challenge them. You can bend things to your will. You can be the hungry vine that strangles all those people you are afraid of."

"I never said I was afraid."

"You don't have to."

Harper placed the tea cup on the coffee table and picked up her trench and bag.

"I wish I could stay longer," she said. "But there is something I have to handle."

Her presence had made Isabelle feel less agitated and she was sorry to see her go so soon. She walked her to the door.

"You must tell me about your younger years another time."

"Unfortunately," Harper paused and looked at her closely. "Sometimes our sins come home to roost."

Isabelle blinked.

Harper's eyes had gone dark and sparkly again, and then she went out the door.

Chapter Nine

AT FIVE AM ISABELLE'S land-line by her bedside table rang for an eternity. The caller ID indicated the call was from the Lennox Motel. It had to be Bastian. Maybe he was calling to brag about his big coup, the capture of Haughton "Hacksaw" Gillespie. A specter that had hung over their lives since childhood.

Isabelle turned over and the ringing stopped. A minute later it started again. She grabbed the receiver and put it to her ear quickly, before she could change her mind. She was filled with a sense of dread. Her hands shook.

"Isa?"

"Yes."

"Your elegant assassin been hanging around outside all night."

"What?" Isabelle sat up.

"That woman," Bastian drilled. "Why she sniffing around me?"

Isabelle was alarmed. Was he talking about Harper?

"I don't know who you're talking about."

"Tall, steely . . . dark-haired."

Definitely Harper.

"The same woman I saw at your guesthouse before," Bastian went on.

"Where's Marcia and Haughton?"

"How would I know?" Bastian sounded glib, but then his tone shifted. "I'm calling to let you know that your fucking Conquistador has her sights on me for whatever reason. Now I don't know what you told her, but . . ."

"I told her what you did," Isabelle said, trying to threaten him. The truth was she didn't understand why Harper would be at Bastian's motel, when earlier she did not think he had anything to do with her parents' disappearance.

"Yuh hear yourself?" He said. "You hear what you're accusing me of? I don't care what bullshit you fed her, but get her off my back. You really don't want me going outside to sort this out."

Isabelle hung up and dialed Harper's number. Her whole body was shaking now. She was in a surreal universe where her worlds were colliding.

Harper picked up. "Yes?"

Her voice had a heavy edge to it, like she was preoccupied and did not care for the interruption.

"Are you outside my brother's motel?" Silence on the other end. "If you are," Isabelle continued, "then I must tell you that is not a good idea. Things could become very unpleasant and that is not what I want. Not for you and not for me."

Silence still.

Then Harper said, "Do you think I'm scared of your brother?"

"No, that's not what I meant," Isabelle said quickly. "I just – don't understand the objective here. I know what I told you, but this is no way to solve it."

"You had a concern. I wanted to see if your concern was justified. Right now I see no indication of your parents anywhere. He could have them someplace else, though."

"We'll figure it out together." Isabelle pressed a hand against her temple. "However, I think it's best for you to go home."

Silence again.

Then came the sound of a car engine starting up.

"Alright," Harper said. "At least now he knows I've got him in my cross-hairs."

The imperious white Cape Cod style home was hidden behind a high wrought iron gate. Junk mail and leaves had begun to pile up. Isabelle stood outside the gate and peered up the driveway to her former home. It had been six months since her parents had padlocked the doors and gate and headed to the woods.

The gate's design featured an iron plant form in the middle. Isabelle placed her foot on one of the branches and pulled herself up. She stuck her other foot in. Before she could start climbing a car pulled up behind hers.

"What if I was the cops?" It was Bastian.

Isabelle turned her head, suspended mid-climb, and looked at him. The iron pressed into the soles of her flats. She grimaced and slowly stepped back down. Bastian came around and sat on the hood of his Cadillac.

"No one's home," he said.

"Where are they?"

"I can't tell you how I know, but I know."

"Because you've been watching us." She spoke flatly.

The smug smile disappeared from his face. "Yes." He did not go on.

Her brother unnerved her, yet she remembered how much she missed him as a little girl. In the midst of her mother's callous behavior and Haughton's grip on their lives, her father's listlessness and her own increasingly chaotic school life, she longed for Bastian to return home. But he was so far away, in someplace she did not even have a name for. At night she'd lay in bed and say dryly, "London, Brussels, Bucharest. Bottom of the ocean." A stark little chant. A call out to him wherever he was before she fell asleep.

She looked away. Stifled tears bottled in her throat and she swallowed hard to release the burn.

"I'm not your enemy, Isabelle," he said finally, sensing her upset.

"What was the point of spying on us? Might as well have stuck around then."

Her voice sounded whiny to her.

Bastian shook his head dismissively and walked back to the driver's side of the car. "I know where to find them." He waited.

Isabelle had unfairly labeled Bastian a monster because for a long time he carried out Haughton's grotesque orders. He did what he was told because he was a boy and no one cared to stop it from happening. Even some of the authorities were in Haughton's pockets in those days. Besides, Bastian had known about their whereabouts for a while. If he wanted to harm Isabelle or their parents he'd had ample opportunities to do so.

Isabelle paused to push her aviator sunglasses up on her nose and smoothed back long wisps of her straightened hair that had fallen across her face. She went to her car to put up the windows and get her messenger bag. Then she slipped into the passenger seat of the Cadillac next to her brother.

By early evening they were in Connecticut. Isabelle did not press Bastian for details on how he knew where Marcia and Haughton were, but it had become quite clear. He had a GPS tracker on them, which he accessed through an application on his cell phone. He had checked it several times as he drove, even informing Isabelle that their parents had moved from their original location. He re-routed the car GPS to follow.

Mostly they drove in silence, pierced only by the chirpiness of the radio. Any attempt at conversation resulted in each of them giving monosyllabic responses and holding their thoughts close to the chest.

When they were children they went everywhere together. Bastian was five years older and he looked out for Isabelle. He was her nurturer and defender. She was an aloof but reckless child who other kids didn't quite understand. He had been the brash, smug know-it-all that other boys despised yet secretly revered. He was loyal, even when brainwashed into that loyalty. Once he changed, Isabelle's love for her older brother fractured. The shattered pieces were like shadows draped over her early memories.

They navigated through a wide-street suburban neighborhood in Hartford.

After a prolonged period of quiet Bastian said, "She seems protective."

It caught Isabelle by surprise, because she had been straining to see into the backyard of a house they passed, where there was a barbecue and the sound of Caribbean music.

"Who?" she asked.

"That woman who was lurking outside my motel."

"I don't know what her intention was," Isabelle spoke honestly.

"You didn't ask?"

"I told her I suspected you of kidnapping my parents."

Bastian's face fell. "You really thought I kidnapped them?"

Isabelle shrugged. "You swore to something many years ago, remember?"

Bastian thought for a moment, looking straight ahead.

"I said one day I would sever Haughton with his own saw."

Isabelle stared out the window.

"I still might," Bastian said chillingly. "Listen, I made sure the old man felt my presence, but I didn't kidnap them."

"Did you burn his stores in Jamaica?"

"I'm not going to answer that."

"Well, I couldn't understand how all of a sudden they disappeared from the cabin," Isabelle said. "I panicked."

"How do you know her?"

He was talking about Harper again. "She came to my party with a friend."

"She came to your party with Caye Wauburg, your girlfriend." He was staring straight ahead as he said this in a matter-of-fact tone, as if Isabelle's explanation required clarification.

"My ex-girlfriend."

"What do you know about her?"

"Caye?"

"That woman."

Isabelle was still sifting through the things *she knew* about Harper, but was not prepared to discuss anything Harper had told her.

"I know she is from a successful family and she is involved with charity work. Besides that I don't really know her."

"So why you hanging around someone you don't know?"

"I know enough." Isabelle pouted. She had contradicted herself.

"You said you don't know anything," Bastian pointed out.

"I'm saying that from what I have seen so far—"

"How much have you seen?"

"What do you mean?" Now she sensed he was trying to get at something.

"You met her the night of your party. You haven't known her that long."

"That's stating the obvious," Isabelle said sarcastically.

Bastian fell silent as his attention shifted to the GPS tracker.

At the end of the block, they turned onto a street with vacant-looking brick buildings. Between the buildings were several warehouses with lowered shutters. Bastian pulled up in front of one of these structures, but at a cautious distance from the entrance. He looked at his phone.

"Last known location," he said.

"Where were they before?" Isabelle asked. "You said they had moved."

"A few blocks away."

Jay Broderick lived in Hartford. If Marcia and Haughton had gone to visit their old friend why didn't they tell her? Now she no longer sensed they were in imminent danger.

Bastian unbuckled his seatbelt and adjusted the weapon in the back of his waistband.

"No." Isabelle stopped him. "I will go."

He scowled and sucked his teeth.

A wave of his hand indicated she should go right ahead.

The shutter was half-open and Isabelle slipped inside. No one was around, but she could make out used tires stacked along the walls and a few rows of racks in the middle of the room, which contained various car parts. It appeared to be an auto shop that sold used items. Dull bulbs flickered in fixtures on the wall. Isabelle moved toward another room at the far end, but the door was locked. She went past it and made her way down a drafty hallway. A Range Rover was parked outside in the impending dusk, but there was no sign of anyone in the yard either. The vehicle appeared empty, but movement came from inside the shop behind her.

Isabelle turned back. An ominous prickle of fear crept across her skin. She went back down the drafty hallway. She hurried past the locked room. Someone shifted between the rows of tires on her right. Footsteps shuffled. When she glanced back no one was there. Was someone hiding between the racks? She picked up her pace to get back to the shutters.

Tires screeched in the distance. Isabelle rushed outside with blood surging to her ears and head, hot and thumping inside her chest. She ran away from the entrance of the warehouse, and then she froze.

The Cadillac had disappeared.

Chapter Ten

ISABELLE RAN WILDLY down the vacant street. How could she have been so daft? She not only went in alone, she trusted an unscrupulous criminal. There was no one in sight and nothing but the brown façade of the shuttered up warehouses. She considered running back to the neighborhood street they had driven down, hoping she might see someone who could help her.

As she neared the end of the block the Cadillac appeared. Bastian slammed on the breaks as he turned the corner. Isabelle had been running in the middle of the road.

She rushed over to him.

"What the hell . . . ?"

"A vehicle came out of the back." Bastian's voice strained with agitation. "I tried to catch up, but by the time I spun around they were gone."

"They came out of that building?" Isabelle's heart was still pounding. She worried Bastian had tricked her and taken off to do God-knows-what.

"Yes. After you went in I cruised down the street to see if there was any kind of activity. Then I circled back up to wait for you. That's when the Range Rover pulled out in a mad haste. I spun again and went after it."

"Did you see who was inside?"

He looked down, away from her eager stare.

"Three men."

"Oh." Isabelle was deflated.

"Get in," Bastian said.

They started back the way they had come. Isabelle waited for her brother to gather his thoughts.

"You shouldn't assume the worst," he said finally.

"I shouldn't assume they were kidnapped and probably will be killed?"

"Kidnapped? You should stop throwing around that word."

"Whatever is going on, I can't imagine they left willingly."

"I recognized one of the men," Bastian said. "Jay Broderick."

"We could call him." Isabelle said quickly. "I have Jay's number written down somewhere back at the guesthouse."

Bastian didn't answer. He had gone into puzzle solving mode. Isabelle was trying to avoid doing the same because she knew she would jump to a dire conclusion. Instead she scrolled through her phone and found Marcia's old cell phone number. She and Haughton had both gotten rid of their cell phones once they left Nutley, but Isabelle called the number anyway. Then she dialed Haughton's as well. The lines belonged to other people by now.

They drove on as the evening darkened.

"Let's go back." Isabelle had an inkling she had missed something. "We'll both go inside and check the place out."

Bastian shook his head no. "Stop and think. You don't have the full picture."

"And what do you think that is? Can you enlighten me?" Isabelle almost added: *I'm no expert criminal.* She thought better of it.

"Do you think your parents are little kids that need your protection?"

Your parents?

"I don't think that at all," Isabelle said defensively. His tone was scolding, irritated.

He had nothing else to say and Isabelle remained quiet for the rest of the drive.

They exited off the New Jersey Turnpike and headed toward a dark back road, flanked by trees. As they approached a train crossing, a loud clanging bell and flashing red lights indicated the train was coming. Bastian came to a stop as the boards descended.

"You know what?" he said suddenly.

"What?" Isabelle's pulse quickened.

Bastian picked up his cell phone.

"The signal is still at the warehouse." He turned the face of the phone for Isabelle to see. Confusion flooded her mind. Her brother's face twisted into a smirk.

"I don't understand."

"They are still there. Well, Haughton at least, was inside the warehouse when you went in. He's still there now."

"You knew that all along." Isabelle was incredulous.

"Yes. What I don't know is what he's doing there."

The bright triangle of lights came closer in the darkness. The train horn sounded, and once it had passed they waited for the boards to go up so they could cross the tracks.

"Why did we waste time going there if not to find them?" Isabelle wanted to ask if he was afraid of the old man, but she didn't have the guts.

"Because something's up." Bastian rubbed the side of his face. "You've got to learn—"

They both saw headlights at the same time. Isabelle sat up abruptly and looked behind her.

"Is that—?"

The Range Rover surged toward them. Bastian swerved left. The truck clipped the rear edge of the Cadillac, jolting them to a standstill. The Range Rover careened off and slammed into the railroad post. The driver wore a black baseball cap pulled low on his forehead and had two other men with him. The truck backed up and swung to the left.

Isabelle screamed. Bastian shot off back in the direction they had come from. Still off balance, the Cadillac skirted off the side of the road onto the dirt shoulder. Bastian finally righted it and they zoomed down the smooth blacktop.

The Range Rover sped up behind them.

Isabelle grabbed her cellphone.

"What are you doing?" Bastian yelled.

"Calling the police."

"We don't need the police." Sweat sprung up on his forehead. He swung right off the road, toward what looked like a ditch within the trees, but soon cleared into a long dirt path. Tree branches slapped against the windshield and sides of the car.

Isabelle looked back. The Range Rover had stopped at the mouth of the woods, waiting like a cat that had a mouse cornered. The dirt path gave way to a bumpy slope and they climbed it. They went right through a veil of trees.

When they came upon a small farmhouse in the clearing, Bastian veered toward it.

"Don't stop in the front," Isabelle said.

There weren't many options for a hiding place, but Bastian maneuvered to the side of the house least visible from the road. A soft external light came on. Isabelle glanced around. No movement came from within the house or its surrounding.

"We should hang back a while." Bastian surveyed the scenery as intensely as Isabelle. "I don't think they'll follow us."

Isabelle got out and stood by the car door to see farther out. In the distance the road stretched past them, as eerily quiet as her life had been just days ago.

Isabelle slipped into her suite and bolted the door. Her legs were gelatinous stilts. She pressed her back against the door and slid to the floor. Once her breathing returned to normal, she crawled across the floor to the window, reached up and dragged the drapes shut. The bottle of rum she had opened when Harper visited was still sitting on her kitchenette counter. She poured herself a shot and collapsed onto the couch.

Bastian was in an empty room down the hall. They had come in quietly after everyone had gone to bed, and before the livelier bar-hopping guests had returned. That her brother meant her no harm helped, but only thinking of Harper calmed her.

It was after midnight. Isabelle called anyway. Harper picked up after the first ring.

"Sorry to wake you," Isabelle said. By now her pulse had settled and she spoke with a composure that belied her true emotions.

"I was still up," Harper said. "Is everything okay?"

Isabelle told her about the trip to Connecticut and the car chase on the way home.

"Did you recognize the men?" Harper asked.

"No, but my brother said one of them was a longtime friend of my step dad's." Isabelle sighed. "I have no idea what's going on."

"Do you feel unsafe?"

"Bastian stuck around. He's down the hall."

"You don't have to stay there if you don't want to."

Isabelle had to admit it was nerve-wracking. "My head is spinning."

"Come to Newport. Spend a few days, clear your head."

"I'm not sure about that . . ."

"Don't worry so much about appearances," Harper said, as if she'd read Isabelle's mind. "Your safety is what's important."

Isabelle was concerned about Caye, but would Caye have given Isabelle's feelings a second thought if the situation were reversed? She knew the answer to that. Caye put her own needs before anyone else's.

By six am a car had arrived to take Isabelle to Rhode Island. Both Bastian and Helene were in her suite, with Helene grilling her in hushed whispers as Isabelle packed a small bag.

"I do believe I am owed an explanation," Helene huffed.

Bastian stood stiffly across the room. He had gone to the window twice to slide the drapes back and peek out.

"It's only a short trip," Isabelle said. "At most a couple days."

She didn't know how long she'd be gone or anything about Harper's house in Newport, but she had to reassure Helene.

"Why so suddenly? Why in the middle of the night?" Helene folded her arms.

"It's already morning."

"You know what I mean."

Isabelle and Bastian exchanged looks. They had not mentioned Marcia and Haughton's disappearance or their trip to Connecticut and the chase.

"I think she's been cooped up too long," Bastian said dryly. "Or maybe it's a curious coincidence."

"What?" Helene asked, frowning at him.

"She leaves as soon as her dear big brother arrives."

Helene glared at him and turned back to Isabelle. "I don't believe you're leaving because of him," she paused and looked at Bastian. "Despite his . . . wily-ness, I suspect there's another reason."

Isabelle let her face fall in mocked surrender.

"Harper and I have become more than friends."

"You were never friends."

"I'm seeing her behind Caye's back." Isabelle hoped this fake confession would suffice. It worked.

"Hmph." Helene looked concerned.

"I know it's wrong."

"Is this some sort of payback?" Helene asked, lowering her voice to a whisper. "For what Caye did to you?"

Isabelle sighed, almost regretting sharing details about her love life with Helene.

She looked at Bastian. "Only unstable people pursue revenge." She was trying to joke with him, but he stood stone-faced and somber.

Helene came closer, still whispering. "Does it have anything to do with what you told me? Ms. Harper and that mess overseas from years ago?"

Isabelle crossed her arms. "In all honesty, this has to do with my own affairs."

Helene looked mystified. She shook her head quietly and the thick drape of silvery hair swung from side to side against her neck. She was wearing a teal robe over a teal nightgown, and in that moment appeared robotic, fortified even.

"I knew there was more to your life than you let on."

"Mrs. Keane, I. . ."

"You don't have to explain right now." The older woman put her hands up. "I'll be here when you get home."

After Helene left the room Bastian hung back, something clearly on his mind.

"Sis, can I get a drink?" he asked quietly, not quite meeting her eyes.

Isabelle poured him rum on the rocks and waited as he paced.

"I don't know where to start." His voice was cautious and hesitant. "It's just been so much lost time, Isa. So many lost opportunities." He looked at her. "What could have been for me, for my life. Time I was absent from yours. You know what I mean?"

She nodded.

"And now this craziness. Everything's just so mixed up and messy."

She wasn't sure what he was getting at, but she nodded again.

"This stuff with Marcia and Haughton. I know in a twisted way you feel like their rescuer."

"I don't—"

"Just hear me out," he pleaded. "You've been looking after them so you feel some sort of responsibility. Don't you see how fucked up that is, after everything they've done? After what that man did to our father?"

"Bastian, can we talk about this later?"

"No!" He stared her down. "We're talking about it now."

His anger caught her off guard and she shifted uncomfortably.

Something in him had come alive. He was wearing an army green baseball cap and matching short sleeve shirt over dark denim. For a moment he looked as he did in the old days – the young soldier with ghastly missions, efficient and unwavering in carrying out his duties.

"After everything they've done," he said with an incredulous tremor, "what repercussions did that man face? None."

"I was alone," Isabelle said quietly. "Throughout all of it I was alone."

"I should have done something back then." He scratched at his chin. "I should have come home..."

Bastian's shoulders contracted, and a hint of something unpleasant played out across his face. The sense of a failure or misstep now smothered the fire that had momentarily flared up in him, and had perhaps extinguished his vigor and stolen his ruthlessness.

"Why do you have this?" He jutted his chin at the painting of the golden candelabra as if it had personally offended him. "It's suffocating."

Isabelle supposed it was. There was something inspiring, yet ugly about the painting. Perhaps that was the dichotomy of the human experience.

"I don't want you to go to Rhode Island." Bastian put his glass down and pulled the chain of magnetic beads from his pocket. He plucked them apart. "I made terrible mistakes, Isabelle. I'm making one now, as we speak."

"I don't know what to do," Isabelle said, her voice breaking.

"I wish I could turn back the clock." Bastian pointed toward his chest with his thumb. "I'm terrified. When have you ever heard me say that? I'm frightened because things are so delicate."

"What are you afraid of?" She asked. The world was shifting beneath her. Her brother, the warrior, was depleted, nerveless even. He was afraid of an old man with dwindling resources and a fading will.

Bastian looked at the palm of his hand as if it revealed the fragility he spoke of. He gulped down the remainder of his drink.

"Nowadays I go toward things that are just broken, buried," he said, lost in his thoughts. "I went to see the ruins of Histria while peddling drugs across Europe like a common haggler. I sat on short stonewall that surrounded what used to be city streets centuries ago. Imagine that – a whole city just sunken. It gave me such a mixed feeling of endurance and . . . decay." He looked at his hand again. "I once could kill a man with my bare hands, and I've done it. But I feel so weak and desperate as I get older."

"You're only thirty-four," Isabelle reminded him, shaken by his admission and vulnerability, and for lack of something more profound to say.

"I don't even know what I'm saying or how to explain," Bastian said. "It's not just about what we did or didn't do." He looked at the painting. "We've got monsters inside, eating away at the goodness in all of us. I'm weak now. I'm a ruin. I don't know how to fix things anymore, but if you stick around maybe we can fix this together."

Isabelle shook her head. She was overwhelmed. Now more than ever she needed to get away.

"Stay here, Isabelle." He looked like a wounded man searching for his resolve.

"I'm sorry," she said. "I can't."

Defeated, Bastian accompanied Isabelle outside to the black BMW with tinted windows. The driver, Sud, had introduced himself as "one of" Harper's bodyguards. He had a bald head and a long, angular face.

He came over, pausing to assess Bastian before he took Isabelle's bag.

"Do you think this is safe?" Bastian asked, after the man had walked back to the car. He regarded the man as carefully as Sud had regarded him.

"Going to Rhode Island? It's certainly safer than being here right now."

"You don't know these people," Bastian said, with sincere trepidation in his voice.

Isabelle understood his apprehension. It wasn't exactly flattering that Harper had planted herself outside his motel two nights ago.

"I'm not concerned," Isabelle said. "It's hard to explain . . ."

"Okay, so what about your mother? What do you want to do?"

"I'm doing it," Isabelle said flatly. "Bastian, I need a moment."

Her brother stared at her. "You are the one who's supposed to care. I don't give a shit about what happens to them."

His eyes showed that he did. Isabelle was relieved. The last several hours had revealed Bastian to be human.

"We'll figure it out," she said. She squeezed her brother's shoulder and walked toward the car, where Sud held the back door open for her.

Chapter Eleven

THE HARPER FAMILY HOME was a charming French country style estate in Newport, perched near the edge of a cliff. Isabelle admired the refined stone façade and pitched roof as the car came around the looping driveway. It had an old world, yet warm essence.

Upon arrival around mid-morning, Isabelle was greeted by a petite man named Frederick. He was the head of the house staff and just as he had summoned a young woman, Lilly, to take Isabelle and her bag to get settled, Harper came bouncing down the stairs. Her dark hair was loose and lustrous across her shoulders. Every crevice of her face appeared to be smiling and that made Isabelle smile too.

Harper stopped short and grabbed Isabelle's bag, which was already in the process of being transferred from Frederick to Lilly. The three of them fussed over it. It was comical, and Isabelle mused at the situation: Frederick's quiet formality, Lilly's confusion and insistence on taking the bag, and Harper's unmistakably flushed cheeks.

Lilly wrestled control of the bag and Harper was forced to face Isabelle. She stiffened. "I am happy you came. I was worried."

"Thank you for inviting me," Isabelle said. "Your home is beautiful."

Isabelle's mind wandered to the asparagus-colored house in Upstate New York. The sparse decoration, the guns and apple targets, the camouflage jacket and boots. Here in Newport the Harper before her was polished and glowing. She wore a loose cream, color-block blouse tucked into white skinny jeans, with a pair of gold flats. A long gold necklace dangled down the front of her shirt. Her nails glistened with blood red polish.

Which one was the real Harper?

They were both awkwardly sizing each other up.

"The last couple days have been bizarre," Isabelle proclaimed.

"We have that in common then," Harper said.

Before Isabelle could ask her what she meant Frederick interjected.

"Shall I take Ms. Bartley to get settled or will you manage?" He had a soft voice and an amicable demeanor.

Lilly had gone upstairs with her belongings and apparently she was supposed to take Isabelle with her. Harper acquiesced.

"We'll talk once you get settled," she said.

Frederick led Isabelle up the curving staircase and down the carpeted hallway to a room with a wide double door. He turned the door handle gently and they went in. The bedroom walls were covered in silk, and the design was soft and feminine, with faint outlines of flower petals. An elaborate armoire and a pair of chaises filled the room. The queen-sized bed was elevated on a marble frame and headboard. It beckoned to Isabelle and she longed for sleep. Frederick pointed out the bathroom behind another set of double doors.

"I brought up some water and tea."

"Sorry?"

"If you need water," Frederick repeated, pointing to the decanter on the night table. "And just in case you were in the mood for tea."

He must have laid them out before she arrived. Lilly had also placed her bag on the wide chest at the foot of the bed.

"Thank you," Isabelle said.

"Please let me know if I can be of further assistance." He patted the intercom on the wall in the sitting area and smiled. Isabelle returned his smile as he left the room.

She washed her face and re-did her makeup. Her hair was still in good shape but she combed it again. She had worn dark blue skinny jeans and a white satin blouse. By the time she had tucked her blouse in, added a slender navy belt to match her flats, and rolled her sleeves a couple more inches up to her elbow, Lilly was at the door.

"Victoria would like to know if you have eaten?"

Sud had stopped so they could grab breakfast on the way up.

"I'm fine at the moment, thank you."

Lilly remained at the door. "Do you need help with anything at all?"

"I don't believe so." The young woman was determined to assist her and Isabelle had the sense she was projecting Harper's unrest. "I would like to go downstairs, however."

Having to say that was strange. It was as if she had been imprisoned in the room and needed permission to leave.

"Oh yes! Of course." Lilly beamed. "Come with me."

Lilly wore a belted gray dress and a green cardigan that matched Frederick's. Her movements were brisk, and she walked eagerly down the hallway with Isabelle in tow. Her right hip jutted out with each hurried step, as if she had suffered an injury.

Once they descended the stairs she made a sharp right and went over to where Harper was sitting in the grand salon, on the edge of a robust looking leather sofa. Lilly smiled, indicating her success, as Isabelle came into the room behind her.

Harper stood and invited Isabelle to sit next to her. As soon as she did Lilly reached for a tray with orange juice and placed it before them on the coffee table.

"Did you report the chase to the police?" Harper asked. When Isabelle hesitated she dismissed Lilly with a nod.

"I would have, but Bastian said not to," Isabelle said. "I thought my stepfather had moved beyond his unwholesome behavior. Now I'm not so sure."

"What do you want to do?" Harper's voice was calm and unassuming, but the question made Isabelle's ears grow hot. Bastian had asked her that question earlier. It had an ominous edge to it, despite their concerned delivery. At moments like this she was fearful of Harper and it befuddled her. "What's wrong?"

"How did you know where Bastian was? Why did you go to his motel?"

"I saw him leaving your guesthouse. Well, I saw him 'watching' your guesthouse, and when he finally left I followed him."

Isabelle was dumbfounded. So Bastian was watching her, and in turn Harper had been watching him. Harper and her brother were alike in certain ways. They were the same age and were clearly similar in their mindset.

"Do you usually do this sort of thing?" Isabelle asked pointedly.

"No." Harper sighed. "These days I feel like a rolling stone. I go to New York, I come here, I go away. I followed your brother because I was curious and because I needed something to occupy my mind. Something that has nothing to do with my own affairs."

Did those troubling affairs have anything to do with Harper's strange entanglement with Caye and her father? Besides her residual problems from the Maramaxe Exposé, there was definitely something brewing between her and the Wauburgs.

"Do you trust him now?" Harper asked.

"My brother? Yes," Isabelle said. "Bastian didn't take my parents."

"Sorry about my little surveillance effort." Harper smirked. "I don't know what I hoped to accomplish."

The crystal chandelier in the middle of the room reflected off Harper's face. She emanated light and brilliance. In this moment she was unsullied, but it was a glimpse at one side of her.

Isabelle let her eyes drift away from the woman before her. The dark hardwood floors and coffered ceiling inspired comfort. Tall windows provided an expansive view of the sea and the sky, and an illuminating sunshine.

Another room adjacent to this one featured a library with white paneled walls and a substantial collection of books.

Her eyes came back to rest upon a portrait on the wall across from where they sat. The woman in it bore resemblance to Harper, with her dark hair and pronounced cheekbones. Her eyes, though lighter, held an imperial glare that bore down on the onlooker. Her lips converged without humor and her slender body was held rigid and steadfast. A bulbous brass pendant hung from a chain around her neck. The image caused Isabelle's pulse to quicken. It was an odd reaction. She had been spooked by a painting.

Isabelle got up and went to peruse another portrait. It featured a man, a face Isabelle had seen before on the Internet, in many of Newport's local newspapers and blogs. He had been a prominent subject in the results of her on-line research. Edward Harper's descriptors in all these write-ups always included "former playboy" or "former ladies man." He also resembled Harper.

"My father, Edward." Harper had come up behind her. "Philanthropist, sports enthusiast, and rampant socializer."

Isabelle smiled, but she was still thinking about the frightful image of the woman with the bulb pendant. She stepped left toward a portrait of another woman with kind hazel eyes. This one Isabelle remembered seeing in a video clip from a TV show. At the time, Patricia Harper had been campaigning to become Mayor of Newport. She came a close second in the elections, but she wouldn't have crossed Isabelle's radar if not for that video that had gone viral.

While campaigning, she had done an interview with a local TV station. After she left the studio, one of the anchors remarked that Patricia and her family were "opulent degenerates," not realizing he was still on the air.

"I take it this is your mother?" Isabelle asked.

"Yes." Harper was only half listening. She was standing before the portrait that had spooked Isabelle. "This," she announced, looking at the terrible image with genuine admiration and reverence, "is my paternal great-grandmother, Eugenie Bradford-Harper. Wartime physician. Healer and savior."

"She sounds fascinating," Isabelle uttered.

"When I was a child my father used to tell me bedtime stories about her. Eugenie was a complicated woman. She started out with a modest dream to save lives. She was one of the brightest doctors in Rhode Island in the nineteen hundreds and served bravely in both World Wars. She was the family champion. No Harper that came after ever measured up."

Isabelle looked into the woman's eyes, frozen in time. "Why was she complicated?"

Harper hesitated and looked at the floor. After a while she said simply, "Her dream shifted."

A light ocean breeze took away the rising afternoon heat. Slow, soft waves folded and unfolded at the base of the cliffs beyond the grounds. Isabelle and Harper had come out to the cabanas by the pool for lunch. Lilly had laid out a large salad and fruits, and a basket of raisin bread with butter.

Isabelle was mesmerized by the sound of the water in the distance.

"You know," she said, nostalgic, "when I was younger I used to hate the sea. It was where my mother went to meet the man she was having an affair with, who's now my stepfather. He'd whisk her away to the country, to Ochos Rios or Montego Bay. Then she would come home and tell me all about her adventures. It was our secret at that time, when my father was still alive."

"What was your father like?"

"My father was much too peaceful." Isabelle considered. "I associated the sea with dishonesty. The sea was where women went to cheat on their husbands."

Harper cleared her throat and looked out at the waves.

Toward the back of the house lay a sunken garden. From this angle, thick hedges concealed much of the plants inside, but Isabelle could make out the low steps leading down and the outline of the border wall. It looked like a sunken plant city and it made her think of Bastian and his meltdown this morning. She felt a mixture of empathy and befuddlement toward her brother.

"Do you know what my brother called you?" Isabelle asked.

"What?"

"A Conquistador."

"A what?" Harper looked at her. "That's . . . odd."

"It was when you were stalking him."

"I was never stalking him!"

She laughed, though her demeanor was a little hesitant and uncertain.

"I thought it was a strange description at the time," Isabelle said, "but now I can see it."

Harper grimaced, even as her eyes were riveted to Isabelle.

"I don't . . . conquer things."

"Not overtly," Isabelle said, teasing. "You have a certain command. It is as if you only need to will something to make it happen."

So easily had Harper willed Isabelle to Newport. So seamlessly had she become Isabelle's confidant in such a short time. So quickly she had won Isabelle's trust.

"I don't think that's true." Harper tilted her head in thought. "If it were then many things would have been resolved by now."

"Like what?" Isabelle asked.

"Like Caye, for instance."

Isabelle perked up. She had been languidly sipping cranberry juice as she teased Harper, but now she was on full alert. "Go on."

"As time passed it just never felt natural." Harper looked out toward the bay. "I only recognized what that feeling was when I looked back months later."

"What was the feeling?"

"Uneasiness, suspicion. Like she was watching me."

"Why would she watch you?"

"I don't know," Harper said quietly.

Clearly she did know. There was more to it than she was willing to share.

"When was the last time you saw her?" She asked, casting an analytical gaze at Isabelle.

"The same day I met with you in Chester," Isabelle confessed. "I haven't seen her since."

"How come you got together?" Harper's eyes darkened and glinted in the sunshine. That look was emblematic of her intensity. It was the same look she wore in Chester before she pulled the trigger.

Isabelle held her nerve. In some strange way, that look appealed to her.

"I was in the city having brunch by myself. She learned I was there and hunted me down." Isabelle paused, unsure of how to divulge the rest of the story. "There was an article about her in the paper and she thought it would upset her father. She wanted me to come along to cushion the blow."

"And did you?" Harper asked.

"I did, but I doubt it did her any good."

"Hmm."

Had she seen the article about Caye and Gergina and their night out on the town?

"I saw that article." Harper shrugged. "Someone brought it to my attention, but we were done. I am done."

"Because of that Gergina woman?"

"Because Caye Wauburg is a fucking spy." Her eyes were steely black stones. This was the Harper of the asparagus house, dressed like the Victoria Harper of the French country estate of Newport. One and the same.

Isabelle pierced a piece of mesculin with her fork. So Harper did not trust Caye. Their relationship had probably started out as a lie. A treacherous lie according to Harper's suspicions, but what was there to spy on? Was Harper entrenched in something of interest to the Wauburgs?

"Why do you think she was a spy?"

Harper looked down, watching a yellow floating device bobble softly in the pool.

"When I came to my senses with Caye I took the time to research Wauburg. He had spent time overseas but it was in Slovakia. I had no connection to Slovakia so I brushed off my suspicions, but I am starting to think Wauburg knows the people who were running the Maramaxe trafficking operation."

Isabelle's mouth gaped open. She tried to utter one of the plethora of words running through her brain. If Wauburg knew the human traffickers, then Wauburg and friends had discovered Harper's whereabouts. Wauburg had likely set up Caye and Harper to date so he could get closer to Harper. To what end? To kill her? Turn her over to his colleagues?

"I like the way your mind works," Harper said quietly.

Could she hear Isabelle's thoughts?

Harper smiled. "I can see you connecting the dots. Though, I haven't fully connected them myself. It seems like a lot, you know?"

Harper looked tired then, and Isabelle shifted closer and rested her hand against her shoulder. The muscles in her back twitched beneath Isabelle's palm.

"Did you love her?" Isabelle finally said.

"No."

The directness of her answer chilled Isabelle and made her stomach sink. Her own reaction puzzled her, but then she understood. Caye was a woman with flaws, but she was also someone Isabelle once cared about. Once loved. It was sad to hear the firm dismissal in Harper's voice. It was not a tone to be doubted. It had a steadfastness to it, as if Harper had long shifted to a different mode where Caye was concerned. It was a tone of action, not reminiscence.

"We should head back." Harper stood. "I'm expecting a phone call."

They strolled back toward the house on the stone paved pathway, walking on in silence as the remnants of their conversation floated around them in the air.

"What do you plan to do if your suspicions prove to be true?" Isabelle asked.

Harper was about to answer but became distracted by something. Isabelle looked up, following her line of vision. A yellow Porsche sat in the driveway.

"We have company," She said.

They went inside to the grand salon where a young man was sprawled out in an arm chair. He was sipping from a glass in his hand and made no motion toward them as they entered.

"Too early for that," Harper scolded.

The young man glanced at the drink and shrugged. He took a long sip. Then his gaze fell upon Isabelle and rested there.

"This is my cousin, Danny Westbrook," Harper announced. "This is my friend Isabelle."

Danny dragged himself over to them and shook Isabelle's hand.

"Good to meet you," he said. He looked her up and down, his eyes coming back to rest on her chest.

"Don't you have anything to occupy your time?" Harper asked, clearly annoyed.

"We were at the shop and we heard you were in town, Cuz."

"We?" Harper's voice went up an octave.

A woman entered the room. She was the female version of Danny, both with bright, quizzical eyes. Dirty blonde coifs framed their narrow faces, only the woman's hair was shoulder length.

As Harper was introducing Isabelle to Cousin Carolyn, Danny leaned in to whisper.

"She's never here," he slurred. "I don't think she likes to see her dear old cousins."

"We have no choice but to ambush her when she sneaks into town." Carolyn smiled as she greeted Isabelle.

"We really don't," Danny said, lifting his arms in a flourish, the drink swirling precariously in his glass as he sat back down.

"It's called the sneak attack," Carolyn continued.

"Alright. Alright," Harper said. Her eyes had been shooting daggers since she entered the house. She observed her cousins like a hawk. Isabelle found her expression amusing.

They were in their late-twenties, twins who had a charming two-headed monster quality to them. The kind of people who were so close in nature and objectives that they could leave one feeling overwhelmed, double-teamed in their presence.

"I just came to see you both," Harper said, mocking them.

"She did not, did she?" Carolyn stared at Isabelle.

"I don't think she did," Danny offered.

"Our cousin is a slippery one."

"Always pulling our legs."

"How long are you staying, Isabelle?" Carolyn asked.

"I think you would make for better company than 'the sullen one.'" Danny grinned.

"Maybe a day or so," Isabelle said, finally getting a word in.

"Only a day?" Carolyn almost shrieked.

"You cannot come to Harper Estate and spend one day."

"We must make her stay longer."

"Victoria, why isn't she staying longer?" Danny shot Harper a disapproving look.

"I bet V has to jet off somewheres."

"Do you plan to leave?" Isabelle asked, though she hadn't meant to chime in. The words simply escaped, as if the chirpy cousins had infected her.

Harper laughed, but her face grew grim as Frederick entered the room and brought her a phone.

"Please," she looked at Isabelle. "Give me a moment."

Isabelle suspected she was apologetic about leaving her with the tweety birds. She went upstairs to take the phone call, and Frederick retreated to the kitchen.

"So where are you from?" Carolyn asked, as she and Isabelle took a seat on the sofa.

"A quiet town in New Jersey. I'm from a small family."

"How nice," Danny said. "We longed for that as children."

"It does your head in to grow up in this place with aunts and uncles and cousins, all vying for their share of the gold mine."

"Consider yourself lucky."

Isabelle shrugged. "No family is perfect."

"But certainly some families are more fucked than others," Carolyn said, winking at her. She wore a trendy outfit – a tennis skirt and Doc Martens, with a negligee top under a sequined jacket – but she appeared disheveled, like she had dressed without care.

Danny went to pour two drinks and brought them over.

"I don't think I should," Isabelle protested. "The day just started."

"Are you fucking scared of her?" Danny glared at her devilishly. His eyes became suggestive, as if he couldn't contain his zestful humor.

"No thank you." Isabelle gave him a blank stare.

Carolyn slid closer to Isabelle. "Does she tie you up and flog you during sex?"

"What kind of question is that?" Isabelle stood, heat flashing across her skin.

Carolyn's face fell. "So you do not have sex?"

"What's the point then?" Danny asked, puzzled.

"We are . . . friends." Isabelle sighed, exasperated.

"Relax," Carolyn said. "It's not a big deal."

"It is a little bit bizarre though," Danny said.

"Alright, Danny, leave it alone."

"I'm just saying," Danny pushed. "Victoria has had a harem of women since she was fifteen. She has never kept a woman as a friend."

"I must admit this is true." Carolyn's face twisted into genuine concern. "I'm guessing you guys will probably hook up at some point?"

It was as if Harper was a sexual creature, a succubus that needed to be fed. Lilly burst into the room as Isabelle was looking for a way out of the conversation.

"I'm sorry," Lilly said. "I came as quickly as I could. I was busy in the kitchen."

"Oh for heaven's sake!" Danny barked.

"Lilly," Carolyn said. "Tell Victoria she is fine."

"She does not need to be rescued from us," Danny said haughtily.

"We're just chatting with her." Carolyn cocked her head.

"I'm sorry," Lilly said again. "Isabelle is needed."

"Needed for what?" Danny stepped between Isabelle and Lilly. He grasped Lilly's arm. "We are in the middle of a conversation."

"Let them be." Carolyn came over and pulled her brother's hand away. "Victoria is always protective of her little secrets. You know how she is, brother."

"We have our own secrets too, you know." He looked like a child then, like a younger sibling trying to measure up to Harper.

"Come on," Lilly said.

She led Isabelle back upstairs to her room, where she was deposited and locked away like a hapless treasure.

Chapter Twelve

BEFORE ISABELLE KNEW it she had fallen into a deep sleep. She had showered and wrapped herself in a cocoon of thick blankets in the cozy bed. In her dreams she fell into the haze of another place and time. She found herself back at the woods near the cabin in New Jersey, gardening, gathering plants or doing whatever she pictured Haughton doing when he went out with his satchel and machete. A rumbling beneath the ground drew her attention and Isabelle ran toward the sound. She found a hatch buried beneath the thick moss and pried it open.

Harper emerged from the hatch and said, "It's coming!" Her face was smeared with soot and beads of sweat dripped from her skin. *It* was unknown. Isabelle pulled her up and they took off through the trees together. They raced out to the clearing as the rumbling noise inched closer. They raced up the dry, brittle flanks of a mountain. Plumes of dust rose up as they slipped and slid, trying to grasp bramble and the rock outcroppings. As soon as they descended the other side another mountain appeared in their path. This mountain was made of red rock with flawless nooks for their feet to climb. They scaled it with little effort and on the other side, the sun streamed down onto a shore and a glistening beach. They dashed across the sand together, splashing into the cool turquoise water. And then the rumbling stopped.

When Isabelle woke up Harper was sitting on the bed next to her.

"You were dreaming," she said softly. She handed Isabelle a glass of water, which she sat up and drank. "What were you dreaming about?"

"You and I."

"What were we doing?" Harper took her hand and a voltaic charge shot up Isabelle's arm. It seemed to signal a palpable shift in the dynamic between them. The attentive way Harper hovered over her now, and the softness in her face caused warmth to spread inside Isabelle's chest.

"We were running from something," Isabelle said, a little breathless.

"Did we get away?" Harper winked.

"We made it," she whispered, not quite trusting her voice.

"My dreams rarely have happy endings."

"How so?"

"Something nasty is always out to get me." Harper's smile was rueful. "Ever since I was a child."

"Your devilish cousins, perhaps."

Harper laughed. "Lilly told me that by the time she got to you they already had you ruffled." She shook her head, regretful. "I wish I could have seen it."

"Really now?" Isabelle pouted.

"It would have been nice to see," Harper said. "You're very pristine."

Isabelle shrugged. She had an opening to Harper through her cousins and she didn't want the opportunity to pass.

"They were making a big deal of your sex life."

"My what?"

"They said you have a harem of women and you don't keep them for friendship."

Harper's eyes went wide. "They exaggerate a lot. I admit to being a bit of a dandy when I was younger, but not anymore. I don't have time for it."

"What you do spend your time doing?"

Harper looked away and Isabelle studied the distant look on her face.

"These days I spend a lot of time tying up loose ends."

"The Maramaxe issue?"

"And more. I want to close a certain chapter in my family's history. Carolyn and Danny can laze around or stir up trouble because they don't have the responsibilities I do. I inherited a burden and . . . "

"And what?"

"I must find a way to sever us from the past and start fresh."

"Is that what your phone call was about?" Isabelle pried.

"Yes. I'm looking out for my friend, Steven Smyth. He is in trouble because of his ties to my family."

Steven was the one who had introduced Harper to the Maramaxe charity. Perhaps he had helped Harper with her exposé, but it sounded like there was more to it than that.

"I'm sorry to hear that."

"Thanks." She shrugged. "I have to figure this out." A low chime came over the intercom. "It's dinner time."

Isabelle changed into a black tank dress that clung loosely to her figure. She did her best to recapture the ordered fall of her hair, since she had fallen asleep without a protective scarf. Her tresses were starting to expand, and she kept smoothing it over sub-consciously. She completed the look with a black cardigan and a pair of black flats.

Once ready, she met Harper outside in the hallway and Harper's eyes immediately went to her hair. She released a sigh, a sound that indicated pleasure. Or was it desire?

They went downstairs together. Harper wore a svelte black tuxedo blazer over a slinky beige T-shirt with a low V-cut neck-line, which showed the rising mounds of her small breasts. Her clothes tended to hug her slender frame in just the right way.

"Brace yourself."

"What?" Isabelle's mind had drifted elsewhere.

"Brace yourself," Harper repeated.

Seated at the table in the dining hall were Harper's parents, Edward and Patricia, Uncle Herbert Harper, and of course the two angry birds, Carolyn and Danny.

Danny let out a slow clap. "Finally, Principessa." He had probably been drinking all day. He still wore the yellow button down Hugo Boss shirt he had on earlier, which by now had become quite wrinkled. "Can we eat now?"

Harper ignored him and introduced Isabelle to her parents and uncle. Patricia Harper had long black hair and a cool, indifferent air about her, as if she was rarely bothered by anything. She looked like a photograph of an actress from another era. Like a black and white image that captured the spirit and constitution of character, with beauty as an after-thought. Her lash-laden eyes were almost dreamy and her mouth curved just enough to let you know she was amiable.

She raised her eyebrows and said graciously, "Isabelle, wel-come."

Edward echoed his wife's greeting. His piercing blue eyes quickly took stock of Isabelle and moved on in a contented way. His broad face was vibrant and tanned, and his thick dark hair was an unruly mop atop his head.

Uncle Herbert however, responded by taking his glasses from the pocket of his sports coat and slipping it onto his nose. He regarded Isabelle keenly, but said nothing in the way of a greeting.

"Uncle Herbert is a little racist," Carolyn whispered. She was sitting to Isabelle's left and inched closer the moment Isabelle sat down.

Danny snickered and Edward cleared his throat to say something, but Patricia's voice cut through them all with its elevated clarity, "Shall we eat?"

Lilly and the cook, Marjorie, brought out chilled cucumber soup with roasted beets. Everyone dug in without much fanfare. Isabelle was grateful there was no need for conversation, and she did not have to present a monologue on herself and her family. Once they were half way through the honey-coriander glazed salmon and ginger rice, Harper, who had been dutifully tending to Isabelle, turned her attention to her mother.

"I put something on your schedule for today," Harper said. "Didn't you see it?"

Patricia looked up, perplexed, yet still with that cool, unperturbed demeanor.

"When?"

"Today."

"I mean what time?" Patricia asked.

"This afternoon," Harper said. "I left a message with your office. I said it was urgent."

"My secretary did not mention it. You cannot put something on my schedule last minute and expect an immediate response."

Harper tensed. On the other side, Carolyn's thigh brushed against Isabelle's. Isabelle couldn't tell if it was to nudge her to witness the drama that was about to unfold, or just unnecessary touching. Isabelle pulled closer to Harper.

"Hence why I said it was urgent." Harper shot her mother a wooden stare.

"What was it about, dear?" Edward asked, his eyes alert. His face was flushed and shiny and vigorous. He had eaten quickly. He had the demeanor of someone who always had somewhere else to be.

"An issue that is becoming more pressing," Harper said.

"That issue is no concern of ours." Patricia spoke up with a new forcefulness, with her elbows propped up on the table and her fingers laced together in front of her. "Why you persist in this hunt, this endeavor . . ." She looked around the table for a word to finish her thought.

"Burying your head in the proverbial sand won't make it go away." Harper met her mother's dismissive tone with resolve.

"Is this about that old Turkey problem?" Herbert piped up. "I thought we had resolved it some time ago. Edward?"

"There are remnants, elements," Edward spat reluctantly, waving his hand. His gaze went to Harper then darted away.

"This is neither the time nor the place." Patricia slowly folded and unfolded her napkin on the table top.

"Which is why I had scheduled a meeting to discuss our course of action," Harper said, glaring at her.

"Put it on my calendar for another day."

"Forget it." Harper clanged her fork against her plate.

"Ugh." Carolyn flipped her hair and poured herself another glass of Sauvignon Blanc. "Such fucking dull conversation. You are all putting me off my dinner."

Danny's head slumped forward as he grinned at Edward. "How's the filly?"

"Mighty sweet," Edward brightened. "The boys gave me a spin today."

"Is your dad into horse racing?" Isabelle whispered. She tried to pull Harper's mind away from the tense conversation with her mother.

"Race cars," Harper said softly. "He's sponsoring a car in one of the North American championships."

Danny and Edward talked about cars for several minutes while everyone else continued to eat in silence. When he realized Danny had fallen asleep, Edward turned his attention to his wife. They glowed with love and attraction to each other. They whispered together and he kissed her shoulder. Patricia sighed.

Harper had been eavesdropping on their conversation. She smiled.

"Looks like I might get my meeting after all," Harper said to Isabelle. Then she turned and kissed Isabelle softly on the lips. Right there in front of everyone.

Isabelle's cheeks flushed and the room blurred. She took a sip of water, unable to look at Harper, although she could sense how pleased she was at having done it. Before she could bask in the sweet tingling on her lips, Herbert rumbled at the end of the table.

"And where is she from?"

Everyone looked at him, except Danny who had passed out on the table.

"New Jersey," Harper said glibly.

"Where part of New Jersey? Where is her family from?"

Harper stared him down, and after an eternity had passed, Isabelle decided she should answer for herself.

"I don't think that's any of your business," Harper spoke up.

Their eyes were locked onto each other's till Herbert broke away and glared at Edward. "What nonsense is this? Can I not enquire about a guest in my house?"

"Our house," Edward said dismissively.

"Precisely. Don't I have the right to know—"

"You don't," Edward interjected. "Not if she's a guest of my daughter's."

Herbert's face took on the color of the salmon on the table.

"This is the same goddamn thing I am talking about!" Herbert said. "Since when does your side of the family rule this house?"

"My side? She is your niece!"

"You damn well are." Herbert looked at Harper. "I deserve some respect here."

Harper softened, but did not say anything. She nodded toward her uncle and looked down at the table. A sense of concession hovered between them. A quiet and tender recognition about each other that drew Isabelle in.

Carolyn's hand slid up Isabelle's thigh. Isabelle flinched. Harper spun around and Carolyn drew her hand back. Isabelle's mind went blank. Her voice eluded her, but Harper read every thought on her face.

She got up and calmly walked around to Carolyn's chair.

"What are you doing?" Harper asked.

Carolyn feigned innocence. Then she took a sip of wine and sneered at her cousin.

"Has something happened?" Patricia asked, standing as well, genuine concern etched across her face.

What hasn't happened?

Patricia had come around the table in a flash, which made Isabelle suspect that certain incidents occurred quite frequently within this family. She stood between her daughter and her niece.

"Victoria, what happened?" Patricia pleaded.

Emboldened now that she had a buffer, Carolyn stood up shakily, having consumed at least three glasses of wine. She waved her hand in Harper's direction.

"What? Did I do something inappropriate?" Carolyn slurred. "Did I take something that wasn't mine?" She shook her head as she said this, taunting her cousin. "No I didn't. I merely grazed my hand against—"

The slap shut her up mid-sentence.

"Arghh!" Carolyn screamed, clutching her face.

"Is that really necessary?" Patricia wrapped herself around Harper, pinning her arms down, but Harper was already calm again.

Isabelle was stunned. Her heart pounded in her chest as Edward dashed over and restrained Carolyn.

"Come, come on now," he said. "Stop this."

He and Herbert dragged Carolyn away as she struggled to lash out at Harper. She stuck her middle finger out before being led out of the room.

In a matter of seconds, dinnertime with the Harpers had devolved into chaos. Adrenalin coursed through Isabelle's body even after everyone had scattered.

Harper did not stick around to talk. She and her mother went off to discuss business in private, leaving Isabelle to wonder if the incident could have been handled in a less ferocious manner.

The older men had invited Isabelle to join them for a cigar in the library, but she politely declined. She retreated to the salon, where Lilly had brought out a Scrabble game so they could play. Lilly tried to reassure Isabelle about the incident.

"Sometimes I think her cousins just want to be her," she said. "They also hate that she got to live with their mother abroad for many years."

"That was just not cool," Isabelle said, still shocked.

"I know." Lilly looked apologetic. She had thin brown hair which she kept pinned in a butterfly clip at the back of her head. Her face was slender and her complexion was washed out, as if she had not seen the sun in months. "It's not an excuse, but Carolyn has this huge chip on her shoulder. There was another cousin who Victoria was besties with when they were young." She lowered her voice. "Herbert's daughter, Edith. Edith and Victoria were around the same age and thicker than thieves in honey. Carolyn was the odd one out."

"So where's Edith now?"

"Nobody's allowed to talk about her." Lilly moved the Scrabble pieces around on her tray. "Herbert's orders."

"Why..."

Danny ambled into the room. The staff had cleared the table after dinner and left him there. One side of his face was imprinted with the floral lace pattern of the table cloth. He mumbled something and threw himself across the chair.

"You missed quite a show!" Lilly said, even though Isabelle shot her a let's-not-rehash-look.

"What'd I miss?" Danny yawned.

"Well," Lilly said, injecting dramatic flair into her voice. "There was the usual bickering."

"Of course."

"But then your sister attempted to fondle Isabelle under the table." The words fell out hastily, as if she could not contain them. She was beside herself with glee.

Danny's eyebrows shot up. "She did not!"

"She did. And guess what she got for her troubles?"

"Don't tell me . . ."

"A stinging slap to the face, that's what," Lilly exclaimed. "Victoria was so upset. I've never seen her so upset before."

"Stupid, stupid girl. I didn't think Sis would be dumb enough to mess with this one."

"Isabelle is very sweet."

"And I'm right here." Isabelle crossed her arms.

Lilly laughed.

Danny pushed himself up from the chair and went to make a drink. Lilly rushed over and pulled the whiskey away.

"How about some water for a change?" She poured a glass of water and handed it to him. He stood there and drank it down reluctantly then came over to watch them play.

After a while he leaned in next to Isabelle's ear.

"Did you like it?"

"That's enough." Isabelle shot him a scalding look.

Danny chuckled and plopped back onto the chair.

For the next hour and a half, the three of them played a silly game of charades and consumed a significant amount of whiskey. Danny was trying to come up with another game when Lilly was called away by Frederick.

Danny yawned and rubbed his eyes. "I'll say this," he mumbled. "Uncle Herbert gets riled up easily, but he's the strongest man I know."

Isabelle seized the opportunity to broach one of the topics that had come up at dinner.

"Do you guys always bicker like this, over house guests and Turkey and what not?"

"Turkey?" He opened his eyes wide, which took a good deal of effort.

"Yes," Isabelle said, filled with superficial courage infused by her drink. "Victoria was pushing the issue and Patricia seemed to want to avoid it."

"Most of us avoid that issue," Danny said, his words slurring. "Victoria is the only one who sees it as some great mission. Unfinished business. She is most like our great-grandmother. Maybe that's why."

"In what way?" Isabelle asked, glancing at the portrait of Eugenie on the wall.

Danny looked at the painting too. "That woman had good intentions that spiraled out of control. She hated to see injustice against the little man. Anyone who couldn't defend themselves, she delivered justice for them." He swung his arm as if it held a sword. His motion was so slow it made Isabelle laugh.

"How?" She was suddenly intrigued by the woman.

"Eugenie had her ways. Legend has it none of those ways were legal."

He turned to Isabelle and grinned. When she twisted her face into a skeptical frown he went on quickly, as if to prove that what he'd said was true.

"For real," he said. "She did . . . stuff to people. Then she started to love the 'work' she was doing."

He got up and teetered toward the portrait.

"It took a lot to do what she did and she ran out of money. Her husband had stopped funding her private medical practice here in Newport, much less giving her extra to go cavorting all over the world." His voice took on a dramatic tone, like a storyteller's, and his arms continued to punctuate. "When Eugenie learned about this venture in Turkey that could get her enough money to do anything she wanted, she packed up and set off for that country with her friends. Everything she had heard was true. Soon she and her crew were bathing in money. They didn't have to answer to anyone.

"Eugenie was away from her family, you know? She was surrounded by people who thought the same way she did and had the same big, self-serving idea of justice. They were fucking unstoppable during that time."

Isabelle was afraid to ask what they did. This story had an ominous feel to it, the way Danny stood transfixed by that frightening woman, and the way the whiskey had loosened his lips.

"What did they do to carry out justice?" She couldn't help herself.

"Eugenie was a doctor," he said, winking. "She used what she had."

Wrong diagnoses? Bad drugs? A scalpel?

"What did she use?" Her head flopped back against the couch.

"I can't disclose that," he said, looking down at her. "Do you know why Victoria was sent to live with my mother, Roslyn, in Turkey?"

Isabelle shook her head and sat up. The sudden shift in topic to Harper caught her off guard.

He came and sat next to her on the sofa, having poured himself another drink, and swirled the amber liquid in his glass.

"When she was a teenager she went through . . . some things. We all did. I think Victoria took it worse than all of us." He took a slow, contemplative sip.

"She ran with a crew that smoked a lot of weed and other shit. They'd go to the mall, for instance, and wreak havoc. Jumping on cars, scratching the paint, slashing tires, being loud and obnoxious. After a while she got bored with that stuff. She seemed to settle down, but I think she was searching for something that could take her to the next level." He smirked. "Something that wasn't so juvenile. When she discovered a bunch of rich kids in the neighboring towns who liked to smoke and didn't have a source – that was her ticket. She supplied them with weed, but it was insane how she mapped everything out. She had this elaborate distribution system even though we were next door.

"I was just a kid, but I helped her out back then. One day she sat me down and showed me her plans to get weed to these kids without being detected. All I had to do was go to the amusement park, get on the same ride as some dude, and slip him the bag. It was so fucking simple, but she made me rehearse like crazy."

Isabelle nodded, unsure of what to say.

"That life wasn't for me though." Danny knocked back his drink. "Carolyn and I run a clothing store our dad opened before he died."

"Who was your father?" Isabelle asked.

"John Westbrook. A studious man who loved artistry. My mom hated him."

"So how come Harper ended up with your mom?" Isabelle asked, ignoring the last part of his statement. "You didn't say."

"As careful as she was, her scheme got busted," Danny said. "Cops caught some kids with weed and asked where they got it from. They ratted her out."

"Did she get sent away to Juvy or something?"

"Not at all. Our family always had the right connections, you know. Victoria also claimed that while it was true she smoked weed from time to time, she had not distributed drugs to anybody else." He smiled. "Anyway, Patricia and Edward had had enough. My mother was a tough woman, and they believed she would take Victoria in hand if they sent her to live with her in Istanbul. She went over there for the summer after she graduated from high school, but something wasn't quite right . . ." His expression turned thoughtful. "She was partying and doing photo shoots, so her parents brought her back and pulled some strings to get her into the academy. By then she'd had a taste of a certain lifestyle and had decided that's what she wanted. She dropped out of West Point and went to Istanbul for a few years. Then out of nowhere she came back."

"What was the lifestyle she wanted?"

He leaned forward and lowered his voice as if he and Isabelle were co-conspirators.

"Going to Istanbul kind of led Victoria down a path she had always thought was her destiny."

"What do you mean?" Her heart thudded against her ribcage with anticipation about this Victoria Harper revelation.

"In her journals, Eugenie had pompously said that her grandson Edward's firstborn was to be the heir to the legacy she started. Edward only ended up having one child, Victoria. So Victoria took it as a sign that carrying on her great-grandmother's legacy was her duty."

Chapter Thirteen

IT WAS TEN THIRTY AND Harper still had not returned from the discussions with her mother. Danny's tales had spooked Isabelle and she excused herself by telling him she was tired. Mostly she wanted a moment to reflect on the day's events, her own muddied affairs, and these new revelations about Harper. She had to admit the details Danny shared about Harper's younger years were not entirely surprising. It was hard to imagine a perpetually good child crashing out of West Point, and later needing an isolated hideout so she could have target practice with all sorts of weapons.

She had been mutinous since she was young. A teenager making questionable choices. A young woman hell bent on rebellion.

Isabelle went upstairs, but when she got to her bedroom she continued down the hallway. Lilly came toward her with a teapot on a tray.

"I considered bringing tea to your room," Lilly said. "Would you like that?"

"Aren't you going to sleep soon?" Isabelle asked, slurring her words. Did the staff work round-the-clock?

"When I feel like it." Lilly shrugged. "This really is like my home."

"Sure. Tea then."

"Chamomile will be perfect. I just brought some to Carolyn."

Isabelle looked toward the double doors they were standing in front of.

"This is Victoria's room," Lilly said. "Carolyn is further down."

She had a twinkle in her eyes and a naughty smirk.

"Not interested in whatever you're thinking." Isabelle rolled her eyes. "I just feel bad about what happened."

Lilly, who Isabelle believed to be around twenty-one, obviously got a kick out of the family drama. "Why don't you go in and see Carolyn? She's whimpering like a kicked dog."

"I don't think that's a good idea."

"Let me take this tray to the kitchen. Be back in a minute."

Isabelle kept going. At the end of the hallway was a cheerful, well-lit sitting area. The bright patterns of the furniture were complimented by a chandelier with gold jewels and emerald stones. This small corner of the house also offered an ocean view, except it was dark outside now. Across the grass and in the distance stirred the hypnotic, gurgling white foam of the sea.

A set of framed photographs sat under the window looking stilted. One of them was a family portrait – she recognized the man as a youthful Uncle Herbert, with a wife and three young children, a freckle-faced girl and two scrawny boys. Herbert looked different, not just in terms of age, but his aura was unbound. Perhaps less rigid than he was now.

An empty teacup was on the coffee table, with lipstick marks the same shade of tangerine Carolyn had worn at dinner. Next to the teacup was a stack of letters in envelopes addressed to Carolyn and Danny with a return address in Istanbul.

Isabelle slipped away. She was worried Carolyn might return and did not want to run into her. She went back downstairs, walking quickly in case Danny was still loitering, waiting to unleash more unpleasant family tales. She'd had her fill for the night. Still, she couldn't resist the urge to get the answers from Harper.

The air in the library swirled with thick cigar smoke. Herbert and Edward were in one corner, hunched over a chessboard.

"Ah, Isabelle." Edward looked up. "Has she abandoned you?"

"She is still speaking with her mother."

"Hmph." Herbert let out a gruff noise. "That sort of business ought to be done with, once and for all."

"Well isn't that what she is doing, Herb?"

"You should have done it years ago!"

Isabelle had not meant to stir things up again.

"I don't want to interrupt your game," she said, hedging back toward the door. "Lilly is bringing me tea."

"Nonsense." Edward waved a hand. "Come and join us." He got up and poured her a glass of scotch as Harper walked in. "Well?"

"I have the go ahead," she said, beaming. "It will be done with soon."

"Good," Herbert said. "And then let's be done with it once and for all."

Edward put his arm around Harper's shoulder and led her toward the grand salon. He listened intently as his daughter spoke, running his hand through his thick hair, and rubbing his chin. It was an intense discussion, but he looked comical. Harper was the more serious of the two. Then again, Isabelle had had at least three glasses of Jack and Coke during the games with Lilly and Danny earlier, and perhaps her mind was turning him into a caricature.

Herbert came over as she stared off into the distance in a bemused manner. He cleared his throat to get her attention. Isabelle turned to him. He was sweating profusely, although the room was quite cool.

"I don't want you to misunderstand my comment," he said.

"Sorry?" Isabelle wasn't sure what he was talking about. It had been a long night.

"My behavior at dinner," Herbert said. "I hope you don't take me the wrong way. I get upset quite often when dealing with my family."

"Oh. I'm not offended." Isabelle's mind was swirling with curiosity about Harper and the tale she was currently telling her father.

"Well, in case you were," he said stiffly, "I do apologize."

"Thank you." Isabelle nodded to him. "I appreciate you saying so."

Herbert was stockier than his brother, and in this light he had a natural and genuine air to him. His hair was cut low and combed neatly to one side. He had removed his sports coat, and was wearing jeans and a white shirt with the sleeves rolled up to his elbow. Satisfied he had cleared the air with Isabelle, he turned and focused his attention on his brother and niece.

"You know." He re-lit a half-smoked cigar and clenched it between his teeth. "For what it's worth, the women in this family all tend to have grandiose ideas. I secretly admire it. Such verve and vigor. It makes me feel encouraged. Uplifted to see what could have been."

Isabelle knotted her brows. "What could have been?"

He looked at the floor pensively, but did not explain.

"V and I squashed our little argument," Herbert mused. "We tend to have these tussles but it's all harmless. Sometimes I'm hard on her. I acknowledge that. I often think of her as my own."

Before she could respond, Harper and Edward came strolling over. Isabelle went to Harper. She was happy to see her and didn't realize how lonely the house had been without her.

"Happy news then?"

"Indeed." She led Isabelle to the opposite side of the room and they stood together next to a wall of books, behind the antique wood pool table. "We've come up with a plan to help Steven. I had to reduce myself to begging my mother to reach out to an associate in Istanbul who can help to extract him from the situation."

"What kind of situation?" Isabelle felt freer about questioning Harper now. Her understanding of her was beginning to take shape.

"Steven worked for an organization my great-grandmother founded. He became a member in the early nineties. Some unpleasant realities have emerged. He's in danger because of his connection to us. It's not safe anymore."

"Are we talking about the organization you referred to before?" Isabelle whispered, having now gathered enough information to know Harper was not joking when she had alluded to it at their meeting in Chester.

Harper held her gaze. "I can neither confirm nor deny that."

Her twinkling eyes revealed she had meant it as a joke, but Isabelle would not let her get away with downplaying things this time. This matter was grave enough to have the entire family worked up and at each other's throats.

"Tell me," Isabelle insisted.

Harper clammed up, and for a while Isabelle thought she might not answer at all.

"Let's sit," she finally said.

They took a pair of armchairs facing each other, next to a window that looked out on the southern end of the property. Isabelle could make out a forlorn stretch of horse stables in the darkness, and closer up the bright tips of flowers in the dimly lit garden.

"It's complicated," Harper said. "I don't know where to begin. I can tell you that Steven helped me with the Maramaxe exposé. I tried to convince him to move to the States. He did so briefly then went back to Europe after a couple years. He's a cultured man of the world and he could not stay still. He managed to be incognito for the longest time, and after several years had passed felt comfortable enough to return to Turkey.

"The problem wasn't just the exposé; it was our history in that country. My great-grandmother's company grew into much more than she had originally intended, and I must admit she never shied away from the benefits. Enemies emerged once huge profits became part of it, and she kind of lost the control she had in the beginning..."

"Anyway." She brushed a hand down her thigh dismissively. "I feel like I've had to pull teeth to get this done. My ways might not always be societally acceptable, but I've done what I needed to do for my own survival. I've never asked for permission to do anything. I've never waited for anyone to tell me what I should do or how I should do it. That's what pisses me off about my mother. She was never cutthroat enough to succeed in the political world. She thought she was above the muck. Yet with me, she can be difficult beyond reason."

"I'm sure she has a reason." Isabelle wasn't sure why she'd said that and she could tell Harper was shocked too.

"Oh yeah? What do you think her reason is?" Harper looked annoyed and amused at the same time, if ever such a thing was possible.

"Foolhardy-ness. Yours."

"Is that a word?"

"Probably not, but I'm sure if there was such a word it would describe you."

"What's gotten into you?" Harper gave a half-smile. "What have you been drinking?"

"Coca cola."

Harper was staring again, a look of unbridled intensity and intrigue. She wasn't used to being tested. She leaned forward.

"If there's anything I learned from Eugenie, it's that you've got to damn the rules sometimes."

"What else did you learn from Eugenie?"

"What else?"

"Hm mm."

"You fascinate me." Harper smiled more broadly. A spark came through in her eyes, as if her mind had wandered elsewhere. She drew a slow breath. "I've learned a lot throughout my life. Time is the best medicine."

"You speak like you've been around through the ages."

"Maybe I have."

Something about the look on Harper's face made Isabelle's breath catch. She brushed her hair from her face and looked down at her hands, which appeared to be floating in her lap. She blinked then forced herself to meet Harper's dark eyes.

"You're quite sure of yourself," Isabelle said.

"Very."

Isabelle stood. She had meant to put on a show of sensual intimidation, but her knees wobbled. She managed a few steps and found herself standing over Harper, sandwiching Harper's knee with her legs, and looking down into her bright, expectant eyes.

"What exactly is your business?" Isabelle asked. "Why are you so entangled?"

Harper held both of Isabelle's wrists firmly, giving them a squeeze. Her fingers were warm and gripped Isabelle with such command that a surge of excitement, like electric currents, coursed through her.

"That's a loaded question," Harper said quietly, almost to herself.

"I need an answer."

"Do you now?" Harper's hands went to Isabelle's hips, transferring the warmth there and holding her in place.

Isabelle nodded, unsure if her voice was still fully functioning.

Harper stood, bringing their bodies so close together that Isabelle froze. Harper pushed Isabelle's hair back with both hands and cupped her neck.

"In time all your questions will be answered," Harper said. "I promise." Her eyes locked onto to Isabelle's lips. "You're in a state," she whispered, entranced.

It was true – Isabelle had drunk too much. Her arms were loose and gooey at her side, though Harper's body against hers was hard and steadying.

She looked toward the other side of the room at the men at the chessboard, the two broad figures like a mirage in the smoke.

When Isabelle turned back to Harper, her insides loosened too. Harper's lips brushed against hers and something billowed inside her. Her eyes fluttered when Harper pulled back, and Isabelle could only see soft edges of her face, as if Harper was under the veil of a cloud.

She was lowered into the chair, and then Harper moved to open the window. The air came in sweetly, like a cool caress across Isabelle's face. A bit of strength returned to her, and when she raised her head Harper pressed a cold cloth against it.

"Never again," Isabelle muttered and squeezed her temples. She had come to Newport to get away from her own troubles, but all she had gained so far was a throbbing, hung-over headache. A copious amount of alcohol was not going to help her clear her thoughts.

She had drunk almost the whole pitcher of water by her bedside before the pain began to dissipate.

"Isabelle?" Lilly was outside her room door. The breakfast chime had gone off a while ago. "Are you coming down?"

"Not sure I can," Isabelle groaned.

"Can I get you anything?"

"It's okay, Lilly." Harper's voice was soft and reassuring. "Thank you."

Isabelle got up and opened the door.

"I'd like to take you out for brunch if you're up to it." Harper was holding a paper coffee cup. She looked casual in a black T-shirt and jeans, and black and white Converse.

"Depends." Isabelle blinked bleary eyes at her. "Is that coffee?"

Harper nodded and smiled.

"Thank you." Isabelle took the cup. She couldn't help smiling in return. "Give me a few minutes."

"Um," Harper hesitated.

"What?"

"I like your hair this way."

"Excuse me?"

"I prefer your hair this way."

"So?"

At certain moments the upper hand was squarely in Isabelle's favor in their strange dynamic, and she derived pleasure out of making Harper's life difficult whenever the opportunity presented itself.

"I was just saying," Harper shifted and cleared her throat, "that it would be nice if you left it like this."

"What makes you believe you get to say?" Isabelle arched one eyebrow.

"I'm sorry." Harper laughed nervously. "I guess I don't."

"I'll see what I can do." Isabelle smiled.

"No." Harper reached a hand toward her, attempting to apologize. "You don't have to."

"First you tell me what to do with my hair." Isabelle paused. "Then you tell me what not to do with my hair."

"I thought you had a hangover," Harper said, smirking. "Here I am feeling bad for you and you're stirring up trouble."

Isabelle ran her hand through her thick curls and batted her eyelids.

"My hair is out of control. So are you."

She shooed Harper away gently and closed the door.

They drove up Thames Street in Harper's 1984 Cadillac Seville. The car had a hunched, razor-back trunk and a long, rectangular mouth. Burgundy leather seats matched the color of the exterior, and it featured a cassette deck, which Harper did not turn on. It was a beautiful and solid vehicle – a classic throwback to a time when luxury had to be substantially displayed.

Victoria Harper was not a classic woman. She was a renegade.

"I'm not sure this car suits you," Isabelle teased.

"Oh really? Why not?"

Their flirtatious rapport had continued throughout the morning, and though Isabelle was well aware she was the instigator, she found it hard to resist.

"You're a twenty-first century woman," Isabelle said. "You're a little more nuanced."

Harper was quiet, as if taking in Isabelle's comment.

"Interesting," she finally said. "It was a gift from Steven."

"Steven Smyth?"

"Yes." Harper smiled as they parked in a lot near the restaurant. "He liked that it was an American car, but it also made him think of his hometown in Spain."

They walked down the narrow sidewalk in silence. Newport reminded Isabelle of other weather-beaten towns – comfortable, unhurried, perhaps even transitory. She was beginning to feel transient herself, like the misanthropic existence she thought was inevitable had been disturbed.

Isabelle and Harper took a table in the far corner of the brightly lit dining room. Their orders of French toast arrived on large plates, topped with fruit under a slathering mound of whipped cream. Slabs of bacon were served on the side. They laughed at the sight of all that food and dug in.

The restaurant was fairly full. It was a mixture of families who looked like they were visiting Newport and locals who greeted the servers and hostesses by name as they entered. A sense of banal familiarity came over Isabelle. She had traveled enough through the States on perfunctory family trips with Marcia and Haughton, and she had come to see how similar people were in their routines and habits. Particularly as a group gathered for a meal in a restaurant at any time, they were all more or less the same. People moved from one activity to another, from one phase of life to another, and in between, the mundane stodge of heaping meals and passing time.

"I thought you might like to get out of that house," Harper said, pulling Isabelle out of her musing. "I'm sorry about Carolyn."

"Why didn't you check on me?"

"Check on you?"

"After what Carolyn did?"

"I handled it. She won't be doing that again."

"That's not what I was asking," Isabelle said softly. "You left me alone in your house after your cousin tried to get frisky with me."

Harper fell silent. Color crept across her face and neck. "I'm sorry. I wasn't thinking." She clasped her hands against her lips. "I was so preoccupied with talking to my mother. I'll make it up to you."

"Apology accepted." Isabelle reached for the syrup. "Has she done that before?"

"My cousins have done a lot of things." Harper smirked and pushed the decanter closer for her. "They really do get on my nerves."

"I totally get it." Isabelle was distracted, trying to work up the courage to raise a topic that had been on her mind since their meeting in Chester. "I've been meaning to talk to you."

"Did I mess up again?" Harper looked sheepish.

"It's about the story you told me. Your memoir project."

Harper stiffened and cut a square of her French Toast. "Go on."

"I've given it some thought." Isabelle hesitated.

"And?"

"Maybe it's best for me to not get involved."

"Why is that?"

"Why do you want me to be involved?"

"Tell me why you're now hedging." Harper put her fork down. "Is it because of my family?"

"Of course not," Isabelle said hastily. "I'm not an investigative journalist. I think you should get help from someone who is more qualified for this kind of work."

"That would be too impersonal."

"Surely, you have friends . . ."

"I'm embarrassed." She shook her head lightly and looked away.

"About what?"

"I'm really having a hard time explaining my intentions to you."

Isabelle waited.

"I like being around you."

"So this is all a ruse to spend time with me?"

"Well, not quite." Harper considered. "I like your writing and I like you."

"My writing is inconsequential."

"I beg to differ." Harper pushed her plate aside. "You're much better with words than I am. I tend to act, sometimes too quickly. Sometimes I act to cover for my inability to express, especially when things are confusing or delicate. I don't even know how to begin—"

"You shouldn't be kissing me," Isabelle blurted.

She was shocked she had said it, and she realized it was another concern that had been lurking in the back of her mind for a while.

Harper's eyes roved over Isabelle's face, as if Isabelle had spoken a foreign language and she was trying to understand. Then Harper took a sip of her coffee and dabbed her lips with the napkin. "If you're finished, maybe we can go for a walk?"

Isabelle finished her coffee as Harper settled the check. They walked to the mostly vacant piers where stores, restaurants, and boutiques lined the waterway. Harper stopped in the shade of one of the buildings and looked out in the distance. The wind tugged at her T-shirt, but she stood motionless for a long time.

The lapping sound of the Atlantic Ocean was its own solemn music. Isabelle's eyes drifted to the sailboats on the undulating water. She'd said what needed to be said. It was wrong of her to get this close to Victoria Harper. Last night in the library the energy between them was pulsating, and Isabelle was afraid of how much it pleased her. The thought of being pleased by this woman's touch or kisses left her feeling bewildered and a little giddy.

"You look cold," Isabelle said. She pulled off her denim jacket, an eighties style bomber, and pushed it toward Harper. Harper turned around and looked at it, then looked at Isabelle. She came closer and took the jacket, letting her hands roam over the fabric. Then she brought it up to her face and closed her eyes. She inhaled. The gesture rocked Isabelle back, but before she could say anything, Harper stepped forward and wrapped the jacket around Isabelle's shoulders.

She remained where she was, entirely too close.

"What were you saying earlier about a kiss?" Harper asked, eyes gleaming. She drew shallow breaths as her lips parted.

"I . . ." Isabelle failed to find the words she needed.

"Yes?"

"You know what I said."

"Why would you say such a thing?" It was almost a breathless whisper. Harper's eyes fell to Isabelle's lips and lingered.

"I don't know how I came to be here." Isabelle's stomach dipped and she had that precarious feeling again, but this time it was accompanied by something else. A smoldering heat shot through her. She attempted to take a step back. Harper was holding on to the lapels of her jacket, deftly keeping her in place.

"It sounds like you teleported." Harper wore a serious expression. She met Isabelle's eyes. "I invited you here and you came."

Isabelle glided closer. She raised her head, bringing her lips a breath away from Harper's. She closed her eyes and the sound of the ocean and seagulls in the sunshine were all she heard.

"I want you to stop kissing me," Isabelle whispered, even as she pressed in so that their bodies fused together.

"Okay." Harper kissed her. Her tongue played across Isabelle's lips then slipped inside, bringing with it a stirring unknown to Isabelle before now. She returned the kiss, her tongue lapping at Harper's, urgent and full of heat. Harper nibbled and sucked at her lips and it sent a sharp trill of desire through Isabelle that made her knees weak.

When Harper released her Isabelle touched her lips as if she'd been bitten.

Harper's face was dark and challenging, her posture alert as if she was afraid Isabelle might run. "I broke it off with Caye," she said hoarsely.

"Why?" Isabelle swallowed to ease the dryness in her throat.

"You're the one I want."

"You can't have me."

Harper's eyebrows shot up. "Give me one good reason."

"It's messy." Isabelle pushed her hair from her face and folded her arms. She was unprepared for the moment and the effect of the kiss. Even as she was being resistant the truth lodged itself in the back of her mind, settled into her. No one else had ever left her wanting more. Not like this.

Harper relaxed and stuck her hands into her pockets. "I wish you could see the way the light plays with your eyes," she said quietly. Then she nodded, as if she had made a bet and lost. "Let's head back."

Chapter Fourteen

HARPER HAD TO MAKE a few phone calls when they got back to the house, and Isabelle used the opportunity to go for a walk alone. She went to the back of the estate, past the aromatic perennials and around the small sunken garden, until she found a stone seat that was really a large gnome-like creature. She sat on its fat belly and thought about the turn her life had taken.

Had she made a mistake from the beginning by entertaining any sort of conversation with Victoria Harper? Perhaps she'd made a mistake coming to Newport, flirting with her. Yet if those were mistakes, how could they make her feel so alive, like she'd come out of a deep slumber? Like she had emerged from a fog that obscured years of her life? Worst of all, how could she explain this to Caye?

Isabelle scrolled through the recent contacts on her phone and tapped Caye's name. It rang for a while, and as Isabelle was about to hang up, Caye answered.

"You never call me these days." Her voice sounded groggy, like she was still half-asleep.

"You know that's not true," Isabelle said. "Did I wake you?"

"I was out late last night." Caye yawned.

"Oh really? Do tell."

"It's not what you're thinking." She laughed like a trickster who'd been caught in the act. "Well, maybe it's partly what you're thinking."

"Who were you with?" Isabelle was more interested in Caye's behavior than who she was with, but she figured it was a good place to start.

"Someone who kind of snuck up on me. She works for a client of ours – a company that manufactures plastic products. They're now trying to position themselves to grab a bigger share of the market. It's going to take a lot to do that because of gaps in the supply chain, poorly managed profit margins, to say the least. When we put the data together—"

"So you slept with this woman?" Isabelle wanted to get to the point.

"It started out as a business dinner. It was all innocent until something shifted."

Isabelle had a good notion of what shifted.

"I just wanted to see how you're doing," she said. Suddenly, she was irritated and regretted calling Caye.

"Checking on me?" Caye sounded pleased. "You still care."

"You behave like a child sometimes."

"Ouch. What did I do to deserve that?"

"I just think . . ." Isabelle felt deceitful and guilty, but talking to Caye made her think she shouldn't feel any of those things. She was conflicted. "You're living your best life, I guess."

"Don't make it sound so dire."

Isabelle laughed. "I mean, you're going to continue to be you, Caye. I have to find something that works for me."

"Are you back in the game?"

"The game?"

"Yeah. Are you dating?"

"I have too much going on."

"I think you're saving yourself for me."

"Oh my God." Isabelle couldn't believe it. "Pompous much?"

"I saw myself marrying you when we were together."

Isabelle fell silent. Caye had never told her that before.

"I really did," Caye reiterated.

"What happened?"

"I get tangled up." Caye sighed. "I've got to put blinders on."

"Maybe you aren't meant to walk a straight line," Isabelle said. "Pun intended."

"Is that so?" Caye laughed. "Maybe I need to be tamed by the right woman."

Carolyn was coming up from the garden. She looked care-free in flip flops and sunglasses, and she carried a book under her arm.

"Are you up for the job?" Caye asked.

"Listen, I just called to see how you were doing," Isabelle said quickly. "I have to run."

"Double ouch."

"We'll talk later."

Isabelle hung up as Carolyn approached.

"Was that one of your lovers?" Carolyn spoke in an airy way, as if it wasn't a real question and it didn't matter if Isabelle answered.

"No." Isabelle tried to conceal her shock. Had Carolyn been listening to her conversation? "A friend."

"I see." She remained standing in front of Isabelle. She was wearing a tank top and a cheeky pair of shorts that showed part of her bottom.

"About last night . . ." Isabelle searched for the right thing to say. She had hoped she would not need to speak to Carolyn for the rest of her stay.

"I fucked up." Carolyn shrugged. "I shouldn't have touched you."

"Why did you do it?"

"Why not?"

Isabelle frowned, perplexed. "That's not how most of us go through life – asking 'why not' and doing whatever the hell we want."

She was getting worked up and she wasn't even sure if it was because of Carolyn.

"Don't preach to me." Carolyn stared her down. "You're with someone who does exactly that."

"I'm not with Victoria."

"Stop fooling yourself. You're not so naïve, are you?"

"What do you mean?"

"My cousin does not waste her time." Her mouth contorted into a smug grin. "If she's invested in you, she's invested."

"What are you implying?" Heat rushed to Isabelle's temples.

Carolyn threw her a snooty glare and looked away, as if she need not participate in a conversation she had initiated.

Isabelle stood. "What are you trying to say?"

Carolyn turned and examined Isabelle's body in a blunt manner.

"I bet I know why she likes you," she leered.

"Why does she like me?" *What was this woman's problem?*

"Besides your body and your face?" Carolyn's bright eyes peered into Isabelle, challenging. She bit her lip and smiled.

Isabelle shook her head. "You know what?" She'd had enough of this conversation. "I don't know what you're on, but you are out of line."

"Maybe it's your innocence," Carolyn said, like she was testing the notion as she said it, to see if it really fit.

"What the fuck do you know about me?"

"Ha!" She cackled at Isabelle's anger. "You're cute when you're mad."

"And you're an inappropriate asshole."

"I also think you're a sexually curious person," Carolyn continued. "What's not to like?"

"Fuck you."

Isabelle walked away as quickly as she could. She was boiling on the inside. She went down a small slope in the land and kept going until Carolyn was no longer in sight. Then she stopped and considered going back. Carolyn was childish and completely out of line.

A thick array of evergreen trees lined the grounds and swayed softly with the afternoon breeze. The house and its surroundings were calming, but everywhere Isabelle turned lately, she was presented with a challenge to her emotional control and peace of mind.

Victoria Harper was a conundrum all on her own, Caye was tone deaf and incorrigible, and this Carolyn person was beyond rude.

Isabelle went inside the horse stables and stood with her hand on her hips. She would leave. No point in spending any more time here. It was doing her no good. She had her own shit to deal with, and she had not spoken to Bastian since she'd left New Jersey.

The horses looked her way, perhaps expecting a treat.

"Sorry." She showed them her empty palms.

"Hello?" A lustrous voice came from one of the stalls.

"Hi," Isabelle said, surprised. "I didn't know anyone was here."

Patricia Harper poked her head out and smiled.

"I'm just grooming Logan."

Isabelle went over to her. She almost didn't recognize Patricia, who wore distressed overalls and a black fedora pulled down near her smiling eyes. It was disarming farm girl chic. Gone was the aerial diplomat from the dinner table last night. Her ability to transform reminded Isabelle of Harper.

"I didn't mean to disturb you."

"You didn't." Patricia took great care in brushing a large chestnut horse. Her movements were slow and languorous, as if this was more of an exercise in reflection and meditation than grooming. "Though I can tell by the way you stomped over here something or someone upset you."

"It's nothing," Isabelle said quickly. "I just wanted to take a walk."

"Has Victoria been a good host?"

"She has." Isabelle nodded. "It was kind of her to invite me."

"It was kind of you to come. My daughter doesn't have a lot of normal friends." She stepped out of the stall, causing the horse to whinny and pinch at her back with his mouth. She laughed. "He doesn't like when I leave."

"What kind of friends does she have?"

"People with a warped philosophy." Patricia picked up a rake and hung it on a hook in the wall. She put the brush away. "Anyway, I'm more interested in you. I understand you have a guest-house and you write."

"I do."

"Do you draw inspiration from your guests?"

"To be quite honest, I have not been very inspired lately."

"Really?" She lifted her hat briefly and smoothed back her dark hair. "Why do you think that is?"

"I've just been . . . buried."

Isabelle followed as Patricia went out.

"Buried how?"

"Blocked maybe," Isabelle said, shrugging. "Cliché, right?"

She found it easy to talk to Patricia. Her easygoing manner was infectious. She had an effortless beauty that was not striking, but rather warm, comforting even.

"Sometimes when I get stuck it's because I'm focusing on external stuff," Patricia said. "Something I have no control over."

"I do a lot of that lately," Isabelle admitted. "I thought this period of my life would be quieter. Well, that was the plan anyway."

"Oh, I see Carolyn's out," Patricia exclaimed, as they went up the small mound and across the lawn.

At first only her gangly legs were visible. The rest of her body was blocked by a freakish object. As they got closer it became clear Carolyn was sitting in the lap of a large bronze sculpture – a Faun. In one hand the mythological creature held a horn. The other hand was outstretched but empty. Carolyn had rested her sunglasses there, in the crook of its beckoning fingers.

"What you got there?" Patricia asked, walking toward her.

Carolyn turned slowly like a spawn of the half-goat, half-human creature, and looked at them with depraved blue-green eyes. She took her time responding to her aunt.

"Márquez," she said finally. "But don't get too excited. I've been on page nine for the last decade or so."

Isabelle moved closer to see the title. *Love in the Time of Cholera*. Carolyn didn't strike her as the type to read serious literature.

"It's a beautiful day for reading," Patricia said, with an upbeat cheer in her voice. "Writing too. I was just talking to Isabelle about her work."

"What do you write about, Isabelle?" Carolyn shot her a sly glance.

"Silly women," Isabelle said dryly.

"You'll find a lot of them here." Carolyn stared.

Isabelle bit her tongue. Carolyn was the silliest of them all. She was bored, entitled, and clearly jealous of her older cousin.

"It's well worth the read," Patricia said, eyes narrowing. "You should try to get through it." She touched Isabelle's arm as she motioned to step away.

"Have a good day," Isabelle said.

Carolyn turned back to her book and did not return the salutation.

"Would you like to sit for a while?" Patricia asked as they approached the lower garden.

"I was about to go inside." Isabelle was exhausted. It had been a trying day and she still had to process her growing attraction to Harper.

"Just for a moment," Patricia said. She led Isabelle down the short flight of limestone steps and into the maze of hedges that came up to their shoulders. Butterflies flittered in the air around them, and the sweet smell of lilies and peonies conjured the joys of the season.

They came out of the maze to a small koi pond where two metallic golden fish swam excitedly toward them, then away again. Their bodies were swift and glistening under water.

"How beautiful," Isabelle said. "I had no idea these were here."

"It's very tranquil down here." Patricia sat on one of the white iron chairs near the water's edge. "An escape from the chaos all around us."

Isabelle kneeled to get a closer look at the fish. They were curious, like they wanted to come to the surface. She put her hand out gleefully.

"To think I had avoided this garden," she said, shaking her head.

"Why would you do such a thing?"

"I don't know." Isabelle sighed. She thought of Bastian. "The idea of it made me sad for some reason."

"Well, I'm glad you gave it a chance." Patricia was watching her closely. "I wanted to apologize for Carolyn's behavior last night."

Isabelle put her hand above the water again. The fish brought their faces up and the little mouths opened. "Thank you," she said, but did not meet Patricia's glance.

"I also did not approve of the way my daughter reacted." Patricia sighed. "Dinner was so pleasant before all that, wasn't it?'

Isabelle chuckled at her sarcasm. "It's fine," she said. Then she thought better of it. "Actually, I had an encounter with Carolyn before I stomped into the stables."

"Ah." Patricia looked at her. "How was that?"

"Not pleasant." Isabelle spoke honestly. "What's her deal, if you don't mind me asking?"

"I don't mind. I know my family can be a bit of a quagmire. Carolyn likes attention. She acts up particularly when we have visitors. It's not personal at all."

"I didn't think it was personal, but it's just odd."

"She has this hang-up when it comes to her cousin. Victoria is older and I think Carolyn saw her as a big sister. She followed Victoria around. Doted on her, and when she didn't get what she wanted, fought with her. It was a constant battle when they were young."

"Did Victoria not want to be a big sister to her?"

"My daughter can be myopic. She's always been driven, even as a little girl. She had no time for Carolyn's whininess, I suppose. She clicks with certain personalities and that's it. She doesn't feed into drama. Victoria's level of intensity shocks me sometimes. She doesn't get that from me."

"Right," Isabelle said, almost to herself. Her mind flashed to her recent experience of that intensity. "I think I have a better understanding now."

"Good," Patricia said. "I apologize again. I will have a talk with Carolyn."

Isabelle wanted to talk more about Harper, but was shy. Patricia might see right through her, but what was there to see? She shrugged.

"Something else on your mind?"

"I . . ." Isabelle stammered. "Was just absorbing what you said."

"About Carolyn's behavior?" Patricia's eyes were astute. "Or about Victoria?"

"Well," Isabelle said, taking a breath. "I'm certainly starting to understand Victoria, but I didn't come here for her. Or I should say I didn't come here to get to know her. I mean, we are friendly, but we are not—"

"It's okay." Patricia smiled. "Victoria told me she thought you could use a change of pace. Coming to Newport is not a commitment to anything."

Isabelle's blush was full on. What the hell? The word "commitment" should not be in play at this moment. It should not be uttered under these bog-like circumstances where Isabelle was snarled by someone in this family at every turn. Not by either of Victoria Harper's parents, and certainly not in reference to their relationship.

Isabelle stood. The calmness brought on by Patricia's presence evaporated.

"Well thank you. It was nice talking to you." She held up her cell phone and backed away. "I owe my brother a phone call."

"Alright." Patricia hesitated, like she wanted to say more.

Isabelle would not give her the chance. As she hurried away, Patricia called out. "Isabelle?"

"Yes?"

"You'll need someone to talk to about Victoria at some point. And I want you to know I'm here when you're ready."

Isabelle went straight to her room and closed the door. She had managed to avoid any potential mines along the way, and that in itself was a relief. She washed her hands and changed out of her jeans, which were muddied at the knees.

She poured herself a glass of water and drank it down. She took a few deep breaths.

You'll need someone to talk to about Victoria at some point.

That phrase replayed in her head as she paced the room. Clearly Patricia thought her daughter was a handful. Bastian was right. She shouldn't have come here. Harper was an unknown. The questions were piling up and Isabelle was afraid of the answers.

She thought about her parents. She was beginning to believe whatever Marcia and Haughton's current circumstances were, it was of their own doing.

Instead of calling, she sent Bastian a text message indicating she was fine and asked how he was doing. He didn't respond.

Isabelle sighed and threw herself on the recliner. So many emotional balls were in the air, coming down all at once. Was she meant to catch them? Something had to be allowed to fall by the wayside. Marcia and Haughton's waywardness? Bastian's incomprehensible objective and psychological trauma? Caye's selfishness? Harper's sudden grip on her and the weighty morass of dealing with her family and her secrets?

Isabelle closed her eyes and longed for a quieter time. The guesthouse was supposed to bring her solitude. It was her personal retreat. Once Caye and Harper showed up at the party it seemed like Isabelle's whole world opened up. She had been sliced open somehow, the bruised and timid heart of her exposed.

❖

Lilly's bony face and bright pale eyes bore into Isabelle. The late afternoon sunlight filled the room, and for a brief moment

Isabelle had to think about where she was. She had fallen asleep in the chair. She was being shaken.

"What are you doing?" Isabelle sat up. "What time is it?"

"Five-something," Lilly said, a little breathless. "Come on, Victoria said to get you."

They went out and down the hall to Harper's room. Harper and Frederick were gathering clothing, toiletries and documents, which they stuffed into a small suitcase. Harper looked up when Isabelle entered.

"Give us a moment," she said.

Frederick zipped the suitcase shut and ushered himself and Lilly out of the room.

"An attempt was made on Steven's life," she said, strained and somber. "He had to flee."

"Oh God." Isabelle reeled back, at once sorry for the man, and shocked that his situation was so grave.

"I've been on the phone all afternoon." She took Isabelle's hands into hers, brushing her knuckles with her thumbs. "We were trying to coordinate his extraction so he could be flown to Wales as soon as possible, but now all of that is up in the air. We lost contact with him."

"Maybe he'll find a way to contact you," Isabelle offered weakly.

"I doubt it." Harper sighed. "I have to go to Istanbul."

Isabelle had known it was coming, and still the words struck her like a punch to the stomach. "This is so sudden," she squeaked. "What can you do?"

"I don't know yet," Harper said, thinking. "But my friends are there, and perhaps we can put our heads together."

"When will you return?"

"I don't know anything. I'm sorry . . ." Her gaze flicked away. "I wish I had more information to share."

How often did she do this – jet off into the unknown like some savior? She was leaving her home and her roots to go sort things out in a foreign country. The place she had fled in fear over a decade ago.

"The flight is in a few hours." Harper's lips twisted with uncertainty as she watched Isabelle. "I've asked Sud to take you home."

"Don't you need a driver?" Isabelle deflated.

"I'll take an Uber."

"It sounds incredibly dangerous to me. All of it."

"I'll be careful."

"I don't understand any of it."

Isabelle's nerves were twisted and tangled with fear. She stared at Harper, hoping to gain clarity, but the woman was content to let confusion prevail.

"I'm not sure . . ." Isabelle paused.

"What?"

"It's just very confounding." Isabelle bit her lower lip. "You won't explain—"

"All I ask for is your patience." She squeezed Isabelle's hands. "I've got a lot to figure out, and I can't explain until I understand where things will go."

"I don't know what to say."

"Give me some time." Harper searched her eyes. "That's all I ask."

She had a whole separate life Isabelle knew nothing of. She had gotten too close to her. This odd attraction between them had moved fast, and in a mystifying way it was as if Isabelle was already a part of this woman's world, whatever that world entailed.

Harper's arms slid around her waist. "May I kiss you goodbye?" She sounded so earnest and heavy with need that Isabelle's heart thundered in her chest.

How could she say no? What if they never saw each other again? She stepped closer and her hands came up to rest against Harper's stomach. The hard muscles shivered beneath her touch. Warmth spread into her fingertips and throughout her body.

"Yes," she said in a husky voice. She lifted her face, and her eyes fluttered shut as their lips met.

She gave Harper space to finish packing and went out to the low perimeter wall at the front of the estate. The waters of the Bay were tranquil now, unlike last night when waves crashed against the cliff, angry and agitated in the dark. Isabelle stood for a while and let the breeze tug at her skirt and whisper in her ears. She studied the blue-black color of the water and wished to be out there, far away in another part of the world.

For most of her childhood everything happened around her. She was a fly on the wall; a piece of furniture or an ornament, while the bargaining and illicit deals were being conducted. Whenever she stepped out of her shell she was clumsy and careless.

For once she wanted to be a force in her own life.

Footsteps approached, and Isabelle turned to see Patricia walking toward her. Another figure shifted in her periphery, and when Isabelle glanced up, Harper stood on a balcony behind them in the distance. She stepped inside once their eyes met. How long had she been watching Isabelle?

"Hello again," Patricia said, as she came to stand next to Isabelle. "Pleasant day."

"It is very pleasant out here." Isabelle lifted her brows.

Patricia crossed her arms. She had changed into a light linen outfit, over which she had thrown a shawl. Her olive skin was fresh and supple in the open air.

"We are never short on drama I suppose," Patricia said.

Isabelle smiled. She was trying to be polite.

"I know you're bothered by my daughter's decision to go to Istanbul."

"I'm not sure I have a right to be bothered."

"You're very different," Patricia said, as if the thought dawned on her in that instant. "When Victoria was young she had a lot of silly crushes. As she got older she dated some oddballs, some flakes who were always on the hunt for something else – money, attention, glamor. None of them really struck me and I imagine it was the same for her."

She turned to look at Isabelle, taking in her face wholeheartedly. It would have verged on unnerving if Isabelle was not used to being studied like this.

"I see it," Patricia said.

Isabelle wasn't sure how to respond so she turned and looked out at the water.

"What do you see?" she finally said.

"You're the kind of woman I once was." Patricia nodded. "I was full of promise but I didn't know how to unearth it."

Was that true? Isabelle had never thought about herself on such deep level.

"I do see the same in you," Patricia continued. "You don't quite know where you stand, which is funny because you exude a kind of brilliance."

"I think you're *sort of* trying to flatter me," Isabelle said sarcastically, smiling.

Patricia laughed and it was sincere. She was quiet for a while then she said, "I don't always understand my daughter, and I am ashamed to admit that."

"You don't know what drives her?"

"Oh well," she shrugged. "It could be a number of things. She is a smart woman, but her choices aren't always logical. I believe she's driven by emotions she has not even accessed on a conscious level."

"What do you think those emotions are?"

"Sometimes I'm not even sure. Victoria is haunted by something she can never change." She drew her shawl closer around her shoulders. "She also takes after her father's side of the family. They like to live in a sort of opaque place. My people are yogis and poets." She chuckled. "We are too tender and holistic for her."

"Why do you help her?"

"What else can I do? I can't make her live the way I choose to, but I also have to keep her safe."

Do you know what she does in Turkey?

Isabelle swatted the question around in her mind. Could she ask this woman about her daughter's clearly shady dealings? People weren't quick to divulge such information about someone close to them. She might think it presumptuous of Isabelle to even go there.

"What drew you to politics?" She asked instead. "That's far from a holistic profession."

"I was influenced by my grandmother, Hiya." Patricia perked up. "She was a remarkable journalist, and had a knack for getting through to the truth of an issue. She emigrated with her family from India when she was thirteen. She was determined not only to be successful in her profession; she wanted to be a humanitarian. In her work, she focused on stories about the dark side of humanity, juxtaposed against stories about people who were led by the light. The light always prevailed in her work. She wanted to relay that a collective consciousness of good could change the world."

"She sounds like an impressive woman," Isabelle said, genuinely in awe.

"I certainly thought so," Patricia said. "I thought I could affect real change in people's lives through politics. It's funny because both Ed and I were greatly influenced by our grandmothers. You see, our parents weren't terrible people but they were practical, and being practical meant you worked night and day in order leave behind a legacy for your descendants. The children either had to fend for themselves or were shipped off to the grandparents. That was one of the things Ed and I had in common when we met." She laughed. "Parental abandonment."

"Our grandmothers were quite different though." She fell silent and avoided Isabelle's eyes. Then Patricia's gaze lifted and dropped to follow a seagull that dipped excitedly at a potential meal at the water's surface.

"Eugenie was his grandmother." Isabelle said it under her breath, for her thoughts has wandered to Danny's stories about the woman and the legacy *she* left behind for her great-granddaughter.

Patricia turned and took Isabelle in. She opened her mouth to say something, then shut it abruptly. "Yes." The confirmation was almost inaudible.

"I don't know what's going to happen," Isabelle said. "Victoria has shown me kindness, but—"

"I don't know what's going to happen either," Patricia interjected, as if she was afraid of what Isabelle was going to say. "But maybe you can show her a better way?"

"Victoria doesn't strike me as the kind of woman that can be led." Isabelle knitted her brows at that insight. The woman had said it herself last night in the library. *I've never asked for permission to do anything.*

"Right." Patricia's thoughts drifted away, as if buoyed by a soft wave. "I haven't given up on my daughter," she said quietly. "She's not the woman I hoped she would be, but I believe she is still the girl I raised."

Chapter Fifteen

HELENE GAVE ISABELLE a quick rundown of events in her absence when she returned to the guesthouse. Things here were still status quo, unlike the course of events in one day in Newport. She was grateful to be back on somewhat calmer soil.

Harper had caught a late flight to Philadelphia, and from there would head to Munich, where she would have a seven-hour layover before another flight to Istanbul. She had a day's travel ahead of her, and said she would call and update Isabelle when she could.

Isabelle spent the next morning researching Eugenie Harper. Her on-line biography detailed her humble beginnings in the late nineteenth and early twentieth century. Born Eugenie Bradford, she married Clifford Harper, who was a wealthy real estate mogul at the time. After becoming a physician, Eugenie volunteered with humanitarian organizations to serve as a doctor toward the end of World War I. When she came home she began her medical practice by opening up a small private office in downtown Newport. However, twice in the nineteen twenties, Newport police launched an investigation into her practice. Eugenie was cautioned against the overuse of morphine. The authorities believed she was prescribing it to drug addicted patients, which was illegal. Clifford Harper used his connections to clear her name.

Eugenie's biography went on to say she ended up under psych evaluation for the first few months after returning home from World War II. Apparently, she had a hard time adjusting to life without the intensity and knife-like edge of the war-zone. For a while she believed she was still at war. No details were given about the facility she was committed to, if any, and no conclusion about her diagnosis.

After living in Turkey for many years, she returned to Rhode Island in the early sixties for good. She would eventually pass quietly at home at the age of seventy-seven.

There was no information to be found about a vigilante group in connection to Eugenie, and why would there be? Things like that were not paraded out in public. Eugenie must have maintained a somewhat professional existence. She had been regarded highly because she was a woman in medicine, and she had served her country. Even if rumors and suspicions existed about her double life, she was clearly never exposed.

Isabelle pulled up a few more results but they simply rehashed the same biographical information.

She got up and stretched. She made a cup of tea and went to look out the window. Did the Harpers have the power to wipe away unpleasant facts about their history from public view? If the group was still active, how come they have not been discovered? Were they still taking justice into their own hands over five decades after the woman had died? It certainly would explain the secrecy from Victoria Harper.

Details on Harper herself were scant, but it likely meant she wanted it that way. She did not have any social media accounts or an on-line life, at least not once she had gotten to the age where she could control her exposure. Still, there weren't even reports about her rebellious teenage years. It was as if their local media simply looked the other way – damaging stories were killed.

Isabelle sat back down, typed in all the phrases that came to mind and parsed through them. "Eugenie Bradford," "Eugenie Bradford Harper doctor," "Eugenie Bradford vigilante group." The last phrase brought up a blog about wartime nurses. It contained pictures and profiles on female nurses who served in various wars. There was no reference to Eugenie's group at all, which was strange since the search result were connected to that phrase. In a section dedicated to Eugenie, this line caught Isabelle's eye: "Eugenie was a salvager who was fond of morphine."

Harper had called her great-grandmother a "savior," which was quite similar to "salvager." It was not a coincidence. It tied into the vigilante aspect. Danny said she used what she had as a doctor.

Had it been morphine?

Isabelle stared at the woman's picture on the website. This image was not quite as harsh as the portrait at the house. In fact, she looked much younger and had a smarmy energy to her. She wore the same bulb-like pendant in the photo.

Isabelle's eyes went wide.

Harper had worn that pendant or one like it at the Grand Machiné restaurant the day Isabelle met her and Caye for lunch.

Now Isabelle was convinced Harper's abrupt departure was not just about flying to Istanbul to rescue a family friend. Whatever Eugenie's organization did in the past or continued to do, Victoria Harper was undoubtedly in the thick of it.

This time Isabelle knew exactly what to look for. She glanced through the image results of "morphine source" as the search words, confirming her suspicion: the bulb-like design of the pendant was representative of an opium poppy bud.

A small flame danced up from the pile on the ground. Secluded at a shrouded end of the property, Isabelle had taken Haughton's documents from the box in her room and set them ablaze. She had left the small handgun hidden in her room since she didn't know how to dispose of it.

Marcia and Haughton had still not contacted her, though she sensed they were okay. A dry cynicism crept into her. They had something going on, some mission her stepfather had planned. Nothing he did was by chance.

She had also not heard from Harper. Whenever she thought of her, a hollow pit opened up inside Isabelle's stomach.

"Isabelle?" Helene called out.

The faint tune of Isabelle's cell phone ring tone played. Then it stopped. She stepped from behind the red oak to see Helene hurrying toward her with her phone.

"Someone is trying to reach you." Helene was out of breath. "Your phone has been ringing nonstop for at least ten minutes."

Isabelle took the phone and checked the call log. It could be Harper, but something about the area code was familiar enough that she knew it was not her. It had to be . . .

It rang again.

She looked at Helene, who was staring off behind her where the small plume of smoke rose from the rubble.

"Well," Helene exhaled. "I'll leave you to whatever it is you're doing."

She cocked her eyebrows suspiciously before turning and swishing back toward the house.

Isabelle tapped the answer key.

"Hello, young sprite."

Jay Broderick. He had called her that since she was young and she despised it.

"Hello, Jay."

"Some friends of mine said you stopped by." His tone was casual.

"Stopped by?" She and Bastian had driven up to a creepy warehouse in Hartford, snooped about the place, and then were nearly run down on the way home.

"Nothing happens in my neighborhood without me knowing."

"Then you must know my parents' whereabouts," Isabelle said, annoyed.

"That's the reason for my call."

Instead of an explanation from him, Marcia's voice came on the line.

"Is everything okay?"

"I should be asking you that," Isabelle said. "I came to the cabin and you guys were gone."

"We went on a little excursion with Jay. Your step dad had a business matter to take care of. We're back now. Why don't you come and see us?"

Marcia's casual tone irked her.

"Did it ever occur to you I might have been scared shit-less?"

"Isabelle, calm down."

"We went looking for you and Jay and his friends didn't seem to like it."

"Who's we?"

"What?"

"You said *we* went looking for you."

"A friend came with me." Isabelle tried to recover. Bastian was technically still in undercover mode, right? Or whatever he was really doing, Isabelle was sure he wouldn't want Haughton to know of his comings and goings.

"Well, you and your friend should pay us a visit."

It was a strange invite, since Marcia and Haughton had been in hiding for so long. Isabelle had been their only visitor in the last six months. Was that even true? Were they holed up at the cabin all this time as Isabelle had assumed? They had certainly made contact with Jay Broderick and friends.

That meant Haughton was back to his old ways.

Benny stood watch over Isabelle as she ate the grilled chicken pesto sandwich he made for her. She took cautious bites, and halfway through she told him she was full. He whipped up a smoothie as she waited in the kitchen, saying it would give her much-needed energy. Food was the furthest thing from her mind, but Benny wanted to be of use and Isabelle did not have the heart to refuse.

Earlier he had driven her to Nutley to pick up her car, and though he eyed the house as they pulled up, he had refrained from asking her who it belonged to.

She had not told Bastian about the phone call from Marcia until she was almost at the cabin. This was something she needed to do alone. She had the unsettling feeling her parents did in fact know Bastian was in town and wanted him to come to the cabin. Certainly the Hartford excursion gave him away. For now, it was best if he didn't accompany Isabelle.

When she told him this over the phone he feigned offense at the thought of his little sister trying to protect him, but he could see it was a sensible decision as well. Haughton knew Bastian had always vowed to "get him." It only made sense for the old man to put security measures in place in case his stepson ever did pop up on him.

Isabelle arrived at the cabin as the evening darkened. The living room furniture had finally been arranged. A throne-like armchair sat in the corner, at the head of a conference formed by the leather sectional, which made an L shape in the other third of the room. One coffee table sat in the middle and held a tray of sandwiches and a pot of coffee.

Haughton, who swallowed up the armchair, had a leather pouch on his lap, his plate of sandwiches, and a handgun next to him on the arm of the chair. The weapon was the same version of the one he had stored away with Isabelle many years ago, long forgotten.

Marcia and Jay sat facing him on the leather couch, and the entire house was filled with the dim glow of kerosene lamps.

Marcia got up and greeted Isabelle as she entered. Jay nodded at her, and Haughton smiled, motioning for her to sit.

"Why were you in Connecticut?" he asked as her mother poured her a cup of coffee.

She had meant to refuse it since the last thing she needed was caffeine this late, but her step dad's question was unexpected and it startled her. Isabelle took the cup from her mother and sipped the hot liquid as she gathered her wits.

"You were missing," she said. "I thought something unfortunate had happened."

"How did you know about that warehouse?" Haughton asked.

"I don't know. I was just trying to find you both." Isabelle floundered. She couldn't think fast enough to come up with an answer that made sense.

"Did someone help you?"

"I didn't need help." She injected fake confidence into her voice. "I did learn some things from you. I suspected you were close to Jay's house and I put it together by chance."

Was there any logic in that? It sounded ridiculous to her as she spat the words out, but her brain was on autopilot.

"Hmm." Haughton shrugged and sorted through the papers in his pouch. Isabelle thought the conversation was over until he said, "I didn't realize you cared so much."

She should say *I do care. I've always cared.* If she said it that would appease him and he might drop this line of questioning. She clammed up. The words wouldn't leave her mouth. Haughton's eyes locked onto hers, as if he could read her exact thoughts in that moment. *She could not say she cared about him.*

"I hope I'm not interrupting anything." Isabelle looked around the room deliberately, and at Jay, who had gone to the kitchen and was back with a few bottles of Heineken.

"We were just wrapping up a meeting," her stepfather said. "Perfect timing, actually. Here's what I need you to do." He paused and leaned forward. "Come to the cabin only when we call you."

"What do you mean?" Isabelle asked.

"Do not drop by. We will call you, and then you can come visit your mother, bring groceries, whatever."

Isabelle looked at her mother.

"What happened to your friend?" Was all Marcia had to say.

"He couldn't make it." Isabelle was still thinking about what Haughton had said, but didn't want to question it. He was generally a calm person, but tended to become incensed when pushed. Isabelle sensed this could be one of those moments.

Jay raised his eyebrows. "Sprite made a new friend?" He had always had a smug aura to him. He wore horrible horn-rimmed glasses, frames he must have had for decades, and a brown tam over his bountiful dreadlocks.

"Sounds that way," Marcia said. "Unless it's someone we already know."

"It's a guest who's staying in town for a little while," Isabelle said. "You don't know them."

"I wish you had brought him."

"Right." Isabelle's frustration was growing. She was particularly irked by Jay calling her sprite. Tonight, it made her feel agitated and angry.

She had never confronted him about the events of the night her father was shot, but Marcia had implied it had been either Royal or Jay Broderick who had pulled the trigger. That incident had upended her already shaky existence, and not until years later had she worked up the courage to ask her mother about it. Marcia's details then were a scanty rehashing of what she had already told Isabelle.

Robert had come in and announced it was time for the men to leave his place, shocking Marcia so much that she was immobilized. Royal and Jay Broderick were protective of their master and had stepped forward to inform Robert they would leave when good and ready. Robert became enraged and dug through one of the large duffel bags that contained a fresh supply of M16s and Glocks brought to the island through Haughton's foreign connections. When he turned the contents upside down a scuffle broke out. One of the men had accidentally shot him in the abdomen.

So the story went. Her father was taken from her, without reason or justice.

Marcia got up. "How about a game of Ludo?" She brought the game board over and arranged the pieces in their respective houses.

Isabelle opened a Heineken, but before she could take a sip, Jay swiped it away.

"I forgot to bring you a glass, sprite."

"I don't need a glass," Isabelle said.

He walked to the kitchen and got the glass anyway, set it down on the coffee table, and poured out her beer.

Isabelle had a terrible urge to smash his face with the glass. She stood and found herself face to face with him. He wasn't a tall man – at most five-foot-seven or -eight inches. His amusement dissipated as she stared him down. Isabelle turned and went to the kitchen to retrieve another Heineken. When she came back she opened it calmly and drank from the bottle.

Haughton laughed.

"Why you bothering her?" he asked. "Both of you sit down and play."

Haughton had been shaking the dice in a little cup, and once everyone settled down he sent them clattering across the board.

Two hours and a couple beers later, Marcia walked Isabelle outside. She stood by the car door so Isabelle could not get in. "Will you be okay to drive?"

Isabelle shrugged. There was so much she wanted to say, but did not know how to begin.

"Take this." Marcia handed her coffee in a paper cup.

"Why'd they chase us? Chase me?"

"Jay and the guys like to play around sometimes. You shouldn't have gone there."

"What are you guys up to?"

"You know your step dad. He can never stay idle for long – he's got something cooking again. We're talking about expansion. Europe is a possibility."

"I thought you guys were done with this stuff."

Marcia threw her hands up. "It is what it is."

"Is that really your answer?"

Marcia's eyes widened.

"Don't be a smart-ass, Isabelle," she said. "This is our livelihood."

"Bullshit. Your livelihood was the restaurant. You left it because Haughton was thirsting for big deals and big game again. So were you."

Marcia looked weary. She sighed and squeezed her temples.

The intensity and fervor she once possessed, that so often captivated others, had long since faded. She'd always had a fierceness lurking beneath the surface that allowed her to step outside of herself and commit acts she otherwise did not seem capable of.

Isabelle remembered the day Aiden Grant had been all philosophical about the little ironies of life. He had pointed out the abstract hummingbird image on the ganja packaging one day when Isabelle stopped by.

"Do you know whose this is?" he had asked her.

"I don't care."

"Well, you should. Take a closer look."

"I don't know, and I still don't care."

"Young lady," Aiden said. "This belongs to your mother."

"What are you talking about?"

"I get my supply from your mother. And here you are, buying it from me."

It made no sense. This was Haughton's world, she had told him back then, but he had just laughed and shaken his head.

Now she knew her mother was clearly entrenched. She was always entrenched.

In the folds of the thick foliage above them, in the quiet, and enclosed within darkness lit only by soft rings of light from the lamp Marcia held, Marcia stared at Isabelle for a long time.

"You know," she said, her voice low and wistful, "when we made the decision to move to the cabin I was worried about you. I told Haughton I wanted you to come with us. He said you were grown, but I was acting like you were a child. He said, 'She is an unfired pistol. A blunt sword. She should be traveling the world. Jet-setting and meeting people as prosperous as she is. If we were her age we wouldn't be holed up in a house with our parents.'"

Marcia moved closer. "You haven't done a damn thing with your opportunities, so don't tell me about my livelihood."

"I've done what I wanted to do."

"I don't think you know who you really are," Marcia said, softening. "You have my fire, but you don't know how to use it." She reached out and touched Isabelle's face.

"I have a lot going on," Isabelle said sullenly, pulling away.

"Why don't you tell me about it?"

"You disappeared without so much as a courtesy phone call."

"I'm right here now."

Her mother was a great contradiction. Marcia could compartmentalize her life and her behavior. Perhaps she could compartmentalize her love too. Marcia had always despised her own mother, who sold produce at the farmer's market in Downtown Kingston. She saw her as a street haggler and generally looked down on that profession.

She had always had lofty goals as a girl, inspired by her father, who worked his way up in an accounting firm. Late in his life he was sent to prison for money laundering. Still, Marcia loved him and thought he could do no wrong. Isabelle had met her grandfather once when she was seven years old. He had been smooth and calculating, and she saw the same traits in Marcia.

These last few years Marcia had tried to be someone else, someone more maternal for Isabelle's sake. But only because she was getting older – her sharper edges mollified by the great sandpaper of time. Grated down so she could now see what she should have been to those who loved her.

But so much time had passed and so much had been done.

"It's late," Isabelle said.

"Come by tomorrow."

"I have work to do."

"Okay, next time then," Marcia said, hesitating. Then she pulled Isabelle into an embrace and kissed her cheek. "Say hello to Bastian for me."

Under the cover of hanging branches, Isabelle got out of her car and squeezed the door shut behind her as quietly as she could. She had driven only a short distance away from the cabin and parked. She scurried past the entrance at the gate, which wasn't a gate at all, but more like an opening between the un-kempt hedges that hid the cabin. She found a spot where the thickets parted and got down on her hands and knees to crawl through.

In the midst of her crawl on the stony ground, it dawned on her she hadn't thought this through and was riding high on in-stinct, alcohol, and sleep deprivation.

She was wearing her black leather jacket. The prickly branch-es tore at it and scratched her hands. On the other side of the hedge stood the woods that flanked the cabin. When she made it through and stood up, the warm lighting inside the house in the distance came from her left. Isabelle headed right, farther in-to the thickness of oak and ash trees.

The flashlight application on her phone led the way enough, and this time she was more at ease. In the winter when the branches were bare, these woods had been exposed. There was nothing sinister around except the typical inhabitants of trees and forestry. A squirrel zipped across the ground as she walked, and crickets added their voices to the dark night.

Then it appeared: the same plank of wood she had seen when she came in here looking for Marcia and Haughton after they disappeared. It was also the hatch from the dream she'd had in Newport, half-concealed under a pile of weeds.

She dug into the edge of the wood platform with the butter knife she had brought with her from the guesthouse. It was the only tool she could find on short notice. Not that she had con-sciously decided to do this absolutely insane thing she was at-tempting to do right this minute.

The knife was on the verge of breaking. The thin stainless steel had bent severely under the weight of the heavy board, but when Isabelle was about to give up, the platform lifted enough for her to fit her hand underneath it.

She opened it and shone her phone flashlight down into the hatch. A wooden stairway led down from the opening. The floor was bare concrete. Isabelle climbed down and looked around. It was a narrow, empty basement with concrete walls.

What the hell was this room?

It was like an underground shelter. With only one direction to go, Isabelle jogged slowly away from the opening. Her flats slapped against the concrete floor and echoed around her.

The room was much larger than Isabelle had thought.

She stopped and looked back. The path behind her was pitch black. Fear peeled away the delirious effect of the alcohol and took her courage with it. Panic set in. Her T-shirt stuck to her skin with sweat. She wanted to run back to the hatch opening and out to her car. The taste of Benny's grilled chicken came into her mouth, sour and sharp. Isabelle heaved. She swallowed hard and forced her legs to move. She ran on. She came upon a metal door, and when she turned the lock she was surprised to find it open. Isabelle peeked inside. Boxes and plastic crates were stacked to the ceiling, all branded with the faint outline of a hummingbird.

Ahead, another set of stairs led to a second opening.

Isabelle climbed up and pushed it open. A surge of water rushed down the hole. She gasped and pulled herself up. She closed the hatch and found herself standing in a shallow pond. She recognized the abandoned aqueduct she had glimpsed on her drives up to the cabin on the back roads. Farther out were the tracks for the freight train, the only one that ran through the area, and the same one she and Bastian had stopped for when they were nearly run over by the Range Rover on the other side of town.

Isabelle was awash with confusion. She sucked in air and tried to right her thoughts. The cabin was not a hideout?

It had never been a hideout.

It was a storage facility. A distribution hub? A means for Haughton to traffic his potpourri of illegal weapons and drugs.

Marcia had always been his partner, participating in and affirming everything he did. Isabelle had uprooted her life and moved here to be closer to them because she thought they were vulnerable. She had bought a house and a business she didn't want. She could have gone elsewhere, anywhere to build a life for herself. She had always longed to see Barcelona. Her body went weak. This time her pesto meal came forcefully out before she could stop it.

At noon the next day Isabelle was still locked away in her suite. Her energy was zapped after last night's sprint back and forth underground and the shock of knowing what Haughton was doing in the woods. She allowed her body to crash and recover, and had only gotten up once to make lemon tea and to use the bathroom.

Someone knocked at her door. Isabelle pulled the covers over her head.

"Isabelle?" It was Bastian.

She remained quiet. What would he say when he found out?

You are a fool. That man has never had a redemptive bone in his body. Why do you think I left? You've wasted your life sticking around with them.

"Isabelle, open the door."

Tears rolled down her cheeks. She got up and opened the door.

She tossed on a pair of black tights and a black button down silk shirt and followed her brother downstairs. The fountain water shone in the sunshine and was a soothing sound in the quiet afternoon. Bastian and Isabelle sat on the concrete ledge and watched the movement of the water.

She told him about her eventful night at the cabin. For a moment he had a satisfied look, but he said nothing.

"Everything is a mess," Isabelle whispered. A couple of guests were on the balcony above them and she did not want them to overhear their conversation.

"There's no mess," Bastian said. "They haven't changed, but you can. Sell this place and get the hell away from them."

"It's not just that. It's . . ."

"What?"

"Victoria is mixed up in something. I wish I could help her, but I can't."

Bastian eyed her contemplatively.

"That woman seems pretty capable to me." He lowered his voice. "And if she is mixed up in something, you might want to keep your distance."

"I feel helpless. I've been such a fool."

"Yes, you have. I think it was all right there in front of you, but you allowed yourself to be deceived. Now you know better than to follow someone like Haughton blindly."

"I didn't follow them. I just—"

"You just like being the docile sheep. The willing captive."

She shoved him. Purely on reflex and pent up frustration. Bastian jerked sideways, but steadied himself.

He glared at his sister. "Snap out of it, Isabelle!"

She got up, angry and embarrassed, but she kept her voice down.

"You have no idea—"

"I do," he said, shaking his head. "You buried yourself in bullshit. Told yourself they need you."

"And what about you?" She spat. "You came back, but do you even know what you want?"

"You're making the same mistakes I did."

"I am not you!" Isabelle snapped, losing her temper. "You left. I'm still here."

"Where?" Bastian came closer. He rapped his knuckles against her head. "Where the fuck are you?"

"Get out of my face." She shoved him again. "Get the hell out."

Helene burst through the door and into the courtyard.

"What on earth . . . stop it."

She half-yelled, half-whispered as she held on to Isabelle's arm.

Bastian shook his head. "A waste is waste, no matter how you slice it."

He turned and went out the back gate.

"Come on." Helene tugged on Isabelle's arm. She brought her upstairs to her suite and shut the door behind them.

"What the hell was that?" She folded her arms and stared as Isabelle plopped down onto the couch. "You were behaving like children."

"Family disagreement."

"Next time can we do that in private?" Helene sighed and sat next to her. "What does he mean by waste?"

"He's trying to say I'm wasting my time here." She sulked. She had known exactly what her brother was going to say and still it shook her.

"Is he saying this place means nothing to you?"

"It's not that." Isabelle ran a hand through her hair, pushing the lustrous curls away from her face. She had not straightened it since she returned from Rhode Island. "I was in search of something when I came here."

"What?"

"Believe it or not. Peace."

"I think it's more likely you wanted to get away from something." Helene leaned back and pulled on her lip as she contemplated. "Would you agree?"

"If that's the case, it's a major fail." Isabelle released a wry chuckle. "Everything seems to be coming at me at once."

"Maybe that's what needs to happen."

"Not you too." She massaged her face. "I can't take another lecture."

"I'm serious," Helene said. "A bit of chaos can be good for you."

"You had a wild life, didn't you?" She turned and studied the older woman. "To be advocating for chaos?"

"Let's just say I had an energetic life." Helene winked. "I certainly didn't sit around hoarding my secrets and shutting myself off from everyone."

"The insults just get better and better." Isabelle hugged a pillow against her chest. "Didn't you warn me to stay out of trouble earlier?"

That warning was in regards to Victoria Harper and the fact that Isabelle was contemplating helping with her project. Now that seemed to be off the table in her absence. Who knew when she would return?

"I did." Helene grinned. Then she turned serious. "I'm not trying to insult you. I just mean to say, this isn't your calling," she spread her arms to indicate the guesthouse, "and you're not writing either. A change of pace might be good."

"I tried a change of pace in Rhode Island. And how do you know I'm not writing?"

"I see everything." Helene rolled her eyes and gave Isabelle's shoulder a playful nudge. "Are you planning to sell the guesthouse?"

"You're an excellent manager." Isabelle sighed and shook her head. "I don't think you need me at all."

"I like your company, but even that I only get in small doses." Helene gave her a cheeky look. "You're in your own world half the time."

Helene was right. Isabelle was shut off even from herself.

Chapter Sixteen

SUD HAD REMAINED NEARBY after bringing Isabelle back home from Rhode Island. He said he had been instructed by Harper to keep an eye on things in her absence. When Isabelle asked him what that meant, he said Harper wanted him to look out for Isabelle in light of the car chase. She had no doubt Harper wanted to make sure she was okay considering how frazzled Isabelle had been that night, but it occurred to her that Victoria Harper was keeping an eye on her.

She was due to arrive in Istanbul three days ago, and yet Isabelle had still not heard from her. She understood circumstances might prevent her from reaching out. Perhaps she had been preoccupied from the moment she landed, but if the situation was dangerous enough for her to feel Steven's life was being threatened, what could Harper do to stop it? How could she keep him safe? How could she keep herself safe?

After an hour or so of absentmindedly staring at the draft of the manuscript she'd started years ago, a copy of which she had kept hidden away in the metal box, Isabelle closed the laptop and ran her hands across the surface of her desk. She had been writing about her father's life and death, in bits and pieces as her nerves allowed. Anxiety took over every time she tried to continue, and this was one of those moments.

Bastian had gone back to the Lennox Motel, or so he said. Their parents were clearly not in imminent danger, and after their little tiff over the situation her brother had drifted off.

Isabelle went downstairs to have dinner with Helene and a few guests in the dining room. She needed a distraction and for now the inhabitants of her house would have to do. At the dinner table, she listened idly to the chatter between her guests. Her thoughts wandered to Harper, whose life was clearly one in a state of chaos, as Helene would put it. So why did Isabelle feel so grounded around her? Common sense would dictate that Isabelle steer clear of Harper, yet an undeniable connection had developed between them and kept Isabelle tethered.

A couple at the table talked about fishing for snappers with such glee it made Isabelle wonder if there was anything she liked doing with that much passion. Mr. Reginald talked on and on about his years managing a jewelry store. He said his best sales were the ones that had meaning: wedding rings, a piece to commemorate an occasion or an accomplishment, or an emblem to solidify a bond between family and friends.

Something occurred to Isabelle. If she could learn more about the opium bud necklace Harper and her great-grandmother wore, she might be able to uncover the name of the organization or learn more details about it. She was curious to know what she had become involved with, inadvertently through her connection to Victoria Harper, even though she already had her suspicions.

When she grew tired of the commentary at the table, she went out into the cool night air and called Sud. He said he had not heard from Harper since her arrival in Istanbul. That alarmed Isabelle.

"Is that unusual?" she asked. "To not hear from her for three days?"

"Not so much," Sud said, in his thick French-African accent. He had playfully refused to tell Isabelle where he was from. "Victoria travels frequently. She reaches out when she needs to."

Isabelle was helpless. She hung up with Sud and stared out at the dark, dull lake water. Before she could wallow in the limitless number of scenarios, Evan came to the front entrance of the house and called out to her. His lanky silhouette was illuminated by the bright light of the entrance hall behind him. He waved and ran to meet Isabelle as she made her way across the lawn.

"Caye Wauburg is in the foyer," he said, out of breath. His eyes were sharp, and he seemed to be judging Isabelle's reaction.

Isabelle's first instinct was to avoid Caye, but curiosity spurred her.

"Okay," she said. She walked back with Evan loping eagerly beside her. At times he acted like her secret cheerleader.

Caye was radiant in the light. She remained as she was when Isabelle entered, with her attention fixed on the small kiosk with local business brochures and reading materials. She straightened and turned slowly, as if on a circular escalator in the middle of the room.

She was dressed in white, with a white blazer thrown over her shoulders. The stuffed shoulder pads gave her a larger than life effect.

"Once again," Isabelle shot her a disapproving glare, "you show up unannounced."

Caye waited, allowing Isabelle to drift over to her. Isabelle hesitated, then moved close to kiss her cheek. Caye held Isabelle's face and planted a kiss at the edge of her lips.

The expression on Isabelle's face must have betrayed how perturbed she was, because Caye perked up like a dog on alert. She laughed nonchalantly and moved toward the stairs.

Isabelle hung back.

"Can we chat in private?" Caye asked.

Isabelle turned toward the couch in the sitting area.

"Come on, now. I won't bite. I promise."

Isabelle looked back at Evan, who was awaiting her decision as well. She had to smile to herself. Caye had style and charm, but she operated in a bubble. She had left Isabelle coldly, enjoyed her many exploits with women, and might be conducting espionage on Harper for some convoluted reason.

Caye's visit tonight was sure to be just as self-serving.

"Let's go." Isabelle walked assuredly ahead of her up the stairs and down the narrow hallway to her room. She opened the door and motioned for Caye to enter. Caye paused, unaccustomed to an assertive Isabelle. She murmured something and stepped into the room as Isabelle closed the door behind them. Her bracelets jangled as she slipped off her white leather wristlet and placed it on the end table by the door. She wore a narrow, high-waist skirt with a tapered button-down shirt tucked in.

"How about champagne?" The excitement in Caye's voice was palpable.

"What are we celebrating?"

"Us."

Isabelle's heart rate elevated. "Pardon?"

"I made a mistake." Caye strolled over and brushed her fingers across Isabelle's cheek. "I should have never left you. When we spoke a few days ago it made me realize how dumb I've been."

Isabelle was flabbergasted. Something was different about Caye: gone was the restlessness Isabelle had become accustomed to. Tonight she was clear-headed. Tonight she seemed triumphant.

Isabelle stepped out of her reach. She needed time to digest what was happening. She pulled a bottle of Veuve Clicquot from the refrigerator and undid the wire slowly, lost in thought. They could have champagne, but there was no 'us' to celebrate. As she reached up into the cupboard for the glasses, Caye slipped her arms around Isabelle's waist. She turned Isabelle's face to her and kissed her.

"Hmm," Caye mumbled, tracing Isabelle's small, plump lips with the tip of her finger.

"We're not doing this again." Isabelle pulled away, frowning.

"Why not?"

"I've moved on."

"Your kiss said otherwise."

"Maybe I'll always be attracted to you." Isabelle regretted saying that the moment the words left her lips. *Was it true?*

"I'll always want you, Isabelle. You see through all my bullshit."

Caye moved close again, but Isabelle put her hands up to keep her at bay. "What changed?" she asked, feeling besieged.

"Nothing." Caye smiled. "You know very well I always wanted you, sweet thing."

"You have a funny way of showing it."

"I'm here now." She took Isabelle's hand in hers. "It's over between me and Victoria."

"Really now."

"She was a good distraction for a while. I don't know what I was thinking."

"And the other women?"

"They mean nothing to me."

"Call her."

"Who?"

"Call Victoria now." Isabelle's pulse pounded in her ears. "I want to hear it from her as well." She wanted to find out how much Caye really knew.

"Don't be silly," Caye said. "That's a little extreme, particularly coming from you."

Isabelle walked over and picked up her wristlet. When she opened it and pulled out the cell phone, Caye was next to her in a flash. She reached for the phone, but Isabelle moved it behind her back.

"Call her or I will."

"I can't call her because she's out of the country." Caye sighed and ran her hand through her bouncy blonde coif.

"Where?"

"Does it matter?"

"It does if you're lying."

"Turkey," Caye huffed. "She is in that ancient . . . mish-mash country. Happy now?"

"How do you know she's in Turkey?" Isabelle's piercing eyes narrowed.

"She told me."

Caye pulled the cell phone from Isabelle's hand and slipped it back into the wristlet. She zipped it shut.

"I'm happy." Isabelle went back to the kitchenette, popped the champagne, and poured two glasses. "But I cannot be with you." She handed Caye a glass. "We are over for good."

"What?" Caye's expression froze over. Her cheeks flushed red.

Isabelle worried she realized she'd been tricked into revealing her knowledge of Harper's whereabouts, but she only said, "You're rejecting me?"

"I'm sorry, but I can't go back. I'm moving on with my life."

Caye's eyebrows shot up and Isabelle feared she might slap her in a moment of madness. Instead she tossed the glass, champagne included, into the sink with a petulant hiss. Isabelle stared at the spilled drink, surprised the glass hadn't broken.

"Overreact much?" she said under her breath.

"You're fucking kidding me, right?" Caye glared at her. "Tell me your kidding."

"I'm more serious than I've ever been."

It was normal to plead under such circumstances, but this was Caye: spoiled and entitled. She was reacting as if it was unfathomable that Isabelle might not welcome her back with open arms. As if that possibility had never even crossed her mind.

Caye turned away, rattled. She pulled off the white blazer and tossed it at the chair closest to them. It just barely caught the back of the chair and hung askew. She glanced around the room, then out the window at the water, thinking.

"You don't understand," she said finally. "I didn't leave you because I wanted to. I did it because I had to."

"Why?"

"It's complicated."

"You saw a gorgeous woman and you wanted to bang her," Isabelle shrugged, being deliberately obtuse. "Not that complicated."

Caye grimaced, exasperated. She reached out and slipped her fingers behind the thin belt Isabelle wore over her dress then pulled her forward.

"What can I do to prove it to you?" She was inches away from Isabelle's face, her dark blue eyes glinting with panic. She dipped her mouth toward Isabelle's, but Isabelle drew back. Her hands went to Caye's shoulders to push out of her arms.

"Please, Isabelle." Caye clung to her waist.

She had never been this earnest, this real before. Isabelle felt tenderness toward her. Whatever the circumstances surrounding her union with Harper were, they were not of her own making. Maybe Caye *had* been coerced into getting close to her.

Isabelle wrapped her arms around her. She wanted to comfort Caye, yet when she thought of Harper a wild panic rose up inside her.

"Please just let it go, Caye," Isabelle said softly. "It's over."

Caye whimpered and held her tighter. "You have to forgive me."

"I do," Isabelle whispered. "I forgive you for leaving."

It all made sense: Caye and Harper's suspicious behavior around each other and Wauburg's reaction to Caye's night out with Gergina Piers. Caye all but admitted her relationship with Harper was arranged. Isabelle was sure of it now. Harper had said they were introduced by someone.

Perhaps Wauburg had decided he needed to get close to Victoria Harper and the best way to do it was through his daughter. Caye supported him in everything he did.

What would be Wauburg's motivation? Harper had implied he was connected to Maramaxe. Isabelle considered what she personally knew about him. Caye had told her how much her father struggled when he first took over the family construction business. He was twenty-eight, with a wife and two young children who depended on him. A move to Slovakia in the early nineties turned things around. He had gone there after learning of prosperous construction bids through a friend, and although it was a risk to uproot his life, it worked out in his favor.

He got a job working on a mall project in Bratislava, which lasted a few years. After that, Wauburg had sent his family back to the states and remained in Slovakia for another two years.

Isabelle had always found that odd. The family had been with him, yet when the project was completed he not only stayed behind, but wanted them gone. At least that was the impression she got when Caye talked about that time period.

Isabelle remembered reading a Forbes magazine article that profiled Wauburg. One of the images featured in the piece was an old photograph of Wauburg as a young man in a Red Sox baseball cap and shabby dress shirt and jeans. He had struggled in those years, but once he got his business going he never looked back.

The article was about his humble beginnings and how his simple quest to carry on the family construction business ballooned into a thriving consulting firm, with some of the brightest minds on his payroll. According to the article his time in Slovakia was transformative.

Wauburg was quoted as saying, "Going abroad was the best thing to happen to me. It freed me and allowed me to truly express myself. My fervor, my strength. My resilience as a business man."

The journalist had made a subtle attempt at delving into the unwholesome aspects of Wauburg's business: the rumors he had once had ties to the Slovakian mafia. He had laughed and shrugged off that line of questioning, too smooth to be dragged into the speculation surrounding him. He said business was ruthless, but there was a line and he never strayed from it.

Considering her impression of the man, Isabelle doubted that was true. He was more than capable of crossing many lines, but he would always smudge the edges. He existed in that vague, sinister world where drive effaced ethics.

Caye had insinuated once that her father felt inadequate among the brazen men his father and uncles ran with. He always had something to prove and he always wanted more. Bigger and better. But perhaps the rumors about him were just that – rumors. He had never been charged with any crime Isabelle knew of. Could he really be tied to the Maramaxe Relief organization as Harper suspected?

The next morning Isabelle went for a walk by the lake. She pondered the Wauburgs' connection to Harper as she plucked at wildflowers along the water's edge. Two small boats that belonged to her house guests were hitched to the dock, and farther out another boat came across the water slowly.

What would Bastian think about Harper's situation? She was afraid to tell him what she knew: about the exposé Harper had attempted many years ago against the Maramaxe slave traffickers, Wauburg's interest in her, the mysterious group founded by Eugenie Bradford Harper, and about Steven Smyth and the reason for Harper's visit to Istanbul. It sounded absurd even to Isabelle when she summed it up.

A gnawing headache pulsated at her temples. She pulled out her cell phone and scrolled through the contacts to the number Bastian had given her to get in touch with him. Her finger hovered over the screen. She needed her brother's acumen regarding these matters if she wanted to help Harper, but she was hesitant. He might berate her again for thinking this was her puzzle to solve.

She glanced up. She recognized the man in the boat coming across the water. Sud. His austere face was set against the gentle spray of water around him as he stood rigidly by the steering wheel. He steered up to the dock and cut the engine. Isabelle looked closely, trying to read the expression on his face, but could not glean much from it. Though she did not sense sorrow in his demeanor, she became nervous.

Once he secured the boat he strolled toward her. His gait was long and efficient. "Good morning, Isabelle," he said.

She returned his greeting with a stunned mumble.

"Victoria contacted me. She learned you were worried." He pulled out his cell phone and dialed a number. "Here."

Isabelle took the phone and listened as it rang on the other end.

"Isabelle?" The sound of Harper's voice made Isabelle's headache dissipate.

"Hi," Isabelle said. "How have you been?"

"Hanging in there." She sounded weary. Isabelle's heart sank. "I haven't been able to sleep much since I got here."

"Victoria, what can I do?" Isabelle asked.

"I could do with a massage."

Isabelle laughed.

"Seriously," Isabelle said. "Just say the word."

Harper was quiet. Her sadness was palpable even through the phone, across the fifteen thousand miles from here to Istanbul. Isabelle wanted to be next to her, to help alleviate whatever burden she was feeling.

"I'm just . . ." Harper paused as her voice broke. "Bewildered."

"What happened?"

"I can't make sense of anything."

"Is your friend okay?"

"He's fine for now."

"Then what is it?"

"There's a lot going on." She paused. "There was a sudden strike against us. It was as if they knew I was coming into town."

"Who struck against you?"

"People who are trying to make our lives hell."

"This is insane." Isabelle was at a loss for words. "Maybe you should come home. We'll figure it out together."

"I can't. I have to see this through."

Isabelle did not like the sound of that. It took on an ominous meaning in her mind.

"Caye knows where you are," she divulged, not thinking.

"What?"

"She knows you're in Turkey."

Silence again. Then Harper said, "I have to go."

"Let me help you," Isabelle pleaded. "There must be something—"

"There's nothing," Harper said quickly. "I can't stay on the phone any longer."

"Victoria—"

"Goodbye, Isabelle."

The phone line went dead, and the vacancy on the other end steeped into Isabelle's heart.

It was a foolish thing to do. To tell Harper that Caye knew her whereabouts in such a flippant manner must have seemed suspicious. Isabelle wished she had thought it through: the uncertainty and stress Harper was feeling as a result of her situation, and the fact that she had called Isabelle for some small comfort only to learn Isabelle had been in contact with someone she did not trust.

It also confirmed that Caye had lied when she said Harper told her she was in Turkey.

"Well, it's better for her to know," Bastian said, when Isabelle finally gave in and told him everything later that day. "The question is, why would the Wauburgs need to know her whereabouts in the first place, and what are they doing with that knowledge?"

"What do they want?" he asked her pointedly.

Isabelle shrugged. She did not want to reveal Harper's suspicion of a connection between Wauburg and the Maramaxe folks. Even though the exposé was done over a decade ago, people had long memories when you crossed them. Isabelle was not ready to speak openly of it to anyone. Not even to her intelligent and resourceful brother.

"That's what I have been trying to figure out," she said.

"Hmm." Bastian rubbed his face. He looked like he had not been sleeping well.

They were sitting on her couch trying to take stock of things, though they did not revisit the conversation regarding Marcia and Haughton. It was clear their parents had thought out and planned their secret operation from the beginning, and Isabelle had fallen for it.

Did Bastian know the story about Jay Broderick or Royal possibly shooting their father? If he did, she could imagine him being deeply angered and enraged. Who knows what he would do. She pushed the thought from her mind. That was one topic she would not broach, not for a long time.

"You need to be careful," Bastian said. "If you're treating this like some sort of game, it's not. Not in my educated opinion."

"I don't think it's a game," Isabelle said, annoyed. "Far from it, but someone I care about is involved, and I—"

"So you need to get involved too?"

"I would like to help her if I can, yes."

He looked at her. "Help yourself."

"Meaning?"

"Meaning whatever interest is driving you to become involved with this woman's affairs, try to snuff it out. It sounds like she's operating in a dangerous world."

"You operated in a dangerous world once. Perhaps you still do."

Her brother clasped his hands together and nodded. "Touché."

Isabelle nodded too. "I still don't know why you showed up. Or why you've done whatever you've done over the last few years, including spying on us from afar."

"Not everything can be neatly explained, Isabelle."

"I suppose not."

She had planned to ask him exactly what he thought Harper's involvement might be, but his sanctimonious lecturing annoyed her. He disappeared from her life for nearly two decades and here he was, scolding her like she was a child.

"Anyway," he said as he stood, "I came by because I thought you needed help, but I think you've got it covered."

He stared at her.

Isabelle got up and went to the window, keeping her back to him. She'd been fumbling through challenges alone for a long time. Finally she was being pulled toward something beyond her small world.

She watched the full and gently-moving water of the lake carry a boat to the other bank, where picnic enthusiasts languished under the bright river birch trees.

When she turned around Bastian was gone, leaving the door of her suite ajar. She walked over quietly and closed it. She sighed. Maybe she had been too hard on him.

She sat back down and tried to connect the dots on her own. It made her head spin. It wasn't just the Wauburg issue. It was also the lawless organization. The necklace Harper wore showed her bond with her great-grandmother and perhaps her commitment to those ideals and that legacy. Isabelle was sure Harper wasn't the only one in her family still brandishing that flag. Her father, Edward, was interested in the goings-on.

She searched through a digital Newspaper database for articles on the Rhode Island area for the last six decades. She looked for any stories that mentioned the Harpers, and Eugenie in particular. There were Harper birth and death announcements, marriage announcements, charity galas, business acquisitions, and a couple scandals driven by extra-marital affairs and family squabbles over money. It wasn't much but it was more than she had found before.

She read again about Eugenie's brave and honorable service for her country, but also about her run-ins with the authorities over her over-prescribing of morphine as a doctor. Isabelle dug in further until finally she came across Eugenie's name in a paragraph from a news story about a man who had been arrested for harassment and vandalism. The man's name was Dezzy Espinosa, and he was identified as a marine who had served in World War II. According to the article, Espinosa had threatened a woman and had defaced her car by writing "SERTURN" across the windshield in yellow paint. The connection to Eugenie? The woman was the new mistress of Eugenie's husband, Clifford Harper. Clifford had moved the woman into the house in Newport after Eugenie went to Istanbul for good. The implication in the write up was that Espinosa was acting on Eugenie's behalf and wanted to scare the woman away. Espinosa's bail was posted by a friend, a nurse named Mary Robinson, who coincidentally had also served in both World Wars.

There was no mention of the word Serturn anywhere else, but Isabelle suspected a huge part of the puzzle had come together. A web search for "Serturn and morphine" confirmed her suspicions. Morphine was discovered by a German pharmacist named Friedrich Sertürner. Could Serturn be the name of Eugenie's group?

Morphine, opium buds, and Turkey all led Isabelle to one conclusion. The resource Eugenie Harper had used to fund her covert missions was heroin.

Harper's great-grandmother was a vigilante-turned-drug dealer.

Chapter Seventeen

ISABELLE WAS GOING to Istanbul. She would no longer tax herself with the burden of emotional wounds inflicted by her parents or worry about her brother, who had done exactly what he needed to do for his own survival. She had to shed the heavy cloak of their misdeeds and of the ways in which their singular view of the world had marred her.

She drove into town to find that Ravi Holder's white rectangular building had been cordoned off and was buzzing with work crews. She spotted Ravi a distance away, leaning against a Chevy truck and talking to two construction workers.

"Well good morning to the Lady of the Manor," he said, grinning. He was wearing beige cargo shorts and a bright green shirt. Perhaps it was the warm weather and the lightness of the season, but something about him was different. The stain in his mouth was no longer as profound.

He had been right about the town waking up in the warmer months. The summer visitors had been robust and vigorous, taking advantage of every bit of adventure the place had to offer.

"What's going on here?" Isabelle asked.

"It needed a new coat," Ravi said.

"It certainly looks like more than just a new coat."

"I gave it strong consideration," he said pensively, "but in the end it had to go."

"Completely?"

Ravi pointed to the bulldozers waiting in the shade. "Everything will be laid flat."

"And your new office?"

"There." He turned Isabelle around and pointed to a statuesque little building. It had reminded Isabelle of a small museum the first time she saw it. Ravi was moving up.

"I bet you're going to miss this little white glob," she said.

"It served its purpose."

She supposed it had. She was transported back to the first day she drove into town and met Ravi inside the white building in the midst of winter, now about to be demolished. That was six months ago, but felt so much longer.

She told him she was leaving, if only for a while, and that Helene would remain with the guesthouse.

Ravi only smiled and touched her shoulder. "I hope we served our purpose."

Isabelle thought about Ravi's comment all throughout running her errands along the plaza, picking up travel essentials. She never took the time to get to know the town and she barely knew the man. He'd been this odd dark figure in an offbeat place, but this was what she needed. A respite, not a complete refuge. After all, the guesthouse had brought Harper into her life.

She smiled as she drove home, and when she came to the fork at the tip of the lake she paused. Her turn to get home was on the right, but she couldn't help peering down the other side. That branch of the road first went down a long hill and finally out from the dark shade of trees to join other roads, which spread out across the unfolding fields past tall, thick blades of grass.

The lonely, once secluded road went forward as if under the spell of a magnetic force until it gradually came upon the hustle and hiss of the unhidden world.

The taxi came to a stop in front of a wide building with a warm-rose color and geometric squares and arches. Ornate designs decorated the outer walls, and long windows in the front were lit by a sparkling light in the early afternoon.

Isabelle counted out the exact fare of thirty-five Turkish Lira plus tip and paid the driver. He wanted to say something, but instead he nodded politely and drove away. Maybe he had hoped to make extra cash off her, but even in her haste to get to Istanbul, Isabelle had done research and thought certain things through. Some aspects of this trip were sure to be beyond her control, but she wanted to be at an advantage where she could.

She had come down highway O-1 and Barbaros Boulevard – named after the great Ottoman naval warrior, Barbarossa – in the cab from Atatürk Airport to arrive at her hotel in Besiktas, one of the Istanbul districts.

The Hotel Garland lit up one corner of a clear, crisp road, which was covered in tiny maze-like bricks along a sidewalk of larger bricks. People strolled by on the avenue as they did in New York City or even the main avenue of her own little hook, shopping, running errands or having dinner.

She inhaled slowly, taking in the heat and humidity of Istanbul. Her hair expanded, and the long curls stuck to her neck.

Bastian had jumped into another cab once they left the airport. He said he owed an old friend a visit and would meet Isabelle at the hotel. She did not know he had friends in Istanbul, but then again, they had missed out on much of each other's lives in the years apart.

She was surprised when he offered to come with her on this trip, and at first she had declined. Isabelle had told him Harper was her friend, and this decision, while brash, was hers to make. She would face the consequences alone.

Bastian had pointed out that Isabelle had barely seen the world, and now she was about to run after a woman whose life she didn't understand.

"This place," he said. "Sometimes it seems to want to step into the twenty-first century and then other times it slides backward into the past. You should know what you're dealing with and you definitely shouldn't go there alone."

She wasn't sure if he meant to scare her off and to get her to change her mind. While it was comforting to know he wanted to protect her, this was something she needed to do. She wanted to branch out like the long, lonely road finding civilization. What better place than the tremendous crossroads that was Istanbul.

As the date of her flight drew close, Isabelle reconsidered and told Bastian to come along. She felt even better about that decision once she arrived. She was confident enough in her capabilities, but having a hardened world-traveler like Bastian by her side could only help.

Isabelle checked into the room, which was modern and eclectic, much like the lobby and the rest of the place as she made her way through. It was impressive – black and white throwback photographs of fishermen on the Bosporus Strait hung on the earthy wood walls, a red comforter over white bed sheets, and a red suede armchair across from the bed. The light fixtures were understated and hung low from the ceiling, complementing the earthy tone of the room.

She showered and changed, and after taking in the room again and studying the photographs, Isabelle sat down to gather her thoughts. She would go to see Roslyn, who lived not too far from her hotel. If Roslyn refused to point her in the right direction, she would call Sud and tell him to let Harper know she was in Istanbul. No way could Harper avoid Isabelle then. It was hardly a solid plan, but considering how limited her options were, it was the best plan.

If Harper agreed to see her, what would she say?

"I, a near stranger you've only known for a month and kissed a few times amidst the chaos of your Rhode Island home, have decided to come all this way to advise you? Rescue you? Force you to come home?"

Isabelle shrugged. It was rash; a great leap. Perhaps one of the silliest things she'd done. Even if Harper's life was in danger, what could Isabelle do to help her? And if there was no danger and Harper was off gallivanting and living her best life, then coming to Turkey was even more idiotic.

What the fuck am I doing?

Isabelle got up and paced the room. She shook her head. She believed her instincts were right in this case. Something had gone wrong. Harper had not told her the full story or explained what she had to gain from this excursion to Istanbul, but she was in trouble. That much was obvious. While Isabelle might not be able to protect her in any grand sort of way, she might be able to convince her to tread with caution and to not feel like she was responsible for everyone involved in the situation, whatever it was.

The best course of action would be for Harper to come home and work with the State Department.

Isabelle plopped down onto the bed and turned the TV on impatiently, not quite convinced. She was annoyed at herself for even entertaining a resolution in such simple terms.

She flipped through the available channels and found a program aimed at tourists. She could not focus on any of it, and after a few minutes she turned to the news. They were in the middle of a story about a notorious Turkish drug lord who had been arrested in the UK for smuggling drugs into Europe from the Middle East.

She turned the TV off and sat in silence for a while. She was agitated. She was eager to do something. She wanted to escape the clouded maze her thoughts kept leading her into.

After she had transferred some essentials – a change of clothes and toiletries – from her suitcase to her backpack, she scribbled a quick note for Bastian and put her sneakers back on. She was anxious, yet a palpable excitement coursed through her.

Outside, the heat enveloped her once again. She wiped her face and neck with her handkerchief and consulted her guide book. Behind her in the distance was Dolmabahce palace, the last residence of the Ottoman sultans, whose empire came to an end in the early nineteen twenties.

Isabelle went toward the shops, past high-end clothing stores, phone and electronic stores, restaurants and cafés. The people were youthful and trendy, but she couldn't help noticing the contrasts. A young lady wore shorts that showed off her large thigh tattoos, and two women in burkas went by with their shopping bags. Men wore close-fitting jeans and T-shirts and had modern haircuts, though they often wore reserved expressions on their faces.

This was a wealthy neighborhood village and not quite what Isabelle had expected. Despite the sizable crowds bustling through, the noise mostly consisted of snippets of conversation and the sound of motor engines. The aroma of freshly-brewed coffee and baked bread and a distinct scent of roasting sesame swaddled her.

She found herself on Sair Nedim Caddesi and was greeted by the beautiful Akaretler row houses. They were all in warm, neutral colors with long rectangular windows and miniature white balconies in the middle. Restaurants on the ground floors kept the theme with neat little tables lined up outside, and were framed by large potted plants.

Lovely as they were, Isabelle didn't stop at any of these places. She went further into the maze of narrow streets where the atmosphere was more like a market packed with places to eat and stores and vehicles and motorbikes and people trying to get by on the small brick street.

Restaurants, cafes, and bars flanked both sides of the confined alleys. Isabelle stopped at a place with a red awning, simply because she was overwhelmed with choices and could not make an informed decision. Her table outside was an arm's length from other passersby and tourists, and the smell of searing meat mixed with the lightness of a sweet hookah fragrance made her smile. She inhaled deeply, feeling an overwhelming sense of fulfillment that comes with experiencing something new and expansive.

The waiter brought her coffee, rich and smooth and black. She let the bitterness of it in while soaking up the sounds and watching a stray cat saunter then pause under a table to lick her paws.

Her dish was served in a small round pot. Cubes of salmon sizzled in a mixture of sweet onions and vegetables with mushroom and herbs and spices.

When Isabelle was done eating she toyed with the idea of going across the street to the bar. Patrons sat on stools in the outdoor, or went in and out, gesturing at a football match being shown on the screens. But it would do her no good to be drunk and lost in this city, despite the adventurous nature it had awoken in her.

Bastian came into the hotel room later that afternoon looking haggard and restless. He mumbled hello and went to the bathroom. When he came back out he took a seat on the armchair across from Isabelle and slowly dried his face and hands with a towel. Then he looked up.

"What's the plan, Detective?" he asked with no hint of humor in his voice.

"Find Victoria," Isabelle said.

"How do you propose we do that?" He blinked slowly, as if doubting Isabelle had a plan at all.

"We could start with her Aunt Roslyn." She pulled out the envelope with Roslyn's address that she had swiped from the house in Newport before she left. "I thought ahead."

Bastian looked genuinely surprised, but he stood and nodded. "Let's go then."

Roslyn's apartment was west of where they were, on the other side of the Besiktas JK football stadium. Isabelle and Bastian stood outside the pink pastel building for a while, trying to figure out how to get in. Roslyn's name was not listed on the building directory. None of the apartments were labeled. What if she had moved?

A child came out pushing a small BMX bicycle and Isabelle and Bastian held the door then slipped inside. They found Roslyn's apartment number in the brightly lit hallway of the second floor. They knocked several times and waited. She was clearly not at home. Disappointed, but still optimistic, Isabelle worked up the nerve to knock on the apartment across from Roslyn's place. A woman came to the door in a red robe with red hair streaming down her shoulders.

"Yes?"

"Hi," Isabelle piped up. "I had an appointment with Roslyn, but she is not at home. I was wondering if you knew when she is expected to return."

The woman looked puzzled. Isabelle thought of the Turkish words she had memorized on the flights over.

"Merak . . . edi . . . ediyorum . . . ?" She pointed to Roslyn's door.

"Roslyn?" Understanding finally dawned on the woman's face.

"Yes," Isabelle said, relieved. She had tried to say she was 'looking for' her friend, but knew she was off.

"Ah." The woman deflated. She pulled her robe closer around her and looked down both sides of the hallway. "Gone."

"What do you mean 'gone'?"

"Left." The woman fluttered her hand like a bird. "Gone."

"Gone where?" Isabelle pressed.

"Quickly. Quickly. Gone."

"She left in a hurry? But why?"

The woman shrugged.

"What is your name?" Isabelle stuck out her hand. "I'm Isabelle."

"Shirley," she said, taking Isabelle's hand. "You friend Roslyn?"

"Acquaintance," Isabelle said, but Shirley did not understand. She moved her palm side to side.

"I see," Shirley said.

"I need to find her."

Shirley studied them both long and hard. "Why you need find Roslyn?"

Isabelle put her hands up in frustration. "I worry. I . . . *korku?*" *Fear* was the only word that came to mind, and it made Shirley's expression freeze over. It might have been inadequate for what Isabelle really wanted to say, but it had an effect. Shirley slipped into her apartment and came back out with a key. She turned the lock on Roslyn's door and they went in together.

The first thing that struck Isabelle was the lighting. An alarming glow blasted them from the orange accent wall as the sun poured through the terrace door glass. Another wall of wood and dark brick grounded the atmosphere, but in between everything else was in shambles. A sleek leather coach regurgitated its cotton inside, having been sliced open. The contents of drawers were strewn across the carpet. A lamp had apparently been thrown against the wood-brick wall and glass splinters dazzled as the sunlight danced across them.

Isabelle, Bastian, and Shirley took in the scene.

"My friend," Shirley finally said, gesturing toward the disaster. "They come one night. They do this, then my friend she gone. Quickly, quickly."

There wasn't much to glean from a smashed up luxury con-dominium, other than the fact that someone had come to Roslyn's place determined to find something. Whoever it was had scared her so much that she fled. Isabelle tried to prod Shirley for more information but the woman was in the dark. Roslyn had not told her where she planned to go.

"My friend, she like to knit and dinner with handsome gen-tlemen," Shirley said, pondering the situation. "Why they do this?"

"She has a niece," Isabelle said. "Victoria. Have you seen her?"

Shirley looked perplexed again.

"Victoria," Isabelle repeated. She put her palm above her head. "Tall."

Bastian dug into his pocket and pulled out a photograph. He smiled smugly at the shocked expression on Isabelle's face. "You're not the only one who thinks ahead."

The photo was worn and he unfolded it and showed it to Shirley.

"Ah yes, Vic," Shirley exclaimed. "She come looking, but my friend gone."

"When did she come here?" Isabelle asked.

"Two day."

"Today?"

"Two day," Shirley said again.

"Two days ago," Bastian offered.

So Harper had come looking for her aunt and had no doubt seen the carnage here. Where could she have gone? Were Harper and Roslyn hiding out together?

Bastian and Isabelle sat on a bench in the last of the sunshine about two blocks from Roslyn's place.

"What's the next step, Captain?" Bastian asked, as he munched on roasted peppers and juicy chunks of lamb he'd bought at roadside setup.

"I'm thinking. I had pinned my hopes on finding Roslyn." She hesitated to pull her "call Sud" card. She needed more time to find out what was going on. It was probably ill-advised, but now that she'd come this far she wanted to come to her own conclusions.

"I texted your friend's picture to one of my associates," Bastian was saying. He wiped his fingers on a napkin and scrolled through his text messages. "He thinks he knows someone who might recognize her."

"Then let's go see him," Isabelle said eagerly.

"Let me call him first."

He got up and walked out of earshot as he dialed a number. Adrenaline coursed through Isabelle's body. She was excited at the possibility of a strong lead, but a sense of uneasiness came over her.

Bastian came back to the bench and sat down, but wasn't speaking.

"And?" Isabelle flailed her arms.

"He definitely knows her. But her name isn't Victoria Harper. It's Jane Reid."

Isabelle was stunned into silence. When she was finally able to parse through her thoughts with logic, she said, "Her name is Victoria Harper of the Harpers in Newport. If she isn't, then every single one of her family members is living under a fictitious name as well."

"You're right," Bastian said. "It's an alias."

"Jane Reid is an alias," Isabelle repeated. Once the shock wore off it all made sense. If Harper used an alias while in Turkey, then it explained why she was able to return to the States after the Maramaxe exposé without facing retribution. Her enemies could not track her down.

Still, her family was well-known in Newport and was in the public eye. How had she existed under the radar for so many years?

"Let's go see your friend about this Jane Reid," Isabelle said.

Chapter Eighteen

THEY MADE THEIR WAY to the crumbling high-rise apartment in their rented Volkswagen. Bastian maneuvered easily through the city blocks past a few men who leaned against a parked car, smoking and telling tales that caused the group to become animated with laughter and spill out into the street.

Isabelle caught the slight nod of her brother's head, a returned greeting to one of the men who turned to look as they passed.

A woman came to the door of the building in a house dress. She looked them up and down. "Merhaba?"

"Merhaba," Bastian smiled. "I am a friend of Decebal."

Without another word she turned and led them inside. She went up the stairs ahead of them, wide and frumpy, and when she reached the top stairs she was out of breath. The hallway was rife with the smell of a pungent meat being cooked.

"Number twelve," the woman said in English, but Bastian had already turned in that direction. He watched her go into her apartment before he knocked on the door. It was yanked open immediately by a scrawny man. The veins on his forehead bulged.

"Come the fuck in," the man said.

"Long time no see," Bastian said dryly as they entered.

The man, Decebal, went over to a flimsy kitchen table and rolled himself a joint. He wore a white tank top and worn out

Chicago Bulls shorts. Isabelle was struck by the familiarity between her brother and this man. Bastian trusted him, but the thought of this Decebal person knowing Harper made her uneasy.

"About the woman," Bastian said.

"Uh huh." Decebal ran his tongue across the joint.

"You said you know her," Isabelle said.

The man looked at her properly for the first time.

"Who's this?" His eyes were like glass, flicking from her face to Bastian's, recognition sinking in even as he asked the question.

"My sister," Bastian confirmed.

Decebal consumed an eyeful before turning his attention back to the matter at hand. "My friend know her."

"Who is your friend?" Isabelle asked.

Bastian shushed her with a look and stepped forward, opening his wallet. "What does he know?"

"He used to took care of her and her friends," Decebal said. "A bunch of long-legged creatures back in the day."

"Models?"

"Yah. Running through the city for night or two of kicks after a job."

"Their drug of choice?" Bastian asked.

"Heroin. Cocaine." Decebal lit his joint and tugged on it. When he released the thick white smoke his gaze steeled over.

Isabelle felt a strong urge to call him a liar, but she knew this sort of revelation was possible in a place like this. She looked around the room at the stacks of newspapers piled up and what looked like sketch books with loose papers and charcoal strewn around an old couch. The décor was sallow and nondescript, and she suddenly felt empty.

"Are you sure it was her?" Isabelle took Harper's picture from Bastian and held it up in front of the man. Decebal nodded honestly, as if he had sensed her disappointment.

"Jane's her name," he said. "I saw her couple times. She came by my pal's place with her friends. Kind of unforgettable because she was different."

"How so?" Isabelle asked.

"She didn't strike me as drug addict."

"So why was she hanging around with a dealer?" Bastian asked hastily.

Decebal shrugged and took another puff. "Beats me. She striked me as someone on a mission. She wasn't there for fun like other dumb bitches."

"Get me Jane Reid's address." Bastian counted out about two hundred and fifty US dollars and handed them to him.

Decebal flipped open his phone and dialed a number. He spoke to someone on the other end in clipped sentences, in a language that didn't sound like Turkish. He scribbled on a piece of paper and hung up. When he held it out Isabelle stepped in front of her brother and took it.

"What do you mean when you say she was on a mission?" she asked.

"She made deal with my friend to get something special," he said. "That was what she came for, not to flirt or have a bit of risky fun and game, if you get my drift."

"And what was that something special?" Isabelle held her breath.

"Morphine," Decebal said, arching one eyebrow up intriguingly.

"Tell me your friend's name," she said, hoping he wouldn't clam up now.

Decebal considered his advantage and Isabelle thought he might demand more money. Instead, he looked defiantly at Bastian and said, "Rasob. My friend's name is Rasob."

Isabelle sucked fresh air into her lungs as they left the building. Harper used to buy morphine many years ago when she lived in Turkey. Dr. Eugenie Bradford Harper had also been a morphine aficionado. The doctor used what was at her disposal. A drug that was lethal in excessive doses, administered by a professional who knew how to snuff out an enemy with it. Morphine had been her weapon of choice decades ago. There was no denying it now – this confirmed Isabelle's research into Eugenie and her group.

Isabelle unzipped her backpack and pulled out her laptop as they walked.

"What are you doing?" Bastian asked.

"I need to look at my notes." Isabelle rested her laptop on the hood of the car. "If I can tie somethings together, then—"

"Or we could just go to Jane Reid's apartment." He looked eager and on edge. This was a stain on his personality. An indelible smudge of tenseness pervaded him. "I'm guessing that would tie some things together."

Isabelle was afraid he might say that. She realized she was stalling once he *had* said it. She was afraid of the truth. Of what she was discovering about Harper. She was a member of an outfit that took the law into their own hands by poisoning people. There was no way around that reality. How far Harper had gone she didn't know, but she was capable of going to the limits.

Victoria Harper was a dangerous woman. That she had known from the first moment she saw her. What was Isabelle doing here in Istanbul? Trying to help a killer? How had she misjudged this situation so horribly? A disturbance stirred in her stomach and she swallowed hard. She had come here to find Harper and now she dreaded coming face to face with her.

"It's too dark now," Isabelle said weakly. "We should go tomorrow."

Soft waves shimmered in the distance, and all along the Bosporus were sailboats and jet skis and lively dots of people swimming. The water had a certain luminance, with its rich blue-green hue; it reached into the imagination and tugged at the most idyllic hopes. All of life's possibilities were laid out across the expanse of the ocean, across this historic through-line between Europe and Asia.

Isabelle had not seen it this up close before. Further downstream, the commercial ships, cruise lines, and ferries powered their way across the water, but she had been too preoccupied with her search for Harper to pay much attention. A search that brought her here, inside Harper's apartment in Yenikoy, where the Bosporus had finally stopped her and made her look.

Bastian had picked the lock once they realized Harper, or Jane Reid, was not at home, and they let themselves in. The building itself was unassuming, concealed, sandwiched between the high-walled waterfront villas and the rest of the residential coastal village. Tinted windows ran across the width of the room and offered a panoramic view of the streets and the sea in the distance, though a couple of the sultanate palaces – under heavy guard – obscured parts of the shore from view.

Isabelle and Bastian quietly soaked up the scenes outside. They had remained by the window, transfixed, after having inspected the place. It was a studio apartment, and all around them was the color of the sea. The bed sheets, the drapes, the small rectangular paintings, and the odd ceramic ornaments. It was clear the decorator had drawn inspiration from the Bosporus. The apartment was certainly more lived-in and treated with more care than the asparagus house in Chester, New York. Yet Isabelle had no doubt this place belonged to Harper. It was as if Isabelle was in center of a magnetic field, drawn in and held by the aura that surrounded Harper at all times. Her perfume wafted up from the sheets alongside the slight fragrance of peppermint, which Isabelle recalled she must have washed her hair with once. It had been as discernible then as it was now.

A quiet breath caught in Isabelle's throat. Her muscles seized up. She willed herself to turn, slowly, and found herself staring into the eyes of Victoria Harper standing in the doorway of her own apartment. Harper looked perplexed, as if she had encountered an unfamiliar foe on a familiar battleground.

"It is almost cinematic," Bastian was saying, his face pressed against the window, both hands cupping his eyes to frame the picture. The sound of his voice drew Harper's eyes to him, away from Isabelle. Here her expression shifted. It became dark, calculating, penetrative. It sent a cold wave down Isabelle's back.

She waited for Harper to speak but she remained silent, and the silence enveloped them both. How had she entered so silently? Why didn't she speak? Why didn't she ask, *What are you doing here?*

Isabelle found her own voice. "I have been looking for you."

Bastian spun around and saw her. His face took on the color of a ripe plum.

"Why?"

It had been said so softly and with such indifference that Isabelle wondered if it had been said at all. Harper's eyes never left Bastian's.

"I came because I was concerned and I wanted to help you in any way I can."

It sounded ridiculous, preposterous, and presumptuous. Isabelle had not thought this through. She thought she had before she got on that flight, but now that it all came down to this moment she realized she hadn't. She clammed up, embarrassed.

"And you?" Harper asked.

Bastian pointed his thumb at his own chest innocently, smugly. Then he pointed at Isabelle as if to say it was all her doing.

"What about her?" Harper asked.

Bastian cleared his throat and stuck both hands into his pockets. It was an odd stand-off.

"He's just trying to help me," Isabelle offered.

"You're trying to help *me* and he's trying to help *you*?" Harper said sarcastically.

"I'll go," Bastian said, smirking.

He went past Harper as if he was in no hurry, then paused and met her eyes. He was inclined to say something, but thought better of it and went out the door.

The tension in the room and in Harper's body deflated as the door shut behind him.

She came toward Isabelle. "Have you lost your mind?" She was more puzzled than angry.

"I know it seems stupid and bullheaded of me to come here," Isabelle said. "But I wasn't sure what else to do."

"Why is it so important for you to do something?"

"I don't know." Isabelle sighed. The fear that overcame her last evening was gone. Her stomach had settled once more. "Because I care about you."

Harper sighed and touched her arm, then gently pulled Isabelle toward her. "You needed to stay at home and be safe. It is the only way you can help. You have no idea what you're walking into."

"Then tell me."

"I thought I could come here and settle in and have enough time to determine how to help Steven." She held Isabelle's hands. "Figure out how to move forward, but I've been running since I got here. My local contacts have scattered. We're in disarray."

"Who are you running from?"

"Remember the people I you told about who ran the Maramaxe trafficking operation?"

Isabelle nodded.

"I knew who they were," Harper whispered.

"Who were they?"

"Members of my great-grandmother's company who split off and did their own thing decades ago. When I was a kid I learned about how they betrayed Eugenie before she died, but that was so long ago. I was more concerned with their operation now. I wanted to strike at them."

"What's their operation?" Isabelle asked.

"I can't get into all of that."

"So you're saying you knew who they were and you sent the report to Interpol as a way to dismantle them?"

"I didn't like what they were about . . . their business involved, among other things, trafficking human beings, children, into sexual slavery. Truly vile stuff." Harper closed her eyes. "I wanted to bring them down."

Isabelle waited. "Do they know you?"

"Yes," Harper said, resigned. "They knew exactly who I was. In other aspects of business I was their competition."

"Competition for what?"

"I can't tell you that either."

Isabelle sighed and turned away. She wanted it to be said. Her suspicions about Harper needed to be solidified, despite how hard it might be to hear.

"Listen, Isabelle," Harper said, coming to stand behind her. "My friend Thatcher can get you a ticket to return to the States. Your brother can find his own way home."

"I'm not going without you," Isabelle said. "Tell me why you were their competition."

Harper came around, cupping her face. "I cannot tell you that, and you will go, because it is for the best. I can't take the risk of letting you stick around to do God-knows-what."

"Same as whatever it is *you* think you're doing," Isabelle protested.

"In time I will explain." Harper led her to the window. The Bosporus was still brilliant – glimmers of sunlight reflected off the waves, and Isabelle was pleased to have made it here and to have found her.

"I've missed you," Harper said.

"I missed you too."

"You're a very brave woman." She slipped her arms around Isabelle's waist.

"Or very stupid."

"No. Not stupid at all."

Harper leaned in and kissed her. She nibbled on Isabelle's lips until they parted. Their tongues touched and Isabelle was ignited. Heat flared across her skin, parching and quelling her at once. Harper's fingers slid up into Isabelle's hair and tugged her head back. She bent her head and claimed Isabelle's mouth again with her own, pressing her against the window. Isabelle clutched at Harper's neck, her breath leaving her in little pants. Her heart hammered as if it might beat right out of her chest.

When their lips finally parted, it was as if they had discovered each other for the first time. Harper's eyes had changed. They were brown, but filled with sparks of light and hazel. Her mother's eyes.

Isabelle's cell phone rang, breaking the stirring trance that had taken hold of them. Harper was still clinging to Isabelle even as she moved to look at her phone.

It was Bastian. Isabelle tapped the answer key and moved the phone to her ear, her eyes drawn to Harper's lips again.

"Get out of the apartment!"

"What?"

"Get out now!" Bastian repeated. "Two men just entered the building. They're packing."

"Did he just say . . . ?" Harper looked as if she had been snapped out of a dream. She had heard Bastian's shout through the phone.

"Two armed men are on their way up."

Harper darted toward the bed. She knelt down and pulled a bag from under it and quickly unzipped it to check the contents. Satisfied, she grabbed Isabelle, and in one fluid motion swung them both out the door and into the hallway. The elevator door slid open and Isabelle caught a glimpse of two conspicuous young men in T-shirts and jeans stepping out.

Harper swung her back into the apartment and locked the door. She stopped abruptly in the kitchen area and pushed aside a small cabinet. Then she slid back a bolt in the wall and opened a compartment that came no higher than their thighs. They stooped to get through the opening. The space led to a narrow corridor that ran between Harper's place and the adjoining apartment. As they hustled, they heard the loud bang of the apartment door as it crashed open. A shuffling sound followed – the men had found the opening and were trying to get through the little hole.

The door at the end of the corridor was barred by a slim metal gate, and Isabelle was sure they were trapped. Harper quickly unlatched the padlock and forced the door open. Clearly she had used this route before.

When Isabelle came out into the sunlight, her whole life was summed up in this heightened moment. Here at the back of the building on a meager ledge, the view was that of other apartments close up. She was struck by the small, crumbling brick buildings and quaint little wood houses juxtaposed against modern structures. By the multicolored hues and the starkness of a humdrum life in this tiny enclave beyond the great grandeur of the stately homes: sheets and clothing hung on lines to dry, wash buckets, a threadbare soccer ball, and a languid cat in the yard below.

Isabelle's heart plummeted. It was only reasonable for her to meet her death here, in this oddly ordinary place.

She scrambled down the flimsy rust-covered ladder behind Harper, acutely aware of her own demise. The smell of rust and sweat and frying fish enveloped her. For these residents it would be fish for dinner then later the alarming spectacle of finding the bullet-riddled corpse of a Jamaican-American girl who had wandered into town on a foolhardy mission.

Tears welled in her eyes, but before the tears could spill they were at the bottom of the ladder and running. The lonesome thud of feet on the ground was all she heard for several seconds then the sound of feet on the ground grew in numbers.

They were still being pursued.

They rounded the corner to the front of the building. Bastian paced the sidewalk. He started toward the back of the building, but when he saw them coming he stopped and ran back to the car. He yanked the back door open for them and jumped into the driver's seat.

Only once they were safely inside and had sped off did Isabelle think to look back. The men faded in the distance, looking longingly after them, gesturing ruefully.

Isabelle's mind flashed back to Bastian on the sidewalk, his gun drawn, with a look of terror on his face until he saw her.

Chapter Nineteen

THE VOLKSWAGEN SPED south along the coastline, out from the intimate streets where beach-goers sat shirtless outside cafes. They went by a market that sold colorful floating tubes in the shapes of animals: alligators, pigs, a cute little cow. As they went on, Isabelle could not get those images of the puffed up animals out of her mind.

She was acutely aware of Harper beside her in the back of the car sweating, whipping her head around as if still being chased, and palming something inside her bag which was quite clearly a gun. Eventually she relaxed enough to turn her attention to Isabelle.

"Are you alright?" She wrapped her free hand around Isabelle's shoulder.

Isabelle nodded. Her throat was dry. She'd had to deal with the consequences of her own mischiefs before, but this took it to another level. They all could have been killed. Harper seemed to realize that too. She pulled Isabelle close and kissed her forehead.

"Are those the people who've been hunting you?" Isabelle asked.

"Yes," Harper whispered.

"Victoria, you've got to put an end to all this," Isabelle pleaded. "Just go to the police."

"I can't."

"You're worse than my brother."

They continued south, zipping along a major highway and through larger cities and business districts. Bastian kept his speed through urban areas, and even as they approached the heart of Istanbul. They sped by ferry boats and the Old City across the water. Fishermen displayed their mackerel bounty on the quay in colorful baskets, and the long silver bodies of the fish glistened in the sunshine. They went through the city cluster, navigating around buses and taxis, until they came out to a clearing and could see the water again.

Harper jerked forward and looked out the window. Her head darted from left to right, this time trying to identify where they were. "Stop the car!"

Bastian kept going, though Isabelle was sure he'd heard her. The cable car went over their heads.

"Stop the car now!" Harper stuck her hand inside her bag.

Isabelle lurched forward. "Bastian, pull over right now."

For a moment she thought he might ignore her as well, but he came to his senses and hedged toward the shoulder, slowing. Harper jumped out before the car came to a full standstill. Isabelle sprang out and went after her. Harper stalked a few paces then turned abruptly, causing Isabelle to run into her.

"What the fuck does he think he's doing?"

Bastian got out of the car slowly, pulling up his pants by the waist.

"What the fuck do you think you are doing?" Harper repeated, glowering at him.

"Saving your ass from some ugly motherfucking goons," Bastian said. "That's what."

"That involves weaving through all of Istanbul, headed to God-Knows-Where?"

"Excuse me, your highness." He glared at her. "You're the one who almost had lead for lunch. Maybe in your haste you forgot to give me your itinerary for this escape." He straightened as a shadow fell across his face. "You got some fucking nerve."

Isabelle knew Bastian was also carrying his weapon. She imagined a Western-like shootout between them, here in this quiet stretch of the city in front of a vacant bus stop, with the gentle moving water of the Golden Horn as a backdrop.

She quickly stepped between them.

"Let's just calm down," Isabelle said, though she certainly did not feel calm.

"I don't trust that fucking Conquistador," Bastian spat, pointing at Harper.

"I don't like his smug face," Harper spat back.

Isabelle went over to Harper. "What is it? This animus between you—"

"I don't trust your brother. That's all."

"Isabelle, let's go." Bastian was coming toward them. "It's not safe around her."

Harper held Isabelle's arm, saying nothing but willing her to remain where she was with a piercing stare.

"Isabelle," Bastian repeated. "I'm not leaving you with this woman."

"Just hang on." Isabelle put her hands up as a barrier or as a calming force. Her voice betrayed her desperation. The tension had shot up and she was torn.

She moved toward her brother to talk to him, but Harper would not release her arm.

Bastian stepped forward. "Let go of her."

"Don't come any closer," Harper said.

"I am her protector and have always been." Bastian's gaze steeled over. "Right now you're not safe to be around. I'm taking Isabelle home."

"If you really wanted to protect her you wouldn't have brought her here in the first place."

"Are we going to have it out?"

"No – this is silly and frankly disrespectful," Isabelle said, her voice shaking. "I don't need to be coddled like a child."

Harper released her arm.

"I came here to help figure things out and I am not going home just because either of you tell me to."

They waited.

"I am staying right where I am, with Victoria."

"Don't be a fool," Bastian said. "You have no idea who this woman is."

"And you do?" Harper asked, emboldened by Isabelle's choice. "Do you know me?"

Bastian smirked and sucked his teeth, dismissing her. "I know you somehow managed to brainwash my sister into thinking you are a damsel in distress. Whatever is going on is of your own doing." He sized her up. "People like you who've got a chunk of change and some standing in your community think you can do whatever the hell you want without repercussions."

"You think you know my family too."

"I don't care about your family." He pointed at her. "And if anything happens to my sister I'm coming after you."

He started back toward the car hastily, in anger. Then he stopped and looked back at Isabelle, his expression a mixture of reproach and regret.

"You're making a mistake," he said, before slipping into the car.

As the Volkswagen sped off, Harper took Isabelle's hand.

"Come on," she said. "Let's get off of this road."

They crossed the street and cut through the park to the other side. The avenue was bustling with shoppers and tourists, and Isabelle and Harper zig-zagged to avoid the crowd. Harper waved down a taxi and directed the driver to take them across the Galata Bridge. Once they were in the Old City they abandoned the main streets and moved along the back alleys.

They crossed several blocks then slipped into a dingy motel that reeked of Lysol and cigars. A tall man with silver-gray hair and beard was at the front desk. He stood as they entered. He and Harper exchanged nods and he pointed toward the back.

Harper led Isabelle down the hall and pulled out her keys. When she opened one of the room doors so they could go in, Isabelle paused and looked at her closely. Did she have a hideout in every corner of every city? Had she been running like this all her life?

Harper seemed to catch Isabelle's train of thought, but said nothing.

She stepped into the room with Isabelle and looked around briefly then half-smiled. "I have to talk with Thatcher. Stay here."

Isabelle did as she was told. She found herself standing in the middle of the room, frozen with her bag on her back. She listened for voices and hints of activity. The motel was quiet, except for the sound of the TV playing in the room next door. Even that Isabelle strained to hear. Several cars went by outside.

Eventually, she sat down on a futon near the door and tried to arrange her thoughts about the events of the day in a way that was logical. The Maramaxe people wanted revenge for what Harper had done to them. Harper and these men were competitors and, judging by the goons that showed up at her place in Yenikoy, they knew where to find her. But why had it taken them so long to deal with her? Harper coming back to Istanbul must have stirred things up again. It was easier to get to her here than it was in the United States. They had known she was in town. She could never expect to be safe as long as she was in this city.

The sound of footsteps sent Isabelle's heart tumbling inside her chest. As the door opened instinct kicked in and she took a quick step to the side, placing herself behind the door.

"Isabelle?"

It was Harper. Relief and embarrassment flooded through her. She would know Isabelle was afraid, hiding like a coward.

Harper closed the door behind her and said calmly, "I got what I came for." She kissed Isabelle's cheek and they headed out.

They were in a taxi again weaving through the city until Harper instructed the driver to pull over. She paid and they got out and walked back toward the direction they had just come from, hidden within the back streets under the approaching evening. Isabelle was exhausted. Her nerves frayed as she tried to keep up. When they arrived at a small lot Isabelle understood. Harper had a car parked here. She found the beat-up Audi with the click of her key fob, and they got in.

"Where are we headed?" Isabelle found the strength to ask.

"Kutahya," Harper said. "We'll take the ferry to get there."

Once they were on the boat and gliding across the choppy water the tension finally released from between Isabelle's shoulder blades. Her heart rate returned to normal. She focused her attention on the distance ahead. The horizon was tinged with a purple haze that filled her with an odd emotion. A sense of hope, crippled with trepidation.

She looked back at Harper, who was sitting inside, covertly arranging items inside her bag and calmly craning her neck to monitor her surroundings. She was sweating profusely, more so than Isabelle. Wet spots seeped through her shirt and she brushed sweat from her forehead with the back of her hand. Her hair was wild, even though she had it in a ponytail. Isabelle gave her a napkin and took a seat next to her. They had picked up turkey sandwiches and coffee on the drive. Isabelle handed Harper a sandwich and a cup of coffee. They ate and sat silently as they looked out at the Sea of Marmara, which seemed to hold all the elements of fate and fear, and even the remnants of dreams.

Shielded under a blanket which Harper had pulled from the trunk of the car, they leaned against each other and dozed for most of the journey. They mumbled and nodded their way through conversations initiated by other riders, wanting to keep a low profile. It reminded Isabelle of how Harper was when they first met at the guesthouse grand opening party. She had been hesitant to speak and was watchful. Now Isabelle was her own version of that mute and paranoid character.

When they arrived in Yavlova in the late evening, they retrieved Harper's car and departed the ferry. Sinking fear returned to Isabelle's body as they ventured out into the dark, speeding along Bursa Yalova Yolu, passing tall buildings that looked like businesses and apartments. They went west, away from the city cluster and highways, and skirted along near Lake Iznik, where the ruins of an ancient basilica was discovered underwater a few years ago.

"What did the man at the motel give you?" Isabelle asked, after a prolonged period of quiet. She had seen Harper palming a yellow flash drive when they were on the boat. Isabelle had noted the care with which she had stuck it in one of the inside pockets of her bag and zipped it shut.

"What?" Harper was distracted, her attention focused on navigating their route.

"The man at the motel. What did he give you?"

Harper shrugged. "Information."

"What kind of information?" Isabelle had the sense she was buying time, trying to come up with an acceptable answer.

"It doesn't matter," she said finally.

"Why not?"

Harper turned and looked at her squarely, before turning back to the road. "The better question is, what good will it do you to know?"

Isabelle's anger rose, but she wasn't sure she was justified in this anger. She had chosen to come here. Was Harper obligated to tell her anything? She glanced out the window into the dark, at the olive and fig trees that surrounded them on this stretch of roadway. She was vulnerable and isolated in this place. Her anger subsided, but she hardened.

"Victoria, I came all the way to Turkey," she said. "I left my brother and chose to come with you. I need to know what information that man gave you and why it was so important."

Harper sighed but remained quiet for some time.

"His name is Thatcher Mowat." She sat up straight and pushed her shoulders back, as if fortifying herself. "He is what I like to call the 'underground CIA.'" She smiled at her own clever phrase, but when Isabelle did not react she went on. "Thatch gets me whatever I need. Personnel records, background checks, police records, dock records. He monitors certain matters and the movement of people of interest to me."

"Why dock records and personnel records?"

"What?"

"You said dock records and personnel records. Why do you need all that?"

"It's purely informational. Sometimes I just like to know what my enemies are up to." She paused. "Or my friends."

"Purely informational," Isabelle repeated, weighing the words.

"You don't believe me," Harper said. "I'm not saying I don't act if I need to, but most of the time I don't do anything with the data Thatch collects."

"So why do you need it?"

"I don't know. It makes me feel protected, I guess."

"What are their names?"

"Who?"

"Your enemies."

"Old Bastards." Harper shrugged. "Two-headed monster."

Isabelle couldn't help but laugh.

They drove on for a long time in a swollen silence. Harper wanted to keep her work and the people she associated with close to her chest. She had competitors hunting her down and threatening the lives of her friends. It was difficult to understand why she would choose this path.

"You said you wanted my help with the project."

"What do you mean?"

"Your memoir," Isabelle said. "I don't see how I can be effective if I am kept in the dark."

"I wouldn't worry about it too much." She winked. "We'll decide on a way forward once we have time to gather our thoughts."

"What do you hope to accomplish in the end?"

"I've not really thought of that, to be honest." She glanced at Isabelle.

"Don't you know what's driving you?" Isabelle pressed.

Harper considered. "I want to build something that's completely my own."

"The way Eugenie did?"

"Eugenie?"

"Yes. It's quite clear you have great admiration for her."

"You know, there was a certain absurdity in what she did. And I think I can tell you this now. She did have a vigilante group – a collection of mentally scarred veterans – that took the law into their own hands. But that was a completely different time. I couldn't bring myself to . . . let's just say I've thought of more sane ways to spend my time."

"What did you want from me?" Isabelle asked. "From the beginning?"

Harper cleared her throat and took a moment to think.

"I was attracted to you," she finally said, her voice reflective. "I wanted to be around you and I wasn't sure how to make that happen. So I asked for your help."

"It was that simple," Isabelle muttered under her breath. Had it simply been a matter of attraction? Harper asking her to come to Chester? Isabelle flying to Turkey like a fool?

She had been around danger all her life, but this was different. She was now colluding with the nefarious. There was no way around that. She had abandoned all she knew to run around like a fugitive in a foreign country.

"Maybe I just wanted adventure," Isabelle said, resigned.

"Maybe you did." Harper smiled with warmth and admiration in her eyes. "Is this adventurous enough for you?"

"It's more than I bargained for."

Isabelle didn't understand her feelings. Hours ago she was in Harper's arms and limitless possibilities unfolded before her. She had discovered something worth grasping, and this discovery promised revival, and a re-imagining of the person she could be. Now they were gliding along a road lit only by the limited glare of headlights, and the impending darkness kept coming toward her.

Or perhaps she had always moved toward the darkness.

Chapter Twenty

IN KUTAHYA, ISABELLE and Harper came along a lone curling road surrounded by gentle, sloping hills. They skirted around the edges of the main square, past the clock tower and the large multicolored ceramic vase in the center of the fountain. The influence of the tile industry in the region could be seen in the decorative choices on many buildings. Shops were closed, but an array of tiles and vases were visible through the windows.

They went past Ottoman-era stucco houses and little museums, as mountains in the distance slumbered beneath the emerging light of dawn.

As they rolled down narrow avenues in town, the structures became a jarring constitution of sturdy pastel houses next to decaying buildings. When they found themselves amid a stack of washed out shabby structures next to a heap of discarded trash and old metal parts, Isabelle feared that might be their destination. She was relieved when Harper drove on, leaving that assemblage behind.

Finally they stopped in front of an isolated, nondescript building reminiscent of Ravi Holder's old place and went inside to a front room with a low ceiling and a bench against the wall. A large Turkish rug covered the floor, and red drapes ran along the walls of exposed brick. Beyond that, the room was completely vacant.

Isabelle expected Harper to announce they would have to wait. Instead she walked to the back wall and stood for a moment, listening. She turned her head slowly toward the lone window in the room, watching for signs of movement outside in the dusty, pebble-filled yard. When she was satisfied, she stooped to the floor and lifted one edge of the rug to reveal a small door in the floor. She punched a four-digit code into the lock and it slid open. As they took the first step and lowered themselves down into the dark room, Isabelle had an eerie flashback of descending into the unknown.

They came to the landing, a surface that was either reverberating beneath her feet or Isabelle was so disoriented she imagined it did. She had to wait for her eyes to adjust to the dim lighting. The cloaked figure of a man approached them. He greeted Harper with a firm hug and said, "Welcome, my friend."

He shook Isabelle's hand apprehensively when Harper introduced them.

"She's good," Harper said in a voice that demanded acquiescence.

The man, whose name was George Clover, was tall and thick, with a pudgy face and slightly balding hair in the front that fell in long reddish clumps down his shoulder. He wore a yellow bandanna rolled up and tied around his forehead. He pulled the hood of his army green trench coat down over his pallid eyes and turned away.

Clover led them through to another room partially lit by blue florescent lights, and again Isabelle had to give her eyes time to adjust. She detected slight movement in one corner of the room, but the person remained quiet. Harper stepped forward and her height and aura filled the room. Two figures emerged from the shadows. The head of one of them was concealed by a wide brimmed, looping hat. Thin lips were visible beneath the shadow. It was a woman.

The other figure was stout and solid-looking, and wore a boxy suit that hung loosely. The person stepped forward and Isabelle was surprised to discover this was also a woman.

Harper greeted the woman in the suit with a warm hug, and then ushered her toward Isabelle. Her brown hair was full and cut into a bob. She looked like an autumnal Louise Brooks.

"This is my Aunt Roslyn," Harper said, smiling.

Roslyn's face was wide and striking. Her intense eyes bore into Isabelle, carrying with them the essence of the woman's sultry strength. Isabelle stuttered, self-conscious about her grand plan to find Harper by finding Roslyn. Irrational as it was, she was afraid they would know she'd been to Roslyn's place just from looking at her. She managed to return the greeting then stood awkwardly silent as the two women continued to chat. Their tone was grim and somber, and Isabelle snapped out of her embarrassed state so she could pay attention.

The other woman had paused to lower something from the wall with Clover's help. It was a desk of sorts that from the look of things they had hastily slid up and folded out of view once they heard visitors descending the staircase. She removed her hat and strolled over. She was a short, awkward blonde with freckles dotting a round, delicate face.

The woman hesitated as her eyes fell on Isabelle. She sauntered over to Harper and held her by the upper arms. She pulled Harper down for sturdy kisses to both cheeks. Isabelle had territorial stirrings she had never experienced before. She wanted this woman, whoever she was, to back off.

Harper turned to Isabelle, her face revealing a slight discomfort, and introduced the woman, whose name was Stuttgart.

Stuttgart? Isabelle almost said it out loud. Was she an entire city onto herself?

Instead Isabelle smiled and greeted the woman diplomatically. As she shook Isabelle's hand, Stuttgart returned the smile with her teeth clamped together, and then she twisted her shoulder toward Harper.

"What is she?" she asked in a muffled French-German accent.

Isabelle started, alarmed the woman would be so rude, but Harper smiled at what was apparently a language barrier.

"A friend," Harper said, placing her hand on Isabelle's back.

"A friend to us?"

"Yes."

Clover stepped across the room. "We verified this?"

"I verified this." Harper stared him down and doled out the same treatment to Stuttgart.

Stuttgart and Clover fell back. Isabelle had the sense the matter was not settled, but for now they had to fall in line.

"We are wasting time," Roslyn said, with the effect of an elderly peacemaker. "We've waited long enough."

"I was delayed." Harper was apologetic.

Clover moved to the desk. He ran his hand over the map and picked up a few push pins.

"We managed to get him to Armenia," he said. "Tomorrow your contact will head out with him to the Georgian border. From there, they must get to Tbilisi and get on a flight to London." He stuck a green push-pin in South Wales, near Narberth. There were green push-pins in the places on the map Clover mentioned, tracking the route. "We can keep him safe in Wales. That's where your family has made provisions."

Patricia, Isabelle thought. The Harpers were helping with Steven's escape.

"Can't he take the train from somewhere in Georgia?" Harper asked. "Wouldn't that allow him to be under the radar?" She looked around the room.

"It present an opportunity for them to follow," Stuttgart said. "The train must take several hours."

Harper would take the hard way, the long way. That much Isabelle knew from traveling with her these last few hours.

"It presents an opportunity to get creative if they run into trouble," Harper said. "An airplane is restrictive." She massaged her chin. "In any case, I need a play by play of the trip until they arrive in Wales."

"To other pressing matters." Roslyn pulled out a folded-up piece of paper from her breast pocket. "Have you seen Thatch?"

"We're exhausted," Harper said quickly. "Let's leave the rest for later."

Roslyn understood, though she seemed uncomfortable, troubled even at a potential delay in discussing whatever she had in mind.

Clover was still studying his map, and Isabelle looked closely. Yellow push-pins dominated Anatolia, southeast from where they were. They appeared to be strategically placed.

A glaring red pin stood in the heart of Istanbul.

Before Isabelle could decipher any meaning behind marking these places, Harper took her hand and led her away from the desk.

The room they were in contained a couch and two large mattresses on the floor. Two smaller rooms were in the back. As they brushed past, Isabelle looked into one of the rooms through the open blinds of a wide office window. There were several computers and communication devices, as well as a refrigerator and a table full of liquor, cigarettes, and a coffee pot.

Harper brought her to the room on the left, where she was greeted by a desk and chair and a small cot on the floor. They went in and Harper closed the door.

"Let's take a moment to gather ourselves," she said, taking a seat on the desk. "It's been a long journey."

Isabelle smiled, but she was struck by memories of her own journey. Her childhood in particular. Her father with his demure, kind ways, snuffed out by barbarians. The barbarians had been winning for as long as she could remember. Barbarians like Haughton and his crew, like Bastian and her mother. They came in many forms. Marcia was proof of that.

Here was Harper. Smug, satisfied. The grand plan coming together.

This operation was serious and solemn, hidden away at the foot of the Kutahya Mountains, deep in the underground of an unremarkable house. The truth of everything hit Isabelle. It was sobering. Sorrow flowed through her. Had she expected something grand? It wasn't that at all. It was the familiarity of the scheme. The secrecy. The spurious way in which things were beginning to unfold.

Oddly, it all reminded her of father's loneliness. Of his death, which she had grieved in spurts throughout the years.

"Are you tired?" Harper asked, watching her closely.

Isabelle nodded.

"Why don't you lie down for a moment?" She pointed to the cot on the floor.

Isabelle threw herself down. "Will you tell me why we're here?" She asked, though she believed she would not get an answer.

She imagined the inner workings of Harper's mind as she considered the question; as she held Isabelle's gaze. She was deciding whether to tell the truth or not. Isabelle pictured the twisted strategies and the endless plotting that had brought Harper to where she was in her life, and to where they were now: Isabelle on a small cot in a dingy room.

Isabelle sighed and put her hands up to stop her before she could speak. "You don't have to answer that."

Harper looked relieved and Isabelle was disappointed. Being with her produced a confounding mixture of sensations for Isabelle: excitement and belonging, and a thread of unease that had been there from the beginning.

Isabelle looked up at the ceiling, which was painted a deep, burnt red. The color of isolation and loneliness. Of worry, and of a rich and penetrating fear. For her, this red reminded her of her fear of the known. The known monsters – red like rust or sulfur – always on the verge of invading like a slow fungus or erupting at the smallest provocation.

Perhaps this red was the color of vengeance and bloodshed. Or the color of dreams within a lost soul, looking for a whole to cling to; a soul lingering at the precipice of darkness, wanting to surrender into the known and the familiar.

Surrender was not graceful and demure. Surrender was singular and sure. Much like the ceiling above her it was pristine in its starkness, the solid red against wood.

The more she stared, the more the darker hues stood out. They were seeped in, leaving eternal stains along the edges.

❖

When Isabelle woke up the room was cool and covered in a soft lamplight. Low voices stirred her. She had fallen asleep on the cot in the little room, and she was alone. She got up slowly and pulled the window curtain aside to see into the main room.

Stuttgart and Roslyn reclined, each to a mattress, while Clover spread his legs out on the couch. They were drinking brown liquor in clear bottles and a sweet, melodic voice came through the speakers in the other room. The smell of roasted chicken and rosemary floated over. Isabelle was starving. She went out, led by her stomach, and Roslyn motioned her over to a low table containing chicken, bread, and green olives in olive oil.

Isabelle ate quietly on the mattress, noting how silent the room was now that she had entered. She kept her composure, as if her being there was the most normal thing in the world.

"How did you two meet?" Clover asked, between swigs of his drink.

"Long story," Isabelle said.

"We got time," Clover said.

Isabelle took a bite of her chicken and regarded him keenly, holding eye contact.

"It's a very long story," she said.

He stared at her, uncertainty in his face. As if he thought he had underestimated her. As if he thought there was more to her than they realized.

"It is a secret?" Stuttgart asked. She sounded silly, like a jealous schoolgirl.

Roslyn lit a cigarette, and the light from the match laid her face bare. It jolted Isabelle, as if the woman had taken off a mask. Isabelle had only perceived her through tales she'd heard from Harper and Danny, and perhaps she had formed an image of her as a nurturing woman. But the woman before her was hard and capable of many things.

"Can I have one?" Isabelle asked.

Roslyn handed her a cigarette and lit it. Isabelle tugged on it and let the nicotine fill her lungs.

Hard and capable of many things.

She liked the sound of that. She looked around the room and noted the desk had been returned to its cavern in the wall. Save for the one playing music, the computers were dark. The outer edges of the room were dark.

Isabelle swallowed the shot of whiskey Roslyn poured for her. She could be a vigilante or an outlaw. She could surrender into the known and the familiar. How different was it than being the daughter of a Don, the sister of a killer? Here she could be aimless and full of purpose at the same time, running from hideout to hideout, plotting escapes and passing clandestine messages. She could carry out secret missions that weren't at all what they appeared to be. They never were. She could lie and live a double life, fooling those closest to her. She could smoke cigarettes and drink whiskey with creeps in a cool basement in Kutahya. Or Istanbul. Or Bucharest. It didn't matter.

"So you're the infamous Isabelle," Roslyn said, after a few minutes had passed.

"Infamous?" Isabelle raised her eyebrows. "That word has never been used to describe me before."

"I've been a captive audience to many rambling conversations about you." Roslyn gave her a half-smile. "I think you present quite a conundrum for my niece."

"How so?" Isabelle asked.

Roslyn lowered her voice. "Well, she's very fond of you."

"I'm fond of her too."

"I've known her all her life and she's always been fond of fantastical ideas. She rarely gave her time and energy to anything else."

Isabelle could see that being the case. Harper was certainly not into romance and domesticity. She also was not fond of constancy.

"I had a good talk with Vic while you were asleep," Roslyn said. "She finds it admirable that you risked your safety to come here. What do you hope to gain?"

"I just wanted to find her," Isabelle said. "I was drawn by a desire to help her figure things out. I know it doesn't make sense. It doesn't even make sense to me. In the short time I've known her she's been a steady force for me. My life is a little murky right now."

"I don't know how much Vic told you, but you can't run away from your problems by running into something you are not built for. This life is complicated. It has its glory and it has its grit. Right now we are in the grit of it."

Isabelle understood. She didn't know if she was built for this, but she had to search for a place of her own. Her life was no longer with Marcia and Haughton. Or Bastian. Perhaps her life was at the guesthouse now. At least that was something that belonged to her.

"I told Vic to send you home," Roslyn said. "But she rarely listens to me. It is hard to do our jobs these days when we are always looking over our shoulder. Our enemies are hot on our heels. We've all become a little paranoid."

Isabelle knew this existence well based on her stepfather's experience. This way of life meant you were always going to be looking back, unable to truly enjoy the fruits of your efforts. She did not know how many enemies these people had made over time, but it was easy for the bodies to pile up. Literally or figuratively. She couldn't say for sure which.

"Frankly speaking," Isabelle whispered, "she doesn't tell me the details, and in the last day or so I have truly questioned my own decisions. I also question whether Victoria knows the end game for herself or if there even is one."

"I can't provide those answers for you," Roslyn said. "I know why I am in this business, but I can't speak for Vic."

Isabelle took a drag of the cigarette. "I met Mrs. Harper. She said she doesn't quite understand her daughter. Do you?"

"Do I understand Victoria?"

Isabelle nodded.

"Yes, I believe so," Roslyn said, but clammed up.

"Could you ..."

"You must speak to her." Roslyn shook her head. "My niece is a complicated woman. At times she is grounded and self-assured. At other times I fear she is fueled by lost causes."

"You mean Eugenie's causes?"

"No." Roslyn was reflective for a while and Isabelle waited.

"It's all so personal," Roslyn said quietly. "I feel it must come from her, because it matters so much to her. Do you understand?"

"Yes," Isabelle said.

How could she even broach this topic with Harper?

Tell me your deepest, darkest motivations?

After all, it was a side of Harper that Patricia claimed not to understand and that Roslyn hesitated to speak about.

Isabelle snuffed out her cigarette. She got up and strolled toward the stairs.

"Where are you going?" Clover asked.

Isabelle paused then looked back. "She up there?"

He nodded.

Isabelle went up and out to the floor above. Harper was sitting on the bench under the window. She was facing the opening in the floor, but the room was dark and from the angle of her head Isabelle thought she might be asleep. As she got closer she discovered Harper was wide awake and was looking at her.

"Are you keeping watch?" Isabelle asked softly, hesitantly joining her on the bench.

"I thought you were asleep," Harper said.

"Did you expect me to sleep all night?"

Isabelle was startled by her own tone. She looked toward the floor then away. Courage drained from her body. The bravado that had momentarily bewitched her in the basement was gone, replaced by weakness and a fluttering stomach. She turned back to Harper to find her watching her, her gaze fastened to Isabelle's face.

"Did you eat?" Harper asked. "And did you drink too?"

Isabelle leaned back against the wall. A flurry of emotions ran through her. She was not built for this. A chill aroused her flesh and she tried to soothe herself by rubbing her bare arms. She was wearing a light scarf over her T-shirt for the purpose of covering her head if she needed to when traveling around Turkey. She pulled it from her neck and wrapped it around her shoulders.

Harper was still watching her with smiling eyes. She was happy. Had she accomplished that much by making it here, to Kutahya? It was as if she had come home.

Isabelle closed her eyes and tried to mentally wipe the smile off Harper's face. It unnerved her. It made her feel jumbled and on edge. Like she could break through these walls and run out onto the street, all caution abandoned. Like she could scream and lose herself like she'd never done before. Never allowed herself to.

A feeling of déjà vu came over her. She had been roped in, beguiled in a way she didn't quite understand. Trapped within someone else's double life again. Trapped like the fountain water back at the guesthouse. It was so vibrant and always mesmerized Isabelle with its freedom, the way it danced despite the concrete enclosure. She thought of Helene and Benny then, living simple, purposeful lives.

"Come have a drink with me," Isabelle said, getting up. She found it hard to sit still. Hard to keep herself from shaking.

"I'm not in the mood for a drink." Harper shifted on the bench and leaned forward, resting her elbows on her knees.

"Drink with me anyway." Isabelle pulled her up.

Harper slipped her .45 magnum into her shoulder holster. She reached for Isabelle's face, but Isabelle did not trust herself in her arms. All of her emotions toward her had become heightened. She stepped back and gave a coy smile, and was thankful Harper did not reach for her again.

"I can drink with my friends." Her eyes darkened as she studied Isabelle.

"Am I not your friend?" Isabelle asked.

"You're much more than a friend." Harper turned to look out the window. "Why are you suddenly afraid of me?"

"I'm not."

"I'm quite happy," she said. "Happier than I've been in a long time, and here you are, terrified."

"I'm not terrified," Isabelle insisted. She wanted to reach out and touch Harper, to re-assure her, but the jumble of emotions came back. Her stomach quivered. She started toward the door. Her legs moved at their own volition.

"Where do you think you're going?"

Harper closed the distance between them. Before Isabelle could turn the lock Harper was in front of her, blocking the door.

"I need air," Isabelle said.

"I'll crack the window. You look pale."

"Because I need air," Isabelle said again, her weakness coming through in her voice.

Harper put her arms around her and led her back to the bench. "Sit down." She cracked the window to let in the night air. "Did they say something to upset you downstairs?"

Isabelle shook her head no. In fact, it was not until she came upstairs and saw Harper that she came apart at the seams like an overstuffed bag of rice. The outpouring of heaping grains of herself washed across the floor.

"It's not that," Isabelle said.

"Then what? What is it?"

"I . . ." Isabelle hesitated, looking up at her. "I think I made a mistake coming here."

It was more than that, but she couldn't put it into words. The depth of her feelings for Victoria Harper shocked and confused her.

Harper deflated. "I see."

"It's hard to explain," Isabelle went on hurriedly. It hurt her to see the disappointment in her face. "It's not you. I don't always understand my decisions."

Harper turned toward the window. "I believe you're feeling overwhelmed," she said in a somber tone. The sight of her leaning against the sill – in skinny jeans with a short-sleeved black shirt tucked in, her forearms flexed with tension and a leather-clad gun at her side – was captivating.

Isabelle cleared her throat and stood up quickly. Being around a contented Harper had rattled her. She had felt safer downstairs under George Clover's suspicious eye.

Harper suddenly turned and held onto Isabelle's upper arm, pulling her nearer. She came so close heat radiated from her skin, making Isabelle's flesh tingle. Harper's breath was warm against Isabelle's ear, teasing against her temple. A supple energy pulsated through her. Heavy-lidded, Isabelle's eyes slid closed.

"I wish I could put you on the first flight out," Harper rasped. Her lips grazed slow and tender across Isabelle's cheek. "But I can't."

A sweet ache rolled up from Isabelle's stomach, tempered only by the sliver of fear that sliced through her. Her pulse raced. She tried to shift out of Harper's grasp.

Someone was coming up through the floor. It was Clover.

Harper released her reluctantly and turned around.

"What is it?" she asked, impatient.

"Rasob is on the line," Clover said.

The mention of that name sent a jolt of shock through Isabelle's body.

"I'll be right there," Harper said.

She turned back to Isabelle.

"I'm serious. Ordinarily I wouldn't object to you going home, but I'm afraid the men who chased us from my apartment might now be able to identify you. They'll know you're with me."

Chapter Twenty-One

THE BASEMENT DWELLERS bustled with activity after Rasob's call. The pace of their work had picked up. Clover and Roslyn were on encrypted phones, while Stuttgart was glued to the laptop. Harper stood watch over everything in the little room, pacing back and forth and giving instructions from time to time. Sometimes they huddled together to analyze a large map spread across the wall while speaking earnestly to each other.

Isabelle had observed all this from the main room for the last two days. She caught snippets of conversation every time the door opened. Harper came out to check on her often, offering her meals and light conversation, but otherwise she was wrapped up in the business of what they were doing.

The business was plainly clear. They were in the process of transporting a product from somewhere in the region, and had hit a couple of roadblocks along the way. Isabelle had formed her own conclusions about this particular product. She had also determined the Kutahya crew was only a small part of the enterprise. Harper had a whole network of people working with her or for her.

Isabelle had kept herself occupied by jotting in a notebook on the couch. In the absence of outside distractions, she had completed an outline for her own memoir, and had begun to piece together the stories of her childhood: her youthful preoccupation with sex then later the demonization of her sexuality because of dogma within her school.

The pervasive absence and dysfunction at home offered no respite. She had been a refuge onto herself for so long. Even the freedom to date women as she got older came with its own shackles, its own hesitancy. She never stood on her own. She had taken steps before and ended up on unsteady ground, so she had retreated. Was she afraid to truly be whole?

That she found herself here now was surreal, but it helped if she viewed these people as characters in an ill-fated drug mafia movie. Harper was the polished but lethal crime boss. The mastermind. Still, it was difficult to frame her as a caricature. To Isabelle she was fully formed and vivacious in her intelligence and beauty. She was smart and resourceful, and surely she was resilient enough to get over Isabelle leaving.

Isabelle wanted nothing to do with this operation, but she wavered when it came to the decision to leave. Though now she knew Harper was not the woman she had hoped she was. That thought conflicted her. What had she hoped? That the story about the Maramaxe exposé had been real? She kept coming back to that one, the first story Harper ever told her. The story that had pulled Isabelle in. That and the fact that she found Harper mesmerizing that day in Chester. She could admit to it now.

Would it be wise to go back to Istanbul on her own? She turned on her phone and pulled up the Google search engine to see where the nearest airport was. Perhaps she would have been better off going with Bastian. She could call and beg him to meet her somewhere. That was if he had not already moved on, gone back to the States or elsewhere.

She resisted the urge to go outside to see Harper, who had thrown something across the room and stormed out earlier over what Isabelle had assumed was bad news. Isabelle had grown tired of hints and half-explanations. A straight answer about Harper's goals here was not forthcoming. The greater issue was that Isabelle could not see herself assimilating into Harper's world the way it was now.

She sighed and went to take her shower in the makeshift bathroom. The shower was tall, like a Porta-Potty made of wood, and had been built up against a narrow door that led from the house. A large iron pipe released a deluge of cold water that beat down on her face and body. Isabelle took her time tonight, indulging in morbid fascination about the lives of Harper and her crew. Were they risking their freedom merely for fast cash? Power?

I could write about this, she thought as the water massaged her body. Wasn't that the pretext under which Harper had befriended her? Well now she could write about them on her own terms. She didn't need Harper's approval to chronicle what they were doing.

Once she had made the decision to memorialize the events of her life in recent weeks, Isabelle got out of the shower and dressed. Harper had given her a couple of shirts and a pair of jeans. Besides her bag with her passport, wallet, and some basic essentials, she had only brought two extra sets of clothing. The rest of her belongings were still at the hotel in Besiktas.

When she came back out, the main room was empty. The others still clung together in the equipment room over a bottle of bourbon, talking in low voices. Harper still had not returned.

Isabelle went outside to find her sitting on a large graffitied rock next to the house. The night was warm and pockets of conversation drifted across from the city. They were nestled far enough away from the sprawling clump of urban life, where pale houses with red roofs extended across the valley. Isabelle had not encountered anyone in Kutahya since she had been there, and she felt a familiar sense of isolation.

She went over to Harper. "Everything all right?"

"Not really," she said, though she was calm now. "There's no loyalty left in this world."

"I'm sorry you're having problems," Isabelle said, feeling impatient.

"And I'm sorry I've been so busy." Harper looked up at her. "There's a lot going on."

"I understand."

"Do you?"

Isabelle shoved her hands into her pockets.

To the right of them, remnants of the Kutahya Castle were visible in the darkening evening. Isabelle could make out its three tiers, scores of towers, and layers of rubble and brick and stone. It was a rampart that the city looked upon.

"I know this is heavy stuff to handle," Harper said. "But you're no stranger to this life, are you?"

"What does that mean?"

"You told me your step dad got into all sorts of antics."

"Is that what you call it? Antics?"

"I'm only joking with you." Harper's voice was shaky. "You've become so serious all of a sudden."

Isabelle sighed. "I'm not sure our goals are aligned."

"What are your goals?"

"Not this."

"I don't think you can say we're not aligned."

"I know this is not what I want."

"This is where you belong."

She said it with such conviction it startled Isabelle.

"You can't be serious." Isabelle frowned. "Is that what you think of me?"

"That you belong with me?"

"That's not what you said."

"It's what I meant." When she saw Isabelle's furrowed brow she hurried on. "Anyway, soon we'll be heading to a place called Konya."

"What's in Konya?" Isabelle was confused and despite herself, intrigued by Harper.

"A lot. We have associates there we've done business with for decades. Descendants of people who worked with my great-grandmother. Things have changed, unfortunately. They made other alliances, essentially giving our organization the shaft. It's not a good way to do business, not when it comes to Serturn."

"What did they do?" The word Serturn set off alarm bells in Isabelle's head and caused her heart to race. She had correctly guessed the name of the group.

"They accepted a better offer. They're working with our competition."

"They're working with the people who tried to kill you. The same people you did the exposé on all those years ago."

Harper nodded. She was deliberately not meeting Isabelle's eyes.

"How do you plan to handle it?"

"First, we'll try the diplomatic route." She brushed at something on her jeans. "Then who knows. I'll do what I have to do."

"Victoria, I didn't get beyond this sort of life with my folks just to wrap myself up in the same business with you." Isabelle tossed back the wild wisps of hair that danced across her face and folded her arms.

"I don't blame you for being worried, Isabelle. It's brought me such comfort having you here. I care very much . . ." Harper looked down at her hands. "I wish I could explain myself to you."

"Try."

"There are things I don't speak of and I wouldn't know where to begin."

Isabelle waited, but Harper was silent for a long time. She seemed to be searching for the right words, but in the end her expression only darkened.

"I'll tell you everything if you agree to be mine."

"It doesn't work like that." Isabelle stared at the castle, trying not to betray how off-kilter she felt. This woman was much too used to getting her way.

"How does it work?"

"I'm not something you can take."

"What I do know is you came all this way to be with me. That means something, even if you don't realize it yet."

"I wouldn't have come if I had known . . . all this." Isabelle spoke honestly. "I would have gone with Bastian."

"That would have been a huge mistake." Harper looked up, raising her voice. "Your brother is not a hero."

"Are you?" Isabelle challenged.

"I'm certainly not a villain."

"That's not for you to determine," Isabelle said, letting her anger and frustration come through.

Harper looked at her with unmitigated shock.

"I have strong feelings for you," she said. "I want you to know that. I didn't realize it until it was too late."

"Too late?"

"Yes – after you were already here. When it became too dangerous for you to leave."

"I can't stay." Isabelle ran a nervous hand through her hair. She was flustered by Harper's possessiveness. She felt a visceral mixture of fear and desire. Her feelings perplexed her, and though she no longer wanted to physically flee, she was having a hard time getting a handle on her swelling emotions.

She concluded that she had strong feelings for Harper too. It was a stark and debilitating realization she had fought to avoid.

"This is your life," Isabelle said weakly. "Not mine."

"If you give me some time I can sort this out."

Isabelle shook her head and backed away. She didn't want to risk being persuaded.

Harper stood abruptly and held on to her. "Come with me."

She led Isabelle back to the front room of the house and pushed the red drapes aside to reveal a door.

Isabelle hesitated, shocked to see there was a room there.

"Come in here." Harper's voice was firm and decisive. It left no room for doubt or hesitation.

The room was bare and much of the space was filled by a full bed. Next to a desk lamp on the floor was a bottle of red wine and two plastic cups. A square of moonlight came into the room through a small window with metal bars on the outside.

"I cleaned it myself," Harper said. "The sheets are fresh."

Isabelle turned away from the bed. A clear vase on a single shelf against the wall held flowers with vibrant orange petals that seemed to glow, with a deep red at their center, the color of ripe red apples.

Had Harper planned for this? For tonight?

She released her shoulder holster and let it fall to the floor. Then she placed a hand on Isabelle's back, in between her shoulder blades.

"Yes," she said softly.

"Yes to what?" Isabelle twisted her shoulders toward her.

The hand slid up and closed around the back of Isabelle's neck. "To whatever it is you're thinking."

With her other hand, Harper pulled Isabelle's body around to face her completely. When she deftly undid a button on Isabelle's shirt, her hand shot up instinctively to stop her. Harper's stare pierced into her – curious, excited, and challenging. Her eyes were like the midnight sky, endlessly dark and twinkling.

Isabelle's knees grew soft as she was pulled closer. She was wrapped up in Harper's arms. Their bodies fused and Harper's leg slid between her thighs. Isabelle's last vestige of restraint fell away and she plunged fitfully to meet the impulse.

Harper's arms tightened around her still. Isabelle's lips were consumed, and she lost all sense of physical place and time. Of where she ended and Harper began. Her body craved more of this magnetism, of the stimuli of hands against her skin. Hands that opened her shirt roughly and pulled down her bra straps. Isabelle was overcome, with little time to react and less time to breathe before Harper's mouth was on her skin. Isabelle's head fell back, at once light and limp. Nails raked across her back, around her sides and down her stomach. A moan stirred from within her. Heat pooled low in her pelvis and her legs wilted. She was sure she was falling, but Harper held onto to her, and led her to the waiting bed.

Isabelle had never experienced anything like she did with Harper. Once the questions in her head had been nullified by passion, her body took over. Frenzied lovemaking gave way to warmth, and a fusing of heart and consciousness all throughout the night.

Then they longed for an end to each day so they could become submerged in each other's arms again. They met in the little room behind the red drapes the following night, and the night after that. Isabelle always resisted at first, finding an odd delight in the tease. Her excitement teemed every time Harper lost herself and pulled her clothes off coarsely or pinned her arms to the bed. Harper's strength and intensity made her feel proud and prurient all at once.

She fell deeper into Harper every time they made love, and deeper into a clamoring twist of fears and desires. She had a notion of dreams she had not fully acknowledged until now; an overwhelming need for so much more than she had envisioned for herself.

The team packed for Konya, moving all their gear out deep into the night. Isabelle stayed out of the way, involuntarily stealing glances at Harper at every chance. She leaned against the desk in the main room as she watched them, preoccupied with her own thoughts, and wearing a short forest green dress Harper had nearly ripped off her the night before.

Passion and fear crossed Harper's face even as she busied herself with gathering items, and this version of her was unrecognizable. Harper was open, vulnerable, distracted. She had tried unsuccessfully to close one of the cases they had overstuffed, and then Clover had taken over the task of tying their equipment grips to the dolly after Harper struggled to secure them properly. Red-faced, sweaty and agitated, Harper had meandered up to the first floor.

Isabelle released the breath she had been holding when Harper had not come over to her. She secured her now unbridled mop of hair into a loose bun atop her head and wiped her face and neck with a towel. She poured herself a shot of bourbon.

Roslyn was eyeing her suspiciously, but Isabelle was faced with larger dilemmas beyond the embarrassing fact that the people around them could tell they had done the deed.

When they were together one night, Harper had woken up in the darkest hour crying out for "Edith." Isabelle had not found enough courage to ask her about her cousin, and she wondered now if she should ask Roslyn.

She forced the thought from her mind and remained rooted to the spot until she felt compelled to go into the little room and unload the refrigerator. Work was a welcome distraction, and as she packed nonperishable goods in a box, she wondered if it was wise to go to Konya to meet with people who had betrayed them. Discussions could take a turn for the worse. They could be ambushed. The stakes were high with what she presumed to be hundreds of millions of dollars involved.

How big was this organization, and more importantly, how had Harper kept her life in the States so separate? The thought of the various levels of secrecy involved made Isabelle shiver, and as they set out on the long stretch of highway in the early morning, her nerves rose to the surface. She was fraught with disillusion-ment and worry.

She'd seen this vault of secrecy in Haughton throughout the years. In his vibrant heyday, and lately, even as his voracity dulled, he had a tremendous commitment to protecting the game and enhancing his illicit business. Such were the workings of deceitful minds. All craft, intellect, and guile had been point-ed to success on a criminal level, at shielding these affairs from discovery by the people closest to them.

Isabelle imagined Bastian living a life of secrecy as well, all those years on his own. He did it so well no one knew where he had gone. And what of love and family in his life? Did she have a sister-in-law out there in the great void? Little nieces and nephews she'd never met?

What if Harper had additional lives? A separate world be-yond all this. Beyond New York City and Chester and Newport. Beyond Istanbul. Another woman somewhere in Reykjavík and little Harpers running around, eagerly awaiting her return. After all, her cousins had painted her as a seductress. There was this Stuttgart woman for starters, who Harper had never quite ex-plained.

Harper's energy beside her in the Audi – the crew ahead in a mini-van – was now confident, self-assured, loving. She had managed to regain her composure.

Isabelle considered all the reasons she should leave, and all the reasons she should stay. She had become entangled with a woman she could never really have, not in the way she wanted. A home. A family. Harper's true love was this grandiose mission to become a drug kingpin. To make a name for herself the way Eu-genie had. To be a self-governing Conquistador.

"Isabelle," Harper said as they drove on, as if she had read Isabelle's mind. "I know you still have questions, but I feel I must protect you."

Isabelle laced her fingers together and twisted them painfully.

"I want so much for us," Harper continued, "but I worry I'm running out of time with you. I worry about your happiness."

"You make me happy," Isabelle said. "When we're alone."

Harper exhaled, a sort of sound between a sigh and a gasp.

"Gottfrieds," she said out of nowhere. "That's their name . . . the men who betrayed my great-grandmother and started up their own side business. They gained a significant amount of leverage. We never anticipated they would become so strong. They used Eugenie's reputation to build a respected and fearsome brand. Everything they've amassed came on the back of Serturn. When Aunt Roslyn and I finally took what was rightfully ours, we were really up against it. They had the gall to fight us over territory. To hunt us down because we take action against them."

She reached over and held Isabelle's hand.

"They're twins. Old men now, but they have their children and their allies."

"At one point you told me you wanted a fresh start," Isabelle said. "Do you remember?"

Harper thought for a moment.

"I do remember," she said, "but that seems so long ago. So much has changed."

"I have to ask you something," Isabelle said quietly, gearing herself up.

"Ask it."

"One night you had a bad dream."

"I did?"

"Yes, and you said the name Edith." Isabelle looked at her. "Who is that?"

Harper's face froze. She shifted in her seat and gripped the steering wheel.

"That's a story for another time." She kept her eyes averted.

They stopped in Afyonkarahisar so the team could reconvene and pick up snacks and coffee for the drive. Harper offered to buy Isabelle breakfast, but Isabelle wanted to go off and stretch her legs alone. Harper looked wounded. She held on to Isabelle's hand as they stood next to the car, entwining their fingers and swinging their arms together.

"Had enough of me already?" She looked bashful, though her eyes were big and open, and had gone hazel in the sunshine.

Isabelle smiled. Harper had a lovely face, but it was one she was not accustomed to seeing with a mopey, love-struck expression.

"No," Isabelle said. "I've been here a week and I've barely seen anything of this country."

"Okay." A milky sadness fell across Harper's face. "I understand," she said. She had a passing look of suspicion and intrigue, and then lust. Finally, she softened, and the lightness of love displayed upon her face. She laced her fingers around the back of Isabelle's neck and pulled her in to kiss both cheeks.

Then she nodded and turned away.

Isabelle watched her saunter toward the market with her head held straight, her shoulders stiff. She seemed to be straining against some emotion within her. She was wearing a worn, sleeveless leather motorcycle jacket, with red bands by the upper arms. Her black skinny jeans were tucked into low cowboy boots, which were covered in a thick film of dust.

Isabelle's throat stung. She turned and took off in the direction of Victory Square with a determined strut, but the bleakness of the morning pervaded her spirit. The atmosphere was overcast and dull.

She slowed down and took in the pockets of tourists who were milling around. A group of kids were taking pictures of an enormous rock situated in the middle of the city in the distance. *Afyon Kalesi* or Afyon Castle in English, sat atop a jarring fortress of rock. The range of crags rose skyward and dwarfed the town beneath it. Remnants of a defensive wall wrapped around the top of the rock, enclosing what remained of the castle. In the foreground in the square, a monument of a Turkish soldier stood over the writhing body of an invader. The image construed violence and rage and territorial might.

Conquest and survival – such was the narrative for many generations of people across the globe. Cities built fortresses to shield themselves from their enemies and to have the advantage when attacked.

Beyond her reserved nature at times, Isabelle had never truly guarded herself and she had never had anyone to do it for her. Despite Bastian claiming to be her protector when challenged by Harper that day in front of the Golden Horn, he'd never had time to protect. He had lost himself so young.

Isabelle had to protect herself now. Flights went from Konya Airport into London, Copenhagen, Amsterdam and Düsseldorf. She would fly into London and spend a night or two, just to clear her head before heading home. Harper had insinuated before that Isabelle would be in danger if she left, but she didn't care. She had lived under the threat of danger before, and now she had made up her mind.

Konya would be her last stop on the Serturn train.

Across the street a crowd had gathered, and Isabelle walked toward them.

She passed a street artist who was fervently working on a portrait of a young woman, his head bent low.

The crowd surrounded a group of Whirling Dervishes near the grounds of the Zafer Muzesi, a museum dedicated to Turkish victory in the war of independence at Dumlupinar.

Isabelle stood still for several minutes, entranced by the rhythmic music of the pipes and drums, and by the chants. The Dervishes released their cloaks, symbolizing rebirth into truth. As they twirled, they became lost in meditation and devotion. Their arms were open and extended, and they became a white blur. Everyone else faded away. Their white skirts flowed and expanded; lifted as if by a lightness of being. Lifted by the cleansing of the ego, which brought them closer to God and love.

Isabelle's inner terrors rose to the surface.

She was gullible and foolish. She turned a blind eye to the things she didn't want to see. She forced herself to take a few steps back, and when she broke the trance her emotions overcame her. Tears flooded her eyes. She left the spectacle and turned back.

She would not think about love now. Love was a terrifying jumble of yearning and heartache. She would focus on making her way out. Away from this place of old and modern, of Asia and Europe and everything in between. Away from these storied oceans and legendary dynasties. Away from everything that would seek to remind her of its foundation in history, and strength, and a conquering nature. She would not allow herself to be conquered anymore. She would lay her own foundation.

As she made her way past the portrait artist again he stood and craned his neck. He was staring off in the direction of the Whirling Dervishes and the crowd around them. His features were alarming, and she thought her reaction to this stranger was odd until she looked closer. He wasn't a complete stranger. She recognized the scrawny frame and bulging eyes. The long charcoal-stained fingers. The baseball cap pulled low on his forehead.

It was Decebal. Unmistakably so. Isabelle stood still. Her brain tried to reconcile what she knew with what she was seeing. Decebal was Bastian's acquaintance who knew Harper and had seen her in an earlier time in her life when she hung around his friend Rasob, buying morphine. Her heart rate catapulted. It made no sense for him to be here now.

Decebal continued to scan the crowd in the distance, looking for someone. Isabelle's stomach fell as he pivoted to his right, for at the moment his eyes met hers she realized the someone he was looking for was her.

He flinched. His pale skin grew paler. For an instant it looked like he might run. Then his countenance changed. He forced his mouth to turn up at the corners. He stepped forward.

"Isabelle, correct?"

She didn't respond. Her throat was dry. A sense of real danger came over her.

"Do you remember me? I'm Decebal. Your brother friend."

She stared at him. When he moved closer Isabelle stepped back. She considered her options. Screaming was the first thing that came to mind, but that wouldn't do.

"What is this?" She blurted.

He knitted his brows and pointed toward his sketch pad. "I am what they call sketch artist."

"How are you here?"

He looked confused. "I don't understand the question."

"Why are you here?"

"I'm working. This is what I do."

It had to be at least five hours by car from his apartment in Istanbul to Afyonkarahisar. It would not be plausible for him to travel back and forth every day, but it wasn't entirely impossible for this to be his job.

"You traveled from Istanbul to Afyon to sketch?"

Decebal shrugged and strolled back to his stool. He arranged the blank canvases and sketch pads in his bag, but he was watching her.

She walked over and stood in front of him. "I'm no fool."

Decebal looked up at her. A thoughtful expression lingered across his face. He sighed and turned to watch the Whirling Dervishes, his gaze fixated in that direction for a long time.

"I am not fool either," he said, keeping his eyes averted and busying himself with nothing.

"I am also innocent."

Decebal laughed. "Nobody is innocent," he said, but her words settled into him. He thought for a moment. "From the first time I saw you, you striked me as a good woman." He wanted to go on, but his demeanor shifted again. "I come here few times every week by car, from Istanbul. I am what they call sketch artist. Look at my work. Don't you want a pic—"

"Tell me the truth."

"I think you should continue about your business," he said, though it was without conviction. "I think you should take yourself and . . . your life. I think you should . . ." He waved his arm in search of a word that escaped him in the end.

"You were honest with me once," Isabelle said. "That day in your apartment you answered my questions about my friend like you were eager to tell."

"I was in honest mood."

"And now?"

He laughed and it was empty.

"Now I am businessman doing my job."

"My brother sent you here, didn't he?"

She pulled out her wallet and his eyes expanded.

"Now I am the one to ask you 'what is this?'"

"You know what it is." Isabelle pulled out fifty-five TL.

"At least try to respect me." He chuckled. "Offer me US dollars."

She pulled out a crisp one hundred dollar bill. He stood and pretended to consider. Then he bared his teeth into a grin and reached for Isabelle's arm.

"Come," he said. "There is a seat."

He pointed to a bench near the steps leading up to the statue. Isabelle avoided his touch but walked with him. They both sat down. Her heart was thumping so loud she had to put a hand to her chest to quiet it.

"You are brave to leave your friends," Decebal said. "How can a woman like you walk alone? Huh? How do I say your skin is like sweet caramel. So smooth like this . . . eyes like honey and the earth. Like a fierce doll. Do you know what I mean? I find you more appealing than your brother."

"My friends?"

He smiled and stuck his hand out. Isabelle gave him the one hundred dollar bill. He stuck his hand out again. She gave him fifty more.

"My dear little Bastian," he said. "I don't think you take me seriously."

"I don't have a lot."

"Information is value, no?"

"That's it." She gave him another one hundred US.

Decebal looked at the ground. He rubbed the tips of his fingers together, where he was accustomed to holding a piece of charcoal. His hands looked battered.

"I am paid, yes." He looked in Isabelle's direction but did not quite meet her eyes. "I am paid to come here."

"To watch me?"

"Bastian told me to come after you."

"Why?"

"He said the woman was a danger to you."

"What woman?"

"You know the woman. The one you ask about. Jane Reid. Your brother told me she was Harper-something. He told me, 'Don't let my sister out of your sight.'"

"Why is she a danger to me?"

"I don't know. This is what he tells me: 'Stay with them as long as you can.'"

"Did you follow us to Kutahya too?"

Decebal nodded. "All the time I watch you. To make sure—"

"I am a grown woman." Isabelle balled up her fists on her lap. "I don't need this. Who the hell does Bastian think he is?"

Decebal shrugged.

"I want you to leave." She stood. "Go back to Istanbul. Tell my brother I found you and I am very upset. He is not to do this again. Do you understand?"

He remained seated, looking at her expectantly.

"Don't you want me to tell more?" He asked cheekily. He stuck his hand out.

"What?"

"I have more." He gestured again.

Isabelle sat down and opened her wallet. Her hands were shaking. When she handed him another hundred dollars he smiled broadly.

This time he looked her straight in the eyes.

"He knew your woman before you knew her."

Chapter Twenty-Two

THE TEXT FROM HARPER was hopeful and succinct:

Meeting in Konya was delayed.
Booking hotel in Afyon for the night.
Getting drinks with the team.
I'll text the address. Come join us.

Be there soon, Isabelle had responded after she received the address for the restaurant. She hadn't moved. She had been staring at nothing for an hour, ever since Decebal had bowed his head hesitantly and left her. He had seemed sad, as if he wondered if he had done the right thing by telling her the truth.

The truth – it was as if someone had picked up the Afyon Kalesi, rock and all, and slammed it against Isabelle's chest. Her breathing had finally returned to normal, but her head was still a whirl of emotions. Her limbs locked up, keeping her rooted to the bench.

She forced herself to piece together the story, details relayed to her in Decebal's excited, rambling broken English:

"Your woman pissed off dangerous people. A notorious drug guy from Bucharest. Do you know this name Gottfried? She mess with them, but I don't know what she did. It was a long time ago. They tried to find her for so long but she disappear. Poof. So finally they send someone. Do you want to know who that someone is? You won't believe, but I will tell you. I will tell the truth to you, Isabelle, because my heart tells me you are good. They send . . . it is very difficult, I'm sorry . . . but they send your brother. They send Bastian. To kill her. Bring her back. I don't know the full story. This is what I know. Your brother told me he made some mistake, you know. He didn't do the job. Something happened to him but he hesitate. And then somehow she found out about him. Maybe her people saw him. He didn't tell me how she found him. Maybe he is no longer good for this kind of work, you know? He only realize she discover him because he saw her with a woman he knew because of you. A woman you were friendly with. A New York woman. Blonde. When your brother saw her with that woman, the next thing he saw was that Harper-something with you. He was so frightened. He placed you in danger. He knew she was close to you to keep him away. To keep herself safe. Do you understand? That's the reason Bastian send me to follow you. He said, 'She has a hook in my sister and I can't go. You must go and watch her. Then tell me all their moves.' Isabelle, I'm telling you this because you are not like them. Bastian broke my face the first time I met him. In the years we become friends. He is a tough man, but he is not the same anymore. Maybe this life caught him, caught up to him . . . if you want me to leave you alone, I will. I know this is terrible. If you want me to leave, I will go back to Istanbul. I will tell Bastian you got away from me. I'm so sorry. What will you do, Isabelle? You are not like them, remember this. I am sorry. I will go. Goodbye, Isabelle."

The short of it: Harper tried to damage the Gottfrieds with the exposé. When it didn't work she fled to the States and hid. They hired Bastian to kill or capture her. He failed – call it a change of heart, a personal crisis, or incompetence. He took too long, and Harper caught on. She befriended Caye to get close to Isabelle. To use as leverage.

To use as leverage so Bastian couldn't harm her.

Isabelle waited for the tears to come. They didn't. She had already cried once today. All the emotions stirred up by the Whirling Dervishes had settled.

"*You are not like them*," Decebal had said. He was a near-stranger but he believed he knew her. The same way Harper believed she knew Isabelle that day they met in Chester.

The clouds became even drearier. A shadow fell across the city. Most of the other tourists had wandered off. A few stragglers sat on the steps, with the darkened images of the soldier and the rock behind them like a gargantuan horror.

Isabelle called Caye. She answered in a bright and cheery voice. Isabelle tried to calculate what time it was in New York.

"Isabelle," Caye said. "My favorite."

"I'm surprised you sound so happy to hear from me." Isabelle smiled sadly.

"I'm always happy to hear from you, although you broke my heart and forgot all about me."

"I didn't forget about you. I've been busy."

"With what?"

"I called because I wanted to ask you something."

"Okay."

"How did you and Victoria meet?"

"Me and Victoria?" Caye sounded hesitant.

"Yes."

"Isabelle, I told you that was just me being dumb. I—"

"I'm not upset with you, Caye," Isabelle said to reassure her. "I'm just curious."

"Okay. Well, let's see. I guess it was just one of those things. I had gone to see a show off-Broadway with some associates. We were just hanging out, having cocktails after the show. She came up to me—"

"She came up to you?"

"Yes. She came over and introduced herself. Offered me a drink and we chatted for awhile."

"I see," Isabelle said.

"Why does any of this matter? Where are you? You sound .. . different."

"I'm just thinking about things. That's all."

"If it's any consolation, what you and I had was better. I loved you. I still do. My relationship with her was odd at times and per- plexing at times."

"What do you mean?"

"I mean, she was beautiful, and she had this great vibe to her, but there was so much more going on, you know?"

"Like what?" Isabelle asked.

"It's hard to get into this stuff over the phone," Caye said. "Why don't you meet me somewhere? Come to the city tonight. I'd love to see you."

"I can't," Isabelle said. "Maybe another time."

Caye was silent. Should she tell her the truth? How would Caye feel knowing Isabelle was in Turkey with Harper? It would break her heart.

"We'll get together soon, Caye. Why don't you tell me what you can?"

"She had connections, Isabelle. She had access to . . . stuff. She was running a whole freaking operation. That night she came up to me, I'm thinking this chick could be a model. She had this magnetic glow to her. The more I got to know her the more it became obvious . . . it was like . . . I don't know. I can't explain."

"What became obvious?"

"I guess I didn't know what she wanted with me," Caye said. "She was distant. At times she was plain cold."

"Did you sleep with her? No, don't answer that. I'm sorry."

Caye was silent again.

"Can I ask you another question?" Isabelle asked.

"Sure."

"That day I went with you to your father's office, what were you guys talking about? He was upset with you after the paper published pictures of you on your night out with Gergina Piers."

"My father is a businessman, first and foremost. He saw an opportunity once I started dating Victoria. He thought I could help him work out an arrangement with her."

"What kind of arrangement?"

"Um. Well, when I told my dad what I'd come to discover he thought it was great. He wanted to get in there and make some money. I tried to schmooze with her on his behalf, but I think it backfired. She started acting jumpy around me. She had like, ze-ro tolerance for ulterior motives. She seemed paranoid, frankly. I still don't think she understood what I was trying to do."

It was Isabelle's turn to be quiet. Everything suddenly made sense. Talking to Caye validated Decebal's story. She also under-stood why Caye and Harper were so suspicious around each oth-er. They both had ulterior motives.

"I'm glad to hear your voice," Caye said. "I know I messed up. Not one day goes by that I don't think of you. My time with Victoria went on longer than I wanted to. I always meant to come back to you. It was just a fling."

"Caye, there's something I must tell you." Isabelle had an inkling the timing might be all wrong, but she needed to get this off her chest. "I've spent time with Victoria. We're working on a project together."

"Huh? What kind of project?"

"It's about her life story. Sort of."

"I don't understand."

"She asked me to help her chronicle her stories."

"And you agreed to do it?" Caye was getting worked up. "When was this?"

"Not long ago."

"You're kidding me . . ."

"She asked me to document—"

"Where are you?"

"Turkey."

"You're there with her?"

Isabelle didn't respond.

"How can you trust her after what I've just told you?" Caye sounded bitter. "But then you already knew, didn't you? You know what she's all about and you're still there with her. Why would you do this?"

"It's complicated."

"Come back to New York," Caye said. "I'll treat you better if you give me another chance."

She could not go back to Caye after her betrayal, and after all that had happened since. Something had shifted within Isabelle's psyche. Being with Harper had changed her.

"Don't you want children?"

"What?" Isabelle was startled. The question was unexpected, and it struck at the core of her.

"We could have lovely children, Isabelle. I want to come and see you to make sure you're alright. Because honestly, it doesn't sound like you are. I think you're in way over your head. It's not what you thought, is it?"

"I'll be home soon, Caye," Isabelle said. "I'm just wrapping things up here."

"Are you coming back to me?"

"I can't discuss this right now."

"I see." Caye exhaled sharply. "I can give you what you need. She can't."

"Goodbye, Caye."

"Good . . . bye. Goodbye, Isabelle."

Somehow, Isabelle had managed to convince herself not to run away. The walk back to the market helped to calm her, though she was still shaken and disconnected from her own body. A cruel trap had been set for her, and she had watched herself walk into it head first. Heart first.

She had changed into jeans and a T-shirt before they left Kutahya, and she had her light jacket tied around her waist. She pulled the jacket on even though it was quite warm, and focused her attention on simply putting one foot in front of the other.

Mavi Restaurant was small and neatly tucked in between a fabric store and a shop that sold a hodge-podge of items. Harper and the rest of the team were at a table in the back playing a card game and chatting over bottles of Efes Pilsen.

Isabelle started toward them but lost her courage and made a beeline for the bar, which was not much of a bar at all, and was more like a small counter enclosing three or four bottles of liquor on a shelf and a refrigerator. The barkeep had been clearing dishes from an empty table, and seemed surprised to see someone sitting on the stool. His eyebrows arched suspiciously when Isabelle ordered a shot of vodka. He smiled and glanced at his watch.

As he poured her shot, Harper rose from the table behind her. The sound of her boots on the floor transmitted a long, steady strut. Isabelle stiffened and down her drink.

Harper came up next to Isabelle and leaned on the counter.

"So what's your name, gorgeous?"

It took Isabelle a moment to register that Harper was flirting, and that she was tipsy.

"I bet it's a sexy one. Like Belle or Isabella. Maybe even Isabelle."

Isabelle signaled for another shot. The barkeep wiped his face with a cloth and reached for her glass. This time he filled it apprehensively.

"I missed you," Harper whispered. "I don't think I've felt like this before. I missed you badly. And we were only apart for a short while."

Isabelle scoffed and downed her shot. She found it difficult to hold eye contact with Harper.

"What were you doing?" Harper asked, looking puzzled.

"I went to see the sights," Isabelle said in a biting tone. "The enormous rock. The grotesque soldier."

"I don't think I would put it quite like that. Those monuments celebrate a period when—"

"How did you find me?"

Synapses had misfired in Isabelle's brain. The highway of nerves that connected her well-controlled thoughts buckled.

"What?"

"How did you know I was Bastian's sister?"

"I don't quite understand what—"

"You knew who I was before you came to my guesthouse for the Grand Opening party."

Harper paled and was stunned into silence. Her eyes glistened. She swallowed.

"How did you find out?"

"I asked you first."

Harper pushed herself away from the counter slowly, holding on to the edge like she thought she might collapse. She bent over and took several deep breaths. When she met Isabelle's eyes again, the steeliness had returned to her face but her eyes still betrayed her. She walked over to the table and picked up her bag.

"Come with me," she said, as she came back and took Isabelle's hand. She led her out of the restaurant.

They walked on in a bloated silence. Harper's body jerked with each step. Isabelle was calm on the surface, but inside she was shaking too. They got into the Audi and drove along the placid streets, passing pockets of people going about their day, laid back and unperturbed.

Isabelle longed for that to be her life. A sense of dread filled her, but not out of fear for her well-being. It was sadness over the dissolution of something that was hard to name.

At the thermal hotel, Harper collected the keys and they went to the room. The décor was a mixture of old and modern, and a succinct expression of the culture of the region. Images of the rock and its crags, of the soldier and its vanquished invader had followed Isabelle here.

Harper closed the door behind them and threw her bag onto the bed. Then she covered her face with both hands. Isabelle thought she might be crying, but when she removed her hands there were no tears. Her face was red and blotchy, and pained.

"Sud saw your brother watching me one day and told me. We carried on as usual, gathering Intel on who he was. We tracked him in return and he led us to your guesthouse. Sud told me you were Bastian's sister. He showed me pictures of you. I thought you were beautiful."

"Please don't—"

"I did. Right from the beginning, but I was helpless. I needed your brother to back off, but I couldn't approach you directly. I don't know why. I was too afraid. Then I saw you with Caye Wauburg and that was an easier in . . . I got to know her."

"You told me you and Caye were introduced by someone else."

"I lied. I can't explain why."

"Because that's what you do."

"Isabelle . . ."

"You lied about Maramaxe . . . about your work. You lied about Caye. Why did you do that? An unnecessary lie."

"I got all twisted up. Amidst all the fucked-up shit that was going on, something about you struck me. You were like that fresh evergreen vine weaving your way into my being. Piercing my defenses. And I was with Caye. And your brother wanted to kill me. And I was deceiving you. I was fucked up."

"You used me as leverage to protect yourself from my brother."

"That was the idea. But it was never about that."

"That was clearly what it was about." Isabelle crossed her arms. "You befriended me under false pretenses. You lured me into your life."

"You came willingly." Harper looked wounded. She stared at Isabelle. "I never lured you. I never captured you. You came here to be with me."

"And it was the biggest mistake I've made in my life." Isabelle wasn't sure how true that was, but she wanted to hurt Harper. To make her feel that momentous wave of disappointment and pain she felt. "I wish I had never come here. I wish I had never met—"

Harper sprang forward and pinned Isabelle against the door. She tugged on the hair at the back of Isabelle's head and covered her mouth with her own. Isabelle gave in, letting the storm of emotions consume her. The kiss was ravenous and frayed, and they both unraveled in the midst of it.

When their lips finally parted, Isabelle tried to push her back. "You—"

But Harper pressed in closer. Isabelle kept her arms in a bracing posture, a futile attempt to keep her at bay. They were at an impasse, and neither one moved.

"I know you want me," Harper said, after a while. "You don't want any of this, but I know *you want me*." Her hands slid under Isabelle's T-shirt. She unhooked Isabelle's bra and covered her breasts with her hands.

"Me," she whispered.

Isabelle let her head sink against Harper's chest. Her resistance withered away like the leaves of an over-saturated plant. Love crept up inside her and overflowed from her heart.

❖

Later that night, Isabelle lay awake in the hotel room with Harper by her side. They had made love throughout the day, engulfed in their anger and hurt, both strangled by a palpable sense of loss.

"I am sorry I behaved the way I did," Harper said.

Isabelle didn't ask what she was apologizing for. So much had happened.

"I'm sorry for the way we came together," Harper continued. "What I wouldn't give to be able to go back and change things. I wish I had just talked to you. I should have been honest from the beginning. I should have given you the choice."

"I had a choice." Isabelle shrugged. "I made it when I boarded the plane to Istanbul."

Harper kissed her hand. "Can you forgive me?"

"I need time." Isabelle spoke honestly.

Harper nodded. Tears brimmed in her eyes.

For Isabelle, love had always trapped her. Love for her mother even when Marcia betrayed her. Love for the notion of family and sticking around, unlike her brother. What good had they done her? How could she stick around for Harper? Harper's family was a lonely band of schemers and killers and outlaws.

"We have a factory in Konya," Harper said suddenly. "We manufacture tiles."

"Tiles?"

"It's how we get our product out. We get it to a major distributor in the UK. That's the extent of our part in the supply chain."

"Why are you telling me this?"

"Don't you want to know?"

"I suppose so." Isabelle no longer needed it to be said. She had known enough for a while now. "Why did you say Wauburg was connected to the Maramaxe issue?"

"I was confused." Harper rubbed her face. "Caye confused me a great deal."

When Harper fell asleep, Isabelle rose quietly and slipped her clothes on. She passed a hand over her hair in the cool room, and then went out into the hallway. The hotel was small and tranquil, and she followed the signs to the spa. A family was bathing quietly in the mineral water, and Isabelle longed to get in.

Instead she went to the window and took in the bright sparks of city lights, and closer up the colorful lighting of the hotel grounds.

The image of the golden candelabra rose from the recess of her mind. Now she knew Harper and Bastian were both the suffocating vine and the faded finery all at once. Where did she fit into their world?

She pulled out her phone and dialed Bastian's number. He didn't sound like himself when he picked up.

"I found Decebal," Isabelle said as a form of greeting.

"I know." He was quiet.

"What else do you know?"

"I always seem to mess things up when it comes to you," Bastian said. "Ever since we were young."

"You tried to warn me."

"It wasn't enough."

"I needed the truth."

"That's not easy. The kind of life we choose . . ."

"You and Victoria are the same." Isabelle closed her eyes. "If you both stop moving you will have to think. And you don't want to think."

"I'm sorry, Isabelle."

"Were you going to kill her?"

"I don't know," Bastian said. "I don't know anything anymore."

"To think I held out a sliver of hope that maybe you came back for me." Isabelle opened her eyes. "To make things right in some small way. That's all I wanted."

Bastian drew a sharp breath. "Tell me how to do that."

"I have to go," Isabelle said. "She's waiting for me."

She hung up before he could say anything else.

Harper was still asleep when Isabelle got back to the room. She sat and stared at her for a long time, watching the slow rise and fall of her chest and the peacefulness in her face as her dark hair cascaded around her. Somehow her features were softer now, unlike the early days of their first meeting.

Her right hand rested under the pillow. On alert with her weapon, Isabelle was sure, ready for an intruder or an invader coming to take her.

Coming to Turkey meant Isabelle had emerged from the hidden woods. She had gone beyond the need to retreat. Beyond the need to preserve any trace of herself by being still and shrouded. Greater still, she had longed to be free from the vagueness that permeated her soul amidst bigger beasts.

She got up and gathered her things, not allowing herself to think anymore. This would be the last betrayal, and the last twist of being taken. The last of Isabelle being timid and convenient.

The bastion of secrecy and lies. Despite how remorseful Harper was now, it had been a grand deceit.

When she was finished, she took one last look at Harper then went out, quietly closing the door behind her.

The front desk clerk greeted Isabelle cheerily in the dreary night.

"A taxi to Afyon Airport, please."

Within ten minutes the taxi had arrived. She paid the driver with the last of her Turkish Lira and his face lit up. She wouldn't be needing it anymore. One hundred TL to get her away from Harper. She'd get on a flight to London and then wherever else her heart desired.

Before she left the room, Isabelle had stooped to the floor and quietly opened Harper's bag. She found a notebook, a cell phone which was turned off, and a small box of ammunition. When she flipped the pages of the notebook, a picture of herself fell out. In the photo, Isabelle was wearing all black, including a fluffy turtleneck sweater that rose over her chin. Her expression was wistful and sad as she stood in the courtyard of her guest-house, watching the water dance.

This was the Isabelle Harper had seen in those early months after they discovered her. An isolated woman who could be tricked and trapped. A weapon to use against her brother.

She took the picture so she would never forget. She took the necklace with the bulb pendant. Then she unzipped the inner pocket of Harper's bag and took the yellow flash drive.

She could be a taker too.

Acknowledgments

WHEN I FIRST STARTED this project I was a lonely writer trying to figure out the craft. I am grateful for my early writers group members, who helped me trudge through concepts and character sketches, and for family and friends whose enthusiasm along the way motivated me. My gratitude to fellow writer and critique partner Andrew J. Peters, whose accomplishments inspired me.

Many thanks to my editor Kelly Lynne Schaub, who not only fixed my wonky sentences and character mannerisms, but also helped me to see the bigger picture.

I am truly grateful to have had the eternal support of Krishna – who deftly coached me on fleshing out my bare bones manuscript – and Tatiana and Byron the last few years of this process. Even when I needed quiet time alone to write, they never stopped rooting for me. If ever there was a time I questioned whether there was a point to all this, they were the reason to keep going.

I am forever grateful to my mother, Merle, for her gentle encouragement.

My sincere thanks and gratitude to everyone who has ever shown an interest in my work. It means the world to me.

About the Author

C.A. CLEMMINGS GREW up in Kingston, Jamaica. She writes general fiction about ordinary characters with an enigmatic and enduring spirit. *The Outlaw's Enigma* is her first novel, and will be followed by the sequel, *The Outlaw's Revenge*. Her short stories, *Placencia* and *Rebirth* were published in eBook format and are available where eBooks are sold. C.A. Clemmings lives in New York with her wife and children. Visit her on-line at www.caclemmings.com[1].

---

1. http://www.caclemmings.com

The Outlaw's Revenge

ISABELLE AND VICTORIA'S intriguing story continues in *The Outlaw's Revenge*. Subscribe to the author's mailing list at www.caclemmings.com[1] for updates about the sequel, and for news and giveaways.

❖

1. http://www.caclemmings.com